LOCKED IN . . .

Willi rubbed her neck again. How long had she been reading? The lights blinked, warning patrons that ten minutes remained before closing time. Her breathing grew labored, almost forced. As the dark shelving closed around her, her heartbeat quickened. Someone *was* watching her.

The lights blinked again. The head librarian called out an obligatory, "Is everyone out?" and doused them.

The great oak doors crashed closed. Willi cringed and yelped. What kind of warning was that? Ten minutes could not possibly have passed since she got up to look for something light to read. Scuttling sounds behind her, then to the side, echoed. She crouched down.

Damn. She was locked inside *with* someone.

Willi crawled to the end of the shelving and headed toward the only source of illumination, the minute skylight in the long corridor. Heat suffused her face. She yelped, stifled the sound quickly and stood.

With eyes widened, she bit her bottom lip. If someone were nearby, he couldn't have helped hearing that screech.

No sooner had the thought formed than a voice, distinct yet grating, rose in an eerie wail to chant a strange incantation. . . .

MORE MYSTERIES FROM THE
BERKLEY PUBLISHING GROUP...

SISTER FREVISSE MYSTERIES: Medieval mystery in the tradition of Ellis Peters . . .

by Margaret Frazer

THE NOVICE'S TALE	THE BISHOP'S TALE	THE REEVE'S TALE
THE OUTLAW'S TALE	THE MAIDEN'S TALE	THE SQUIRE'S TALE
THE PRIORESS' TALE	THE BOY'S TALE	THE CLERK'S TALE
THE SERVANT'S TALE	THE MURDERER'S TALE	

PENNYFOOT HOTEL MYSTERIES: In Edwardian England, death takes a seaside holiday . . .

by Kate Kingsbury

ROOM WITH A CLUE	DO NOT DISTURB	PAY THE PIPER
SERVICE FOR TWO	EAT, DRINK, AND BE	CHIVALRY IS DEAD
CHECK-OUT TIME	BURIED	RING FOR TOMB SERVICE
DEATH WITH	GROUNDS FOR MURDER	A BICYCLE BUILT FOR
RESERVATIONS	MAID TO MURDER	MURDER

GLYNIS TRYON MYSTERIES: The highly acclaimed series set in the early days of the women's rights movement . . . "Historically accurate and telling."—Sara Paretsky

by Miriam Grace Monfredo

SENECA FALLS	NORTH STAR	THE STALKING-HORSE
INHERITANCE	CONSPIRACY	MUST THE MAIDEN DIE?
BLACKWATER SPIRITS	THROUGH A GOLD	SISTERS OF CAIN
	EAGLE	BROTHERS OF CAIN

MARK TWAIN MYSTERIES: "Adventurous . . . Replete with genuine tall tales from the great man himself."—*Mostly Murder*

by Peter J. Heck

DEATH ON THE MISSISSIPPI	GUILTY ABROAD
A CONNECTICUT YANKEE IN CRIMINAL COURT	THE MYSTERIOUS
THE PRINCE AND THE PROSECUTOR	STRANGLER
	TOM'S LAWYER

KAREN ROSE CERCONE: A stunning new historical mystery series featuring Detective Milo Kachigan and social worker Helen Sorby . . .

STEEL ASHES	BLOOD TRACKS	COAL BONES

All signs point to
Murder

⚨ ⚹

Kat goldring

BERKLEY PRIME CRIME, NEW YORK

This is a work of fiction. Names, characters, places, and incidents are either the product of the author's imagination or are used fictitiously, and any resemblance to actual persons, living or dead, business establishments, events, or locales is entirely coincidental.

ALL SIGNS POINT TO MURDER

A Berkley Prime Crime Book / published by arrangement with the author

PRINTING HISTORY
Berkley Prime Crime mass-market edition / August 2001

The Penguin Putnam Inc. World Wide Web site address is
www.penguinputnam.com

ISBN: 0-425-18029-8

Berkley Prime Crime Books are published
by The Berkley Publishing Group,
a division of Penguin Putnam Inc.,
375 Hudson Street, New York, New York 10014.
The name BERKLEY PRIME CRIME and the BERKLEY PRIME CRIME
design are trademarks belonging to Penguin Putnam Inc.

PRINTED IN THE UNITED STATES OF AMERICA

10 9 8 7 6 5 4 3 2

ACKNOWLEDGMENTS

Pilamaya. Heartfelt thanks to the first wonderful storytellers—Joyce and Pete Goldring—who instilled a respect for all and a curiosity to discover something new each day. To Jay and Holly, thanks for letting me know how important it is to pursue dreams. You two were my first ones. For giving me the honed skills to write the stories, blessings on the most dedicated of The Writerie members: Glenn Diviney, Jim Minter, Glenna Jarvis, Shirley and Mac McKee. For allowing me a venue for testing those abilities and learning about marketing my writing, thanks goes to DFW Writers' Workshop. Most think that DFW stands for a certain metroplex, but such is not the case. The DFW stands for Damned Fine Writers, and I'm most proud to be a member. And the Bordeaux brothers, Leland and Jim, of the Rosebud Sioux Reservation, *pilamaya, K'ola.* To colleagues and students encountered over the last twenty-five years at Alvarado High School, *muchas gracias* for putting up with this strange teacher with the weird sideline—writing mystery novels. Thanks to Cleburne PD's Citizens' Police Academy, which taught me so much. To all who've helped me on this path and been a positive blessing, *pilamaya, pilamaya ye.*

K'eya Kimimila Win
(Butterfly Turtle Woman)
Kat Goldring

CHAPTER
I

"THE blood—could you believe all of that *blood*?"

"It was real enough. That gosh-awful stink."

"Yeah, I didn't know blood had a smell, either. What got to me, though, you know, was the sight. *Mucho*. So much blood."

"How could one tiny . . . how could it have so much?"

Willi Gallagher, in her best English teacher pose, tried not to look like she was peering between the books on the high school library's shelves. Two of the fluorescent lights blinked, sputtered and dimmed. A lone ray of sunshine which broke through the murky cloud bank outside the library window veiled the room in an amber wash. A shiver coursed down Willi's spine.

She had given up eavesdropping. Sure she had. Like she'd given up breathing. Thirty-plus years and she still hadn't followed Mama's advice to keep her nose out of other people's business. Face it, two freshmen mentioning *blood* roiled her curiosity like fermenting yeast. Her blue-green eyes gleamed, a sure sign she was on the scent of a good tale, one likely to catapult her into trouble of some kind.

She spread the books on American Indian myths and legends apart in order to see better. Two texts—*Coyote Myths* and *Animal Totems*—toppled out, and she caught both before they hit the floor. With the extra space open, she could finally see. Ah, yes. D'Dee Oxhandler and Adela Zeta, girls Willi liked.

"The whole initiation, like you know, was horrible." D'Dee glanced upward, closed her eyes and sighed. Freckles stood out against her pale complexion. "Horrible." Her whisper came out as loudly as someone calling across to the next table.

Willi smiled. The girl was definitely an Oxhandler. When any of the Nickleberry Oxhandlers whispered, they talked as loud as most folks did in normal conversation, and if an Oxhandler spoke in what was *normal* to them, their voices boomed and ricocheted off the walls.

Adela said, "We've got to escape, D'Dee, but how? *Ay*, once in the circle, you can never leave."

"Uh, come on, come on. Don't be silly, Adela. It's just a stupid club. We"—D'Dee's voice faltered as if she were trying to convince herself—"*can* get out. We can. Like I said, just a stupid club for fun and games."

Willi edged closer for hints of what had brought the sense of urgency and panic to Adela's voice when she'd said *escape*. This was not just idle curiosity. Any teacher worth her paycheck would do the same.

"*Ay, sí.* Since when do you like games with *blood*?" Adela asked.

"Don't worry." D'Dee grinned, some of her impish composure obviously restored. "I know who the leader is. Now don't be so lame."

"No way, D'Dee. No one knows him."

"Okay, okay, but like I know someone who does, though."

The fluorescents fluttered to life for a moment and

crackled, but finally went out completely. Under her breath, Willi cursed the antiquated wiring. The amber wash turned to a dismal gray and the air seemed heavier, harder to pull into her lungs.

"Keep your voice down, D'Dee. How's knowing him going to help us get out of the circle?"

D'Dee opened a compact and applied blush to her freckled cheeks. "All we do is let this guy know we want out or . . ."

"Or?"

"Or else we'll tell."

A braying voice broke into the conversation's rhythm. "May I help you, Miss Gallagher, or were you just eavesdropping again?"

Willi gasped and jumped back from the shelf. "No, I can find everything myself."

Hortense Horsenettle, the Nickleberry High School librarian, gawked over the tops of her bifocals. Her glasses were rimmed in shiny red like satiny ruching around Valentine's boxes. She adjusted them and peered at the ceiling. "That makes five bulbs to go out this week. Put in a work order, though, and what do you get? A two-week wait just for some lightbulbs."

She focused on the book in front of Willi. "*Grue . . . so me.*" Hortense had a tendency to draw words out into a nerve-stretching bray. "Interested in classic horror, I see. Let me point out one or two recent purchases. The students wear these out so fast or just don't return them; we have to constantly reorder. *Hauntings of Hill House* isn't what you want. Ah, here we are. *Dragon Tears*. This is really *gruesome*. Ought to offer an interesting foil to your other choices." She snapped a lacquered nail against the Native American books Willi still clutched.

"I hadn't really planned to read these. They just—"

"Nonsense. Finally, you're getting brave enough to look into your Indian background."

"I don't think so. That part of my blood has been so diluted by the Scotch-Irish, I really don't believe—"

Hortense shoved her glasses farther down her nose and put her hands on her hips. "I saw you admiring *The Council Grounds* painting in Tendall's law office the other day. And what about that Navajo jewelry you've been drawn to lately? Huh? These things are calling to you, Willi. Your mother was always proud of her Comanche blood."

"Well, yes, but—"

"So, these books came to you right when you needed them. Enough said."

"Yes, perfect, Hortense." Willi sighed. Blast the busybody woman. And the words! Hortense's word of the day was obviously *gruesome*. Well, that was an improvement over yesterday's *moribund* and last week's *malignant*. Okay, the words she could handle, but the brays—something to do with bad sinuses—that interrupted Hortense's speech every few sentences were hard to ignore.

Willi said, "Thanks. I don't need anything else. Don't let me keep you from helping others."

Hortense didn't budge.

Willi kept a tight smile in place and walked to the checkout desk. Glancing once more toward the girls, she cocked a receptive ear, but dark-headed Adela and freckled D'Dee leaned closer together. She couldn't approach them. They could make up any kind of tarradiddle to cover what they'd said. Nothing could disguise their fear, though. That was real. Damn Hortense's interference. Willi sighed and checked out *Dragon Tears*. She'd better not bring the book back unread. Hortense always wanted to discuss the selection.

Devil's eyes, she might never discover what D'Dee and Adela seemed worried about. She clamped her hands around the book as she sauntered slowly toward the door. Maybe she was overreacting. In all likelihood, the girls might be rehearsing for the spring play or going over the plot of the newest soap opera. Sure, and terrorists didn't roam the world, and metal cans didn't take five hundred years to rot. No doubt about it, there was fear in Adela's voice . . . no, she wasn't overreacting.

Another lightbulb snapped and crackled, sputtered back to life for a heartbeat, but then fizzled to leave a darkened corner where the two girls huddled.

All of that blood?

RUBBING the back of her neck did nothing to alleviate Willi's tension or sense of foreboding. At any rate, she couldn't mull the matter over now, not with third-period English class waiting for her. She pushed back the mental storm warnings, ignored the whispered breath against her spine and in her typical Capricorn fashion focused on problems she *could* solve, like three more classes and guests for dinner, one of which she'd prefer to be a no-show—Dan Oxhandler, D'Dee's cousin. She pushed him to the back of her mind through fifth period, but finally her mental berating surfaced. Why she'd ever let herself get involved with an ex-student ten years her junior was beyond her.

After setting aside the notes from her sixth and last class, she counted items off on her fingers. Her housekeeper, Elba, and Elba's sister, Agatha, were preparing the breaded cutlets, the creamed spinach and the carrot cake. Bless their Betty Crocker hearts. Elba, in her usual manner, had even uttered an incantation over the recipes.

Fondly, Willi envisioned short, round Elba and lanky Agatha, who practiced the Old Religion, white witchcraft. Sure, Willi loved them but never knew if they'd have a

Tarot deck spread out with her evening meal or a cup of tea leaves nearby.

Sometimes they had predicted strange things which uncannily had come to pass. At thirty-two she did well to manage what life tossed her, but occasionally the *witch* sisters could be a handful.

Shoving the sixth period essays to the back of her desk, she put Dean Koontz's book along with the Native American ones in her satchel and headed for the car and the supermarket.

NOW, what had Elba asked her to pick up on her way home for the dinner party, a festivity in honor of Auntie moving back to Nickleberry after thirty years in Tyler, Texas? For the life of her, Willi couldn't recall, so she strolled through the Nickleberry Market aisles and hoped she'd remember. She did. Horseradish for the cutlet sauce.

Satisfied her memory banks weren't totally deleted, she stood in line at the checkout counter. She wiped at a trickle of perspiration on her forehead and stared at the heavy clouds spoiling for a rain.

In front of her, Caprithia Feather, the high school guidance counselor, stared at the gossip tabloids. Willi craned her neck to see the glaring headlines. BOY EATS PLAYMATE, SATANIC CULTS INCULCATE VIRGINS, WOMAN MEETS THE REAL HULK and ZODIAC ZONKED ZUCKERMAN.

Gray-haired Caprithia shifted and glanced behind her. "Willi Gallagher. As I live and breathe. The star signs. Interesting, aren't they? I'm the 'goat,' and you, too. I saw the faculty birthday list." She tapped the bottle in Willi's hand. "Horseradish. Good for poultices, isn't it?" Caprithia continued in a breathless twittering, all the while patting and fussing with the lace on her bodice as if she were drawing attention to a great treasure, if anyone cared to notice.

Dry lightning ripped across the sky and Caprithia jumped, bumping into Willi.

"Excuse me, dear. Don't you hate this kind of weather, Willi, like it's trying to suck the breath from everyone and everything and oh, the mugginess, but never a drop, never a drop of rain?"

"I know what you mean." Willi clutched the horseradish and tapped the label.

Caprithia took a big breath and said, "Mama had to have some more . . . necessaries. Of course, she loves her baby oil and powder. Bought her favorite candy, too. Lemon drops. I don't like her to eat them since, well, you know."

Willi did *not* know, but smiled encouragingly.

"Oh, my, my," Caprithia said, "when Mama choked on that drop last year, why, I was scared to death. Don't know what I would have done if Dan Oxhandler hadn't known—now what is that called where you squish someone's middle and make them regurgitate—*Himmler's Maneuver?*"

Caprithia didn't pause long enough for Willi to correct her.

"But, Mama is an invalid, poor dear, and one must give in to a few things, and she does so love her lemon drops, and—"

As most people did after a few minutes of Caprithia Feather's ramblings, Willi tuned the voice out and nodded in time with the general cadence.

That whispering along her back had become a cold iciness. CULTS INCULCATE VIRGINS, she read and imagined a horrid scene of young girls held by cloven-hoofed and well-endowed Satyrs. She rubbed the cool bottle of sauce against her temple.

Girlie, you're imaginative, Daddy had said. *You visualize. That's part of your mama's Comanche sensitivities coming out in you.*

Willi grimaced. She really wasn't the type to go delving into any of her bloodlines. She was a more here-and-now person. But the voice from the past wasn't going to let her rest.

What with my Irish, you get a double dose, my girlie. Most merely sense something if they are aware of happenings at all. Nothing to worry about because your ideas take shape in the form of pictures in your mind's eye. Some call them visions. Your mama and her mother had them. They'll get stronger as you mature. Your daughters will have that gift, too.

Caprithia's rise in voice startled her. Willi jerked and tried to pay closer attention. Poor woman had nursed her eighty-two-year-old invalid mother for so many years everyone had lost count. The least she deserved was polite attentiveness.

The twittering halted, and by the look in Caprithia's eyes the counselor had just asked a question.

"I'm not sure." Willi tried to sort out an answer.

"Oh, I think it's going to be grand, grand, grand."

"Me, too." That seemed a safe response.

"Imagine, the whole week in Galveston."

Now assured of the conversation's direction, Willi picked up her end of it as the cashier lifted items from Caprithia's basket. "Sand and salt air sounds fine to me."

"Tomorrow night we'll be on the beach, won't we? I'm so glad I was asked to help chaperone the Honors Club," Caprithia said.

"I'm looking forward to the tours, but not the big group of students." Tucking a strand of hair into her French braid, Willi raised an eyebrow. "About twenty kids per teacher."

"Oh, didn't Hortense tell you, now? She corralled more sponsors. Jerald Stanley from the history department. He teaches world history, you know. And the math department will be represented by Paul Undel. Oh, and there's someone else. Fun, it's going to be fun, fun, fun."

Sure, Willi wanted to say. Fun for the kids, pure hell for the chaperones.

Rubbing her neck, she asked, "What about your mother?"

"The sitter is to stay the whole week. Isn't that wonderful?" Caprithia followed the box boy out and said, "Yes, yes, yes, CaShawn, I have the application for UTA in my office, dear. Now, remember to make plans for the SAT and ACT, and while you're at it, you can look at the available scholarships. Oh, such wonderful, wonderful, *wonderful* possibilities await you. Look, everybody, the sun has finally broken through. Lovely, lovely."

CHAPTER
2

WILLI made it through the meal without one fearful thought.

"The cutlets, my dear, were *muy sabrosos*," Rodrigo said. He was Auntie's most recent and youngest lover, and his sienna skin and shock of white hair allowed many to mistake him for Charlton Heston. Auntie called Rodrigo her El Cid, a throwback to one of Heston's famous roles.

The other two men, Dan Oxhandler and his Uncle Ozzie, seemed as satisfied as Rodrigo. Seated side by side on the sofa, they looked like their namesakes, strong yoked oxen.

At seventy, Ozzie was graying and stoop-shouldered, as if he'd been harnessed to one too many heavy loads in life. Certainly, ownership of the Oxhandler Barbecue and Emporium had to be a burden at his age.

Dan rubbed his stomach. "Good meal, Willi. Your aunt can't say she's not been properly welcomed back to Nickleberry."

"Thanks." She tried to use her most professional voice, not too friendly, but not too cold, either.

Ozzie, toothpick dangling from his mouth, slapped Dan's knee. "You got that right, nephew. Willi, I might have to wheedle that recipe from Elba for my restaurant. Mighty tangy, but not bitter."

Willi managed not to cringe at his loudness. Heavens, she'd been around Nickleberry's Oxhandlers all her life, but sometimes she was caught off guard.

Willi nodded. "Thanks, fellas. The compliments should go to my neighbors, Elba and Agatha. All I did was *play* hostess. They did all the real work."

She refused to refer to the eccentric Kackelhoffer sisters as housekeepers or cooks. Most thought they were family, anyway, and few knew that Agatha had once married and used the name Carstairs. She insisted on the use of her maiden name. Rumormongers had it that she was interested in the attentions of the county's finest, Sheriff Brigham Tucker.

Willi continued. "They're going to entertain us this evening, too."

She glanced at Auntie and furrowed her brow. Auntie was uncharacteristically quiet tonight. Seventy-plus years and as sweet-looking as a Mrs. Santa with bouncing white curls, she seemed out of sorts. Not once had she run her fingers over the velvet sofa and sighed, or commented on the scent she wore or what emotions it brought forth, and if anything, Auntie was aware of the sensual . . . in everything. Perhaps the fortune-telling she had arranged with Elba and Agatha might brighten her up.

After lanky Agatha had settled everyone with cups of cappuccino, she headed toward the small nook full of books. Agatha wore a red silk skirt that swirled around her bony ankles. Her purple blouse sported a design in green sequins. If she weren't such a quiet person, Willi would have found it easy to think of her as a brightly plumed parrot. Agatha swished through the door and sank her frame upon a stool in front of a Herculon recliner.

Elba stayed in the living room, chose a table about as round as herself and sat in one of the two chairs drawn up to it. The chair creaked as she adjusted her generous rump.

She announced, "I'm as ready as pones fresh from the oven, as ready as a virgin on prom night, as ready as—"

"Elba is going to tell fortunes," Willi interrupted. One day she'd have to break the old woman of her habit of making audacious and often randy comparisons. Sure, and that would be as easy as getting Texas Bubbas to give up beer and boob ogling.

Willi swept her hand toward the crystal ball placed on top of the embroidered tablecloth and doused all lights with the exception of one.

"And," she said, "in the reading nook, Agatha will favor us with palmistry." She indicated the door to the tiny alcove covered from floor to ceiling with books.

After getting candles lit, Willi dimmed the lights there, too. Undulating flames sent shadow dancers across the walls and ceilings. Somehow the shifting display seemed grotesque and frightening—anything but relaxing. Shivering, she reached to turn the lamps back on, but halted when her aunt spoke.

"Exciting," Minnie said. She settled her granny glasses on her pert nose. "Isn't it, my El Cid? Sort of like being in an Indian tent around the cozy fire."

"My dearest." Rodrigo bent over Minnie's hand to kiss her skin, soft and virtually unwrinkled. "I understand now where Willi's overactive imagination comes from."

Willi lounged in the inky shadows to study her aunt. The septuagenarian had refused to move into the rambling farmhouse with her after making the change from Tyler to Nickleberry, Texas.

Auntie wanted to be where *the action* was, so she chose

the Bluebonnet Apartments, located a street behind the high school.

Probably Auntie was beginning to realize Rodrigo wouldn't be quite so near to hand. That sentiment could account for her unexpected silences and the palm she placed across her heart from time to time during the evening. But then Auntie's laughter drifted across the room, testimony that she wasn't suffering at the moment.

Dan Oxhandler strode closer, his beastly shadow looming over her. Pretending not to notice, Willi approached Agatha. The tactic failed.

"A penny for your thoughts," Dan boomed.

"Thinking about how things change."

"Between us, you mean?" His voice carried to all corners of the room.

Raising her chin, she played it like everyone wasn't listening. "Dan, no, not at all. By the way, I want to tell you something about D'Dee and—"

He held both palms in front of him. "Nope. I refuse to discuss my cousin's school antics after hours. If we can't talk about you and me, our life toge—"

"Don't, Dan. Not here. Not now." She knew her cheeks were flaming in embarrassment.

"Fine by me." He nodded to Agatha and dropped into the Herculon recliner as he extended his hand. "Do your stuff. Tell me Willi isn't going to ditch me. If that's not in the palm lines, let's hear the worst and get it over with, Agatha."

The slender-fingered woman took his hand in hers, swished her skirts aside and piped out, "You have a long lifeline, Dan Oxhandler." Candlelight caught and flashed against the green sequins.

"Great. That means I get to suffer longer, right?"

Willi turned up the corner of her mouth. He could damned well get in a huff and have a pity party, but she would not stay to listen to it. She left to tidy the kitchen and wandered back to the living room only in time to hear the tail end of Auntie's fortune.

Auntie tilted her nose in the air and placed her hand on her bosom. "Well I'll be damned."

Willi frowned. Blast Elba, she was supposed to make the evening fun and entertaining. "Auntie, this is just a parlor game, not worth taking seriously."

Elba pushed her arms underneath her hefty bosom. "I beg your ever-loving pardon. This is not a *game*." She snorted and faced Minnie. "Another female will try to get your man. Might succeed. Bookish woman but man-hungry as a she-wolf in heat, as hot as a cat—"

"Elba!" Willi had no time to admonish more. The doorbell rang. She hurried toward the entrance and ran into Rodrigo, who carried two fresh cappuccinos. No one could be more attentive than Rodrigo was to Auntie. Elba's crystal ball was cracked this time. Willi opened the door.

Hortense Horsenettle rushed inside, gasped at the shadowy figures, the flickering candles, the crystal ball. "A little séance perhaps? Any gruesome ghosts show up?"

"No, we're not trying to commune with specters, Hortense. Just having some entertainment for Auntie's homecoming."

"Well, whatever." She pushed her red-framed bifocals upward. "I must have the book back. Someone had put a reserve on it for the spring break." Grudgingly, she said, "My mistake."

"The book?"

"Koontz's *Dragon Tears*."

"All righ . . . uh . . . really?"

Ushering Hortense through to the living room, Willi assured the librarian there'd be no problem and thanked God she wouldn't have to read the horror novel immediately. She loved Dean Koontz as much as the next aficionado but preferred to choose her own time.

Hortense paused long enough for introductions and continued, "I promised to pick the book up and return it within the hour."

"Don't say another word." Willi retrieved all three texts from her desk and returned to find Rodrigo setting the extra cup of coffee close to Hortense rather than taking it over to Auntie.

"You must not rush so, pretty lady, no." He enclosed Hortense's hand with his own.

"Pretty? Uh . . . how . . . gal-*lhant*." Hortense didn't retract her left hand from his grasp. But with her right she removed her glasses from her sloping nose and slid them into her purse.

"So you teach with Willi?"

"I'm the librarian." She sat up straighter, crossed her legs and hiked up her skirt. "And you?" She fluttered her lashes over her myopic and bulging eyes.

Willi slapped all the books down on the sofa between them. "Here you are, Hortense. I'm sorry you're in such a *rush*."

"I'll just take a minute to catch my breath." Peering at the texts, she picked up *Dragon Tears* to stuff into her purse, but handed back *Animal Totems* and *Coyote Myths*. "You'll need these two."

"Need?"

Hortense sighed all the way down to her painted toes. "Yes, for some reason, I feel it's so important for you to get in touch with your Native American roots."

Aunt Minnie said, "She *is* right about *that,* Willi. Your mama always wanted you to learn one of the Indian languages along with your study of the Spanish language. You've always said yourself that no knowledge is wasted, and that you can't know others if you don't know yourself. Your mama's and my Comanche blood may be diluted through the decades, but it's still there, and I'm as proud of the connection as she was."

"Fine." Willi grabbed the books. She smiled and hoped neither her aunt nor Hortense could hear her teeth grinding.

"Perfect," the librarian said. "Now, I can visit for a few minutes with this delightful gentleman."

Minnie, finished with her crystal ball session, whispered in Willi's ear, "That's the piece of baggage, I bet. A double-dime bet."

"I beg your pardon, Auntie."

"You heard Elba's prediction. That female is giving all she's got with both gams." Minnie glared. "Isn't she a sight long in the tooth to be making eyes at my El Cid?"

"Auntie, Hortense is forty-something, I guess. She's being polite."

"You'd think a woman her age would know better than to wear a frosted shag and bangs. Looks like the wet, sticky mess is glued to her head."

"I have to agree, Auntie, she does overdo it on the mousse and spritz."

Hortense placed her hand on Rodrigo's shoulder.

Minnie narrowed her eyes. "Like the crystal revealed. Bookish and damned right hungry-looking."

"Now, this is mostly in fun. Don't take the reading so seriously. Perhaps we should try the palmistry."

"Damnnab right I'm going to try some *palm*istry on that horsey face." Hand raised, Minnie stalked toward Rodrigo and the librarian.

Willi grabbed her arm to guide her gently but insistently toward the nook. "Wait here. Don't do anything you'll be sorry for later."

A weariness settled over her. Bright lights and laughter were suddenly an agitation.

In a few moments Hortense uncrossed her legs, sighed,

and picked up her purse. "You did hear the announcement before you left this afternoon, didn't you, Willi?"

"Pardon?"

"You won't believe what the kids found after this evening's baseball game. Really gruesome. They'd just called the sheriff before I came over. Bet the squad cars are surrounding the school right now. Possible health hazard, you know."

"What's the health hazard, Hortense?" she asked. "Asbestos in the ceiling again?"

Hortense opened her eyes wide, blinked as she replaced her glasses, refocused upon the world at large and flipped her shaggy hair ends. She brayed once, covered her mouth and frowned.

"Why, the *bodies,* of course."

CHAPTER
3

AFTER Hortense's announcement, everyone clambered into their own vehicles and in less than a quarter hour, Willi stood beside the sheriff. Moonlight glinted off his silver badge.

"Ah-choo!" Sheriff Brigham Tucker worried a yellow bandanna over his bulbous nose. Willi's father—Phidias Gallagher—lawyer, farmer, and tall tale twister—had worked with Tucker for years and been the first to suggest bandannas rather than mere handkerchiefs for the sheriff's use. Seemed natural for Willi to serve as *gofer* between their two offices during her early teens, and at Phidias's request, Sheriff Tucker hired Willi as substitute secretary-dispatcher-photographer during her college years. In Nickleberry, being the county seat, and a small town to boot, that meant that Willi was well accepted as one of the law that enforcement team. She had been accused many times of working undercover as a teacher at the high school.

"But," Willi now said, "don't you see, Sheriff? The blood the girls mentioned could be connected with this." She pointed toward a group, including her dinner guests, milling outside the yellow-taped area.

"Now, Miss Willi, I don't think—"

"They mentioned death, blood and something tiny." She put her hands on her hips.

"Ah-choo!" He folded and patted the large handkerchief before putting it in his pocket. "I appreciate you sharing that conversation, but really, unless you come up against more reasons, don't fret yourself none. You and me both know you tend to let your imagination run now and again."

"Yeah," Dan said, stepping over and tapping his cap brim, "she has a tendency to fantasize. Lots of women do."

With great strength of will, Willi ignored him.

A strong whiff of ozone wafted around her. She peered up at the nighttime cauldron of gathering clouds, obscuring the stars here, leaving patches twinkling there.

Sheriff Tucker looked upward, too. "Yeah, this dang weather needs to break and soon. Just go and rain and get it over with."

A hundred yards to the side of the school parking lot and to the left of the baseball field, Sheriff Tucker walked underneath the crime tape and into dense shrubbery, mostly holly bushes.

"Don't worry. We done checked for prints here." Bending down, he pointed.

She knelt beside him. At first she couldn't see due to the distortion created by swiveling lights. Sheriff Tucker directed a steady beam from his flashlight to the center of one bush, and she gasped.

Two tiny bodies, a small cat and a miniature dog of some mixed breed, were hanging from rough cord around their necks. Both had been gutted. Blood matted the fur.

"Figure they been here nigh on to twenty-four hours. After the baseball game, kids saw the flies buzzing and reported this."

Perspiration beaded on Willi's forehead but dried quickly in the evening breeze. She shivered, jerked and peered over her shoulder as if expecting some madman to jump out from the shrubbery, but only Dan pulled on his cap brim and hovered too close for comfort. Auntie and Willi's other guests visited with folks in the crowd.

At the sheriff's signal, a deputy wearing surgical gloves approached the tiny bodies.

Moving a step closer, Willi wiped her forehead and shut her eyes for a moment. Those tortured remains had turned her stomach into an internal washing machine on fast spin.

There was the other feeling, too, that always plagued her at times like these. The itch to know why and who and all those other Ws.

With an explosion of air, she blurted, "Why is the Sheriff's Department using men and resources on the deaths of a couple of animals?"

"Reckon that's tactical information at the moment, Miss Willi." Tucker grabbed a bandanna and screwed up his face for a sneeze that never arrived. "Uh-whee. I sure do hate when that happens."

Her eyes sparkled, and she tapped a finger lightly on her retroussé nose. "Tactical?"

"Can't be divulged at this time."

"What you're saying is you think there's a cult on campus, don't you, but you don't want to state that officially?"

"Miss Willi, Miss Willi. Don't let your imagination run like a loose-necked goose." Sheriff Tucker finally sneezed. He pulled out his yellow bandanna. "You couldn't be further from the truth. We think somebody sure wants us to believe that right here in Nickleberry we got us some satanic *problemos,* but we're one step ahead, yes, ma'am." To the crowd he said, "Now, looky here. Don't the rest of you step past the tape, please."

She bent and peeked under the bushes again just as Dan Oxhandler had the same idea.

"Pitiful," he blurted.

"Cults or covens, there's some sort of satanism in Nickleberry, Texas, Dan."

He placed an arm around her shoulder and a hand over hers. "Don't be an alarmist, Willi. Kids did this, but not a cult."

She pulled out of his embrace. "Last month a police officer from Midlothian talked to the faculty about the possibility of satanic cults developing in this area. Might be some creep trying to get schoolkids involved."

"What do these dead animals have to do with *involving kids?*" he asked.

"Don't men ever listen or does everything go in one ear and out the other?" she snapped. "Cults work on kids' feelings. Feelings of insecurity, of not being loved and all the rest. In fact, I overheard this morning—"

"Stifle the womanly worries, Willi. Really, you need this vacation in Galveston, don't you?" Dan pulled his cap down and strode away. "Gonna check with the boys on the baseball team. Be right back."

Her face flushed. She wrung her hands and counted. ". . . eight . . . nine . . . ten . . ." Blood pounded in her temple. His own cousin could be involved, and he didn't give a rat's rear. She rubbed her forehead and tried Spanish. ". . . *tonto . . . idioto . . .* "

Lightning singed the clouds. Thunder crackled and Willi swirled around.

"*Perrón* might be a little stronger. Or if you prefer Lakota, *waglula.*" The man's deep voice was as startling as the thunder.

She stared up into piercing black eyes set in a square-jawed face. His gaze was *too* intense and as intimidating as the dry lightning had been earlier in the day, as fierce as the streaks now illuminating the scene. Light-headedness hit her, and she averted her glance for a moment. When she looked up, his lopsided grin made her smile in return.

He stepped back a pace. "Didn't mean to scare you." His black eyes never wavered.

This time she managed to keep her own blue-green eyes steady and said, "Crazy Texas weather. Spring is the *loco* time of the year. You could see tornadoes or snow."

"Yeah. Those farmers over there"—he thumbed across her shoulder—"are fussing up one side and down the other about knowing whether or not to plant, and the rednecks across the way are worried about a cancellation of a rattlesnake roundup."

He lowered his chin and tapped the brim of his hat. "I'm Quannah Lassiter. That's with two N's and two S's. You're the type who needs to know those nitpicky details, aren't you?" His quirky grin took the sting from the words. "I'm visiting Uncle Brigham." He nodded toward Sheriff Tucker.

"Right, I remember you coming for summers when you were a kid." Indian on his mother's side. Willi squinted in concentration. Little Feather—that was her Indian name. She was married twice to white men. The first one was Ben Tucker, the sheriff's brother, but she opted to live on the reservation when she was widowed in her twenties. "Your dad was Ben Tucker, but Strom Talking Stick Lassiter adopted you, right?"

He narrowed his eyes, took his hands from his jeans' pockets and folded his arms in front of his massive chest. *"Han, hecetu yelo."*

"Huh?"

"Not *huh, han. Yes,* you're right. Lakota language." He made the words sound grim. "Partly right."

"Oh?"

"Strom was my natural father. Guess you could say Uncle Brigham unofficially adopted me when Strom left Mama and me, which is okay since Uncle Brigham has Comanche blood like my mother. I'm a half-breed no matter how you look at it. Sioux and Comanche. You, too, have roots from The People." His perception and steady gaze were starting to unnerve her.

She was hoping for an interruption when she saw the deputy bend down toward the holly bushes. Willi said, "Oh, look, he's getting the animals."

With tiny clippers, the deputy bagged the collars—one pink, the other a simple chain. Sheriff Tucker asked the crowd to step back. Folks complied as the officer, with more gentleness than skill, untied the small remains from the branches.

Dan returned to her side. His presence seemed as intrusive as the proverbial leech, but she tried to be civil to him. "They will catch whoever did this, won't they, Dan?"

"With us on the case, of course."

"No way."

"But, Willi, someone in that building is the culprit, and who better to discover them than you and I?" he insisted.

"A female investigating?" Quannah Lassiter laughed. "If she was my woman, I'd keep her barefoot and pregnant."

Sheriff Tucker stepped up. "Don't let my nephew rile you none, Miss Willi. He's with a special branch of the Texas Rangers. Sort of an investigator hisself." He winked at her.

"*Miss* Willi?" Quannah raised an eyebrow.

"Yep. What I've called her since the first time she run away from school. Had to pick her up for truancy in first grade."

He cocked a finger in her direction. "Must have gotten her on the right track. Miss Willi, I sure would appreciate it if you and Dan kept your eyes and ears open at school."

"No." She tapped her foot. "Absolutely not. At five in the morning I'll be chaperoning close to seventy Honors Club members on the bus to Galveston. Too bad you can't go, Dan."

"But," Dan said, "I thought I might because—"

"Your Uncle Ozzie is in charge of the rattlesnake roundup, right?"

"Sure, but—"

"But me no buts. Not you or the sheriff. You, Dan Oxhandler, won't have time to investigate. Ozzie expects you to help with the crowds showing up for the roundup and cookout. Are you going to disappoint him?"

Lightning pierced through the cloud banks and thunder clapped so loud the crowd, en masse, stared upward.

Shrieks erupted somewhere in the crowd. Oh God, someone had been struck by a bolt.

"Now, what in tarnation?" Tucker shouldered his way through the gathering, and she and Dan followed in his wake.

Willi noticed that Quannah Lassiter seemed to have disappeared.

A woman had a stranglehold on a girl and both were screaming. "You ain't going to do this stuff no more, you hear me, *niña*? You hear me, Adela?"

Willi had thought only Oxhandlers could blast out like that. When Dan, she, and the sheriff reached the two, Mrs. Zeta had twisted Adela's arm behind her.

"Turn loose, woman, and calm down a mite. Mayhap we can help you all," Sheriff Tucker said. "You the girl's mother?"

Mrs. Zeta huffed, pulled strands of unwashed hair out of her face and pushed Adela away.

Willi caught the girl. Adela, shivering, stood in the circle of her arms. One ear bled where an earring had ripped through the tissue. The other earring tinkled merrily against her cheek. Willi tilted her nose at the first strong scent of rank sweat coming from the girl, but kept her comforting hold on Adela's shoulder.

Up close, she studied the piece of jewelry, which consisted of a dozen or more tiny crosses. She brushed Adela's dark cap of hair back to check closer, but the girl pushed her away.

"What's all this rigamarol about?" asked Tucker.

"Private family business, Sheriff. *Familia.* That's all," Mrs. Zeta said.

"This young lady is bleeding and scared." He let the thought hang in the evening air.

"She went out. Don't tell me where. *Ay,* she drives me *loca.* You think I let my *niña* run wild?"

Rubbing her earlobe with one hand, Adela placed the other on her hip. "I wanted to know what was happening at the school. From our house all the lights are easy to see."

She pointed to the north toward her home, one of many in a tract of three-bedroom clones which began around the baseball field's perimeter and continued into the horizon. "Mama was drun . . . asleep. Figured I'd be a few minutes. *Ay,* she didn't let me explain before she almost ripped my head off." She bent down, retrieved the broken earring and glared at her mother.

Mrs. Zeta looked sheepish. "Okay. So maybe I overreact. If you have a fourteen-year-old girl so pretty as my Adela, you worry, too, huh, Mr. Sheriff?"

"Most likely, ma'am, most likely, but I don't want no more bruises and bloody ears on this here young lady."

Adela, red-faced, approached her mother but looked at Sheriff Tucker. "Mama didn't mean to do this, Sheriff, okay? Let's go, Mama. I've got to catch that 5 A.M. bus, *sí?*"

Mrs. Zeta nodded. Touching Willi on the hand, she asked, "You going on the Galveston trip? You watch out for my Adela, okay?"

Willi couldn't deny the sincerity and worry in Mrs. Zeta's eyes, eyes bloodshot from a close encounter with José Cuervo, nor could she ignore the pleading look from Adela. The girl was resilient. Damned sad—no, worse than sad that any kid had to struggle each day against the painful knowledge of a parent's self-inflicted illness. Adela and her brother, Trujillo, were intelligent and deserved better in life.

"Sure, Mrs. Zeta, I'll take care of her."

Willi swallowed and tried to smile politely at Mrs. Zeta, but her heart wasn't in it.

Dan slapped his cap on. "All the excitement is over. Guess I'll head out. Coming, Uncle Ozzie?"

The crowd dispersed. Willi sauntered toward her car. As she touched the door handle's cold metal, a prickling of fear skittered across her. Her heart fluttered. She rubbed the back of her neck and lifted her head to survey the nearly empty parking lot, the baseball field and finally the copse of woods edging one side.

At the sight of the lone figure, she opened her eyes wide and wrapped her arms about herself in a protective hug. What did he think he was doing? Even at this distance and despite the fact she couldn't see his eyes, she quailed before the intensity of his wolfish gaze. Yes, completely focused and calm as a wolf surveying the lay of the land.

Arms crossed over his chest, legs apart, he blended in with the strong oaks, seeming to become one with the woods.

Her heart pounded. For a moment his face was highlighted by the moon until swiftly scudding clouds obscured the milky orb. Suddenly and as surely as she recognized the nose on her face, she understood why she feared him. Somehow, Quannah Lassiter, special investigator, knew her inner musings, her most private secrets, and could put thoughts—words—into her mind.

Han, hecetu yelo.

CHAPTER
4

THE next day, after spending hours with a busload of teens pumped up by anticipation and sodas, Willi was elated when they finally reached their destination. Galveston was often called the Oleander City because the shrub bordered almost every street and home. With her luck, half the kids would be allergic to the plant, and hadn't she heard somewhere that oleander was poisonous? *Gallagher, no negative thoughts. Be happy. Have fun.* She hid a jaw-popping yawn behind her hand. Her gritty eyes burned, and she rubbed her temples where her head throbbed.

Unpacking seemed to take forever, but at last she lay down for a quick nap, from which she awoke with that dry, gummy, aspirin aftertaste, which hadn't done a dang-blasted thing for her headache. A quick shower did little to restore her spirits.

By then it was late afternoon and a definite coolness had drifted in from the Gulf. Willi donned warm slacks and a soft cotton turtleneck, loafers and comfortable socks. She studied the itinerary and the Galveston city map. Uh-huh. *There's where Paul Undel told everyone to meet for the ferry ride.* She hailed a taxi from the hotel and reached the dock just as the ferry was about to embark.

"Ms. Gallagher, come on, come on," D'Dee yelled.

Adela grabbed Willi's hand and raced along beside her down the planking. "Like, maybe we can talk tonight, *sí*, just for a little bit, huh? I think I might be in some trouble."

"We can talk now, Adela. Let's stand over—"

"Sure," D'Dee said, "as soon as we're back at *The Flagship*."

Waning sunlight softened Adela's eyes, shone on her cap of dark hair and glinted off the inverted-cross earring.

D'Dee nudged Adela. "Come on, come on, let's watch the water along the edge. I told you we'd talk to her after the movies at the hotel tonight. Later, Ms. Gallagher."

Willi grinned. "Later. You two be careful."

Standing on the pulsating deck, she tried to shove away an encroaching weariness. She reveled in the disquieting glimmers of the descending sun, the dance of shadows created on the waves which mesmerized with a silent counterpoint created against the noise of the engines.

Her thoughts hovered around Dan. His attentions had become stifling, but each time she tried to break away, she was thrown together with him at school or community functions.

Caprithia strolled up to her. "Thinking about a certain coach-cum-biology teacher, perhaps Dan? Yes? Yes, I thought so." She had to raise her voice from her usual twittering to a more throaty screech.

"Yeah, I've got to tell him how I feel."

"Yes, yes, yes. And how do you feel?"

"Bottom line? Well, in Auntie's vernacular, Dan and I *don't suit.*"

"Such a shame. He's so handsome."

"I suppose."

"But," Caprithia said, eyes twinkling. "But?"

"He's stopped growing, isn't curious about anything, and . . ." Driving along the highway, she'd spot a side trail and want to investigate. He'd be bored. Get to where you're going and get there by the straightest route possible, that was his motto.

"I can't live with mental blinders, Caprithia. You miss out on all the surprise of life with that viewpoint." Hugging herself against the breeze, Willi said, "Sorry. You don't want to hear this on your time off from counseling."

"Nonsense, Willi. I saw this coming months ago. Accept your feelings. You'll be happier by following what's right for you, and so will Dan. Now, have fun." Caprithia moved away.

Flocks of gulls cawed and cackled overhead, dipped down to catch the bread thrown by the passengers and swirled above to repeat the maneuver moments later.

With a hand shading her eyes, she squinted at folks in the off-bounds area which the captain had insisted passengers avoid. Students, no doubt. She ambled in that direction until she spied a larger shadow approaching the kids. The person, who wore a generic windbreaker, had the collar turned up and was unrecognizable. Willi couldn't even be sure if it was a man or a woman.

Fine with her. She rubbed her neck. Someone else could take care of the troublemakers tonight. Walking away, she tried to recapture the sense of peace the waves had brought her.

Instead, hairs prickled on the nape of her neck. She twirled around and peered across the long deck past cars and bicycles. Two figures, barely discernible, stood in the gloom. One of the students must have been getting a real dressing-down, if jabbing hands and body language were reliable indications.

Movement to her left caught her attention. No, it couldn't be. A broad-shouldered man, his back toward her, ducked behind the crowd and at the same time pulled off a Stetson hat. She blinked. Lassiter was *not* on this ferry. He was in Nickleberry visiting Sheriff Tucker, right? Sure. Blast it all, she was jumpy. Probably her overworked imagination had gotten the better of her along with a chill from the strong Gulf breeze.

The ferry executed a smooth turn. A grind sounded belowdecks. Expecting the ferry to lurch, she grabbed hold of the railing and braced herself. Still, she wasn't quite ready for the sudden pitch of the ferry and she jumped back, jamming the heel of her foot on a length of chain holding down a rusty car. Heart thumping, she yelped. Damn. She moved gingerly around the chains.

A raucous wail rose above the clashing pistons; a lone bird returning to roost for the evening called to its mates with a screech that scraped along her nerve ends. A shriek echoed. Goose bumps tap-danced over her arms. She jerked and searched in every direction. Good grief, that was one of the kids. That scream had to be human.

No one else appeared alarmed. Okay, maybe that yell just *seemed* human. The birds' cacophony increased, escalating into an ear-splitting screech like chalk scraping across a blackboard. She covered her ears. As the captain berthed the ferry, the seagulls drifted away into a white and blue blur on the horizon. Sounds receded as if she were in a gossamer cocoon, able to observe, but only from a distance, able to react, but only slowly. Something was awfully wrong.

She walked with the other chaperones, who followed the birds' example and headed the club members toward home—toward The Flagship hotel.

Moonlight, almost as powerful as the sun, guided her. Despite the illumination, she stumbled against Paul Undel once. She apologized, reached out and pushed herself away from him.

"You okay?" he asked.

Still encased in that gossamer cocoon, she nodded and smiled. Along the seawall, huge fluorescent lights helped bring the world back into alignment. A strong wind blew her toward the hotel at a faster rate than she'd anticipated.

Paul Undel grabbed her arm when she would have fallen without his support. He kept a strong hold on her elbow and to the group said, "Hey, you all. I listened to the weather." He pointed to the small earphones around his neck and the cord leading to his pocket, where his transistor radio peeked out. "You all know they expect gale-force gusts up to sixty and seventy miles an hour?"

Caprithia Feather fluttered her hands. "Dear, dear, dear. Let's hope the duty teacher tells us everyone is back when we finish herding this group into the hotel. Oh, my, yes, yes."

Hortense nodded and pushed her red eyeglasses up her sloping nose.

"Look!" Caprithia grabbed Paul's other arm and pointed seaward. Waves broke one upon another, frothing the beach. "Such force. Oh, the grandeur—the—the *power*." Her awed voice caught and held on the last word. "Yes, my yes, my yes, the *power*."

CUDDLED up in a warm chair in the private lounge accorded to the Honors Club and its sponsors, and having changed into a fleecy jumpsuit, Willi drank a cup of hot chocolate. She poured another and stared at the cups.

Every teacher seemed to have their own talisman drinking vessel. A Leaning Tree design of an Indian woman, hair blowing in the wind, decorated Willi's cup, a gift from Aunt Minnie. The caption read: "The hand that holds this cup rules this teepee." Paul Undel's, a huge tankard, boasted an A&M University logo. Caprithia's was a black cup which seemed at first to have nothing on the outside.

Turning the cup around, Willi touched a gold-embossed astrological symbol with "Capricorn" written above. Hard to believe she and Caprithia shared the same sun sign. Goats of the zodiac were fierce climbers in career and social circles. Somehow, she couldn't see the self-effacing Caprithia, who cared for her invalid mother day after day, as being aggressive.

A bloodred goblet stood tall as if defying any other cup to approach too near. She picked up the glass to read the etching on the bottom. The name Jerald Stanley didn't surprise her, but the Waterford imprint did. Well, one never knew who had the bucks.

She'd always wondered what made Jerald tick and why he taught. An almost elegant man in his speech and dress, Jerald never wore jeans. Even today he'd had on casual slacks. His snowy hair looked frosted like a model's, and his body could handle the job, too. Only thing scholarly about him was those bifocals.

Willi pulled her legs up underneath her and stirred the hot chocolate in her cup. One problem with Jerald. He hated kids, had admitted the fact, and yet he had volunteered for duties as an Honors Club sponsor. Maybe he was a snob. The Waterford pointed in that direction. A loner, he'd never involved himself in any of the cliques or groups around town, choosing to live as Auntie did, in the new and accessible apartments by the high school, The Bluebonnet. She had asked once about the unusual spelling of Jerald's name.

"Jerald?" he said. "Not unusual, just the letter change from *G* to *J* when Mother studied linguistics. When my first sister came along, Mother embarked on learning geography. Tasmania hates her name. My first brother came when Mother embroiled herself in Spanish history. Fritz has always kept his name secret, although I think he got the best one, Frederico. Now, that's a strong name. Denotes intelligence. Power.

"She had a baby girl who died. A sister I never knew. Named her Arlighta Witchsmoke." He tilted his head and the silver highlights shone. "Mother had a *spell*—forgive the pun—when she read the Tarot and every type of book about the occult. I'd always wished she'd had me during that time. I would have done well with Mandrake or Warlock."

"Any others?" she queried.

"My second brother's name is Chippewa Dakota Stanley."

Even at the memory of that conversation, Willi whispered, "Indians." She replaced the crimson Waterford on the countertop.

Hortense stepped through the door and grabbed her tumbler, a light blue ceramic with her name painted across the side. Hearts and flowers surrounded the handle. Filling the cup with strong black coffee and pulling her fingers through her bedraggled shag cut, she chose a chair, picked a mousy brown strand from her shoulder and placed it in her pocket.

Raising an eyebrow, Willi grinned lopsidedly. "Trash can is over there. For the hair."

"Oh? Well, yes, but you don't want to leave things like hair or fingernail clippings for a malevolent creature to find."

"I beg your pardon?"

"Sorry. Guess I've been reading too much about voodoo and witches." She brayed, but didn't throw the hair in the wastebasket. "Can you believe a storm brewing on our first night?"

"Has everyone checked in?" countered Willi.

"Almost everyone. Except that little vixen, D'Dee Oxhandler."

"What? She was on the ferry with us." Willi tapped her finger across the tip of her nose.

"You know that girl. Oxhandlers own half of Nickleberry businesses and the best farmland. Gives them the idea they can do what they please when they please. D'Dee's no different. She's probably soaking in the tub and oblivious to everything but the music on the radio. They'll find her. No *malevolent* demon has slithered from the ocean to give the little hellion her due." Hortense pulled her shaggy style up, wound a rubber band around a couple of times, and let the band snap into place.

"That's been such a difficult word to work into conversation today." She shoved her glasses up the slope of her nose. "Oh, yes. Undel warned us about a possible power failure. The kids are staying in the video center or in their own rooms. Well, anyway, we shouldn't worry about D'Dee, especially since Adela Zeta and that Norris girl are poking around everywhere to locate her."

A wicked wind howled; rain slashed against the hotel. Willi jumped up, and with one hand on her hip said, "What if she's out in this storm?"

"Stop it, Willi. Lance saw her come inside. She's probably playing stupid games. You know, like running through the halls with that fake blood all over her trying to scare everyone. I heard her and Adela—or was it Betty?—talking about something like that on the ferry."

CHAPTER
5

ADELA zeta shivered. "I hate *blood*. I dream about it, smell it. *Ay, Dios.*"

After starting to check the rooms on the sixth floor, Adela eyed Betty Norris and sniffed. If colors had scent, then pink would smell like Betty's bubble gum. Lately, she either chewed it or had something to eat in her hand. Round-faced and good-natured, agreeable with whatever happened, Betty often tagged along with her and D'Dee.

"Gosh. The other kids are downstairs watching a video and playing pool," Betty said.

"Don't whine. We'll find D'Dee and go down, too, but none of your whining. Not tonight."

"Honest to God, Adela, you've really been the pits lately." Betty wiped bean dip from her bottom lip, shoved a Dorito in her mouth and chomped. She threw the empty bag in a hotel trash can between the Coke machines.

"We ate an hour ago. You keep stuffing like that, you're going to look like a *puerco*," Adela said. "A pig, okay?"

Betty's eyes teared. "You know . . . why . . . if anybody should . . . understand—"

Adela said, "Hey. Out of line. Okay, I'm sorry. *Ay, ay,* I'm worried about D'Dee." She fingered the broken earring in her pocket and shook her head.

"Yeah, I understand," Betty said, hesitating. "I saw D'Dee on the ferry, honest to God. And Lance—he lied."

"Lied?" Adela frowned. "To D'Dee?"

"No. To the teachers. He said he saw her come into the hotel. He didn't. Now he's worried, but won't tell the sponsors."

Adela tilted her head and sighed. "She wasn't with me but for just a few minutes after we got on the ferry. First time today we'd been apart."

"She made gooey eyes at Mr. Stanley. Why, I don't know. He's old."

"Huh-huh. Not forty yet. Premature gray, that's all."

"White, Adela, the man's hair is white."

"*Ay,* who cares? We're looking for D'Dee."

"Right," Betty said. "Anyway, she acted silly with Mr. Stanley, and then Mr. Undel fussed at her for going to the wrong end of the ferry."

"Undel is like . . . like . . . *greasy*. Can't believe D'Dee wouldn't come and tell me. He is a nasty creep. The *perrón*."

Betty raised her index finger and pointed it in Adela's face. "I know you. When you get really scared, you get mud-mouth. Honest to God, it's not impressive, Adela. Why don't you quote some of that guy's poetry you like. What's his name? Like you do to calm down when your parents go all weird and strange?"

"Quoting Poe won't make me worry less, Betty. Most of his poems are about death, horrible death like being buried alive in a tomb by the sea."

"Stop worrying. We'll find her. We'll find her," Betty prattled on.

Striding down the corridor, Adela ignored her. She smoothed her cap of hair, and the one earring slapped against her face in a rhythmic tinkling. She rubbed her bandaged earlobe, which throbbed. "Damn D'Dee. If she hadn't pulled me away from Ms. Gallagher, I could have told her what was going on, you know?"

The wind's thin wail infiltrated the walls of the hotel. "*Ay, Dios.* Where could D'Dee be? She should not have opened her big *boca*." Adela covered her own mouth when she halted. The corridor of plush carpet was empty.

"Betty? Where are you?" She sighed. "*Dios.* Girl probably had a chocoholic attack."

Ceiling lights winked off, then on and off again. She held a hand to her heart. She whispered, "Where in hell are you, D'Dee? *Mierda.*"

The teachers had warned about a possible power failure. Great. Really great. Now the chalk pushers would get their chance to say, "We told you so," and she'd have to stand there and listen.

The hallway lights flickered, and Adela sidled over to the wall. A moment later darkness shrouded the corridor. The tall building shuddered in the high winds. "Maybe it's a hurricane. Be just like dumb Undel to say high winds when the radio said hurricane." She triggered the switch on her flashlight, angled the beam through an open doorway and stumbled inside.

She directed the weak beacon ahead. A shadow crossed the path of light. The shadow of a person? Who?

"Yo, D'Dee? Hey, that you, Betty?" She hit her knee on a table and yelped. "*Caramba* and damn. If you're playing games, they aren't funny. You're going to be in deep *caca,* southern fried shit. Come on and check in with the duty-teacher. D'Dee?"

She examined the bathroom, too, but no one was there—no person and no shadow. "*Caramba,* now I'm seeing things." She stumbled out and knocked at the next two rooms, but the doors were locked. Taking a deep breath, she banged on the last door, which stood partially open.

Skittering her hand across the wood, she pushed, and the door with the tiny peephole yielded. Staring at that security eye scared her as if someone, something, glinted in its depths ready to clutch her. She shut her eyes and shook her head. She had to get her *caca* together, big time. She walked inside.

The corner room had a floor-to-ceiling window which offered a panorama of the tempest outside. Mesmerized by the building's protest against the storm's assault, she leaned against the cold pane.

"Bitchin' awesome." Her heart hammered against her chest. Looking down, she blinked against her light-headedness.

Dios mío.

Waves had turned into vicious tentacles—tentacles which tried to rip the hotel from its moorings.

"Bet Poe saw the sea like this."

Shivering, not from the chill but from a fear piercing through her, she swallowed the cotton-candy-turned-sour taste invading her mouth. Something—*someone*—breathed behind her.

Ay, Dios. If she'd been in bed, she would have covered her head with the pillow until the childish prickling went away.

"D'Dee? Betty?"

"No."

One syllable spoken roughly. Not D'Dee's booming voice. Not Betty's whine.

Adela shut her eyes, and tears pooled in her lower lids. One hot tear escaped and slid down her face. She tried to suck in air.

"Wh . . . who . . . who are . . . ?"

Her legs wouldn't move, she couldn't turn, and her breaths became gasps. Her heart pounded as if she'd just awakened from a suffocating nightmare. Finally, her limbs reacted. She shook so violently the crosses on her earrings clicked together like dry bones. When she managed to move, she sobbed.

"Please, don't hurt . . . me."

A figure blended into the shadows.

"Wiccan?" Adela whispered. Tears cascaded down her face as fast as the rain drizzled across the glass pane. She twisted around.

Holding her hands in front of her, she backed toward the window, but the move came too late. With one violent wrench, the hooded figure grabbed her, spun her back around to face the floor-to-ceiling glass and shoved.

Adela's arms burst through the pane, and she screamed—a primeval scream—that lost strength in the relentless storm, the rasping waves and the metal pilings below.

SHERIff Tucker sat behind his massive desk and sucked on a Luden's cherry cough drop while he studied the reports sent from Galveston.

Willi had never been so glad to see him, tuberous nose and all. The last hours had been a disjointed nightmare. Numbed, she stroked her face with the back of her hand and stared blankly at the hardwood floor.

D'Dee Oxhandler's and Adela Zeta's parents sat across from her. Other than the difference between Hispanic skin and Anglo blue eyes, the parents were mirror images— frozen figures of listless limbs and shocked faces. A doctor had administered mind-dulling drugs before leaving them. A faint scent of rubbing alcohol remained and mixed with the smell of cherry cough drops.

D'Dee Oxhandler had been found five hours before the group left Galveston. Her mangled body, one arm ripped away, had floated to the top of the water, where one of the ferry's mechanics spotted her. The arm had not been recovered.

Feeling faint, Willi placed a hand on her forehead. Too much had happened too fast. No sooner had the instructors received news of D'Dee, then a couple of beachcombers, wet and bedraggled, burst into The Flagship.

The woman had shouted, "Some loony just jumped from a third- maybe fifth-story window."

Adela had been pulled from the pilings—pilings she'd been impaled upon for less than half an hour. Willi shivered, kneaded her fingers against her arms to generate some warmth and considered the sheriff.

"Accidents," said Sheriff Tucker. "Galveston authorities have ruled both deaths as accidents." He ran a meaty finger across the bridge of his nose and shook his head like a massive lion with a tick lodged in its ear.

She understood his discomfort. She had told Mrs. Zeta she would take care of Adela.

This was the way the session in Nickleberry had begun over an hour ago and now it had come full circle. At last a matron escorted the families out and around the corner to the morgue.

Suddenly, the tiredness washed through her, and her head fell forward. She jerked upward and trembled. Her intuitions and visions had not been wrong the last few days. The problem had been in not acting on them properly.

Her heart pitter-pattered and she shuddered. What was the matter with her? She peered over her right shoulder and stiffened.

A deep voice intoned, "Reading the messages is a slow

process, one of trial and error, confirmation and reconfirmation." Quannah Lassiter, hands clasped together behind his back, rocked on his boot heels while he stared at her . . . and smiled gently.

Get out of my head. "You," she said, tilting back to see him better, "you were there on the ferry."

Quannah frowned. "No, ma'am, you're mistaken."

"But I thought . . ." She rubbed her temples.

Shaking his head, Quannah bent over her and placed a hand on her shoulder. "Are you all right?"

"Miss Willi? Miss *Willi*?" The sheriff said her name a number of times.

"I . . . I'm fine. Just tired."

Sheriff Tucker scooted his roller-chair backward on the smooth wooden floor, rose and opened a file cabinet.

"Best you get on home and get some shut-eye."

Facing him and ignoring his nephew, she said, "I promised to meet Auntie and Rodrigo for drinks in the Bluebonnet Restaurant." She shrugged her shoulder to force Quannah to move his hand.

Shaking his leonine head again, the sheriff said, "The Bluebonnet Restaurant. Ain't been there myself. Since it opened two months ago, I've been expecting calls about them *mojados* that work in the kitchen." He yawned and stretched, pulling at his earlobe. "But anyway, Miss Willi, you shouldn't be out by yourself."

"I'll escort the little lady, Uncle Brigham."

"Good idea," Sheriff Tucker said. He grinned and stepped out the door.

"The *little lady*? Now, just a min—" She pushed the chair away and faced Quannah.

"We could talk about the case." His somber gaze held steady and locked with her glance.

Oh, shoot. He knew that she wanted answers and was too tired to argue. "Sure, let's go."

CHAPTER
6

INSIDE the Bluebonnet Restaurant Willi and Quannah had ordered and sat at the table across from her aunt, who was decked out with a pink rosebud arrangement tucked in her cotton-ball curls.

Rodrigo leaned toward Willi and sighed. "So, now you are on another case with the sheriff, *verdad*?"

"No, not at all." She pushed back the salad. "According to him there isn't a case, but . . . well . . . I think he's wrong."

She eyed Quannah, who was aloof from the others while concentrating on a hefty sirloin and a baked potato oozing with butter.

Damned stubborn Indian. Was he ever going to say what he meant by *the case*? No guidance coming from his direction, she said, "I'll . . . uh . . . think about this weekend in Galveston. Something might come to mind when I'm not so tired and beleaguered by horrid dreams."

"Dreams?" Quannah asked, his eyes suddenly boring into hers.

"Last night. Dreams about spiders, crawling all over me. So—?"

"So?" he asked around a bite of salad.

"I thought Big Chief would know what spiders were all about."

"Spider is powerful Medicine with many messages. Spider weaves many things and brought the alphabet to The People. Maybe you're getting too close to some web of intrigue—or maybe writing is about to become very important. Perhaps you should stick to grading papers?"

"Right. Just what I expected. Turn your information against me. I guess that's your way of saying get off the case."

"Case?" Aunt Minnie piped up. "So, you're investigating? How exciting. How may we help?"

Quannah jabbed at the potato skin sliding in the melted butter. With an impish grin he said, "*She's* not investigating anything. Women can't really do the things needed in an investigation. Emotionally wears them out, especially if it turns out to be a murder case. Hunting killers is a test of stamina, intelligence—which I admit Willi seems to have—and downright bullheadedness, which I hope she doesn't."

Edging away from the touch of his knee beneath the table, she fumed. Out of the corner of her eye, she studied Quannah's pseudo-innocent face. That blameless appearance did nothing to hide his devilment, especially since his dark eyes twinkled good-naturedly. Well, he wasn't fooling her. She'd suffered his piercing stare when he stood at the woods' edge. Even then she'd realized he knew, *really knew,* her inner thoughts, her pitiful secrets, and the fact bothered her because . . . because damn it, she felt vulnerable.

She'd act like what he said didn't bother her. The tactic worked with students, so despite the weariness she said, "I am perfectly capable of maintaining my emotional equilibrium, Lassiter, in the face of—"

"In the face of the hideous deaths of two of your students?" His eyes narrowed, pinning her with their sharp glance.

Damn him. He'd been leading up to this all along to force her out of the cocoon of pain, the bone tiredness, by making her rise to the bait and . . . what? . . . fight back? Cry?

And she'd fallen for that bait, that opportunity to show her control over the situation. Well, no one could accuse her of being ungracious in defeat. She sighed and offered a lopsided smile. "Yes, even then."

"I could be wrong. Seems you've got some color back in those pretty cheeks."

Well, she'd see if Lassiter would take a bit of ribbing with grace. "Auntie, you know, come to think of it I don't believe Sheriff Tucker has mentioned any famous cases which his nephew has been—"

"Cases in the papers all the time," Quannah said, "but security measures dictate I keep a low profile. Wouldn't do much good undercover with my mug all over the news, and—"

Hortense strode up to the table. *"Hello."* If one could bray sensuously, then Hortense Horsenettle did just that when her glance encountered Rodrigo's.

He stood and pulled out a chair for the librarian.

Willi arched her back. The last straw could be putting up with Hortense this late at night.

The librarian fluttered her lashes, and Minnie adopted her huffy attitude with her nose in the air. Daddy had often said Willi got *her* put-upon look from Aunt Minnie. She didn't believe that, of course, because she never appeared haughty.

Quannah leaned forward and whispered, "You and Auntie are a lot alike, aren't you?"

Sitting up straighter, she tilted her nose in the air. "I beg your pardon, Lassiter."

"I rest my case." He placed his napkin beside his empty plate and got up. "Time to take this body for some shut-eye."

"But . . . but we were going to discuss the case."

"Nope. Time isn't right." He placed his hat on his head at a jaunty angle, flicked the wide brim with two fingers and sauntered away.

"Indian giver. Jerky eater. Arrogant ass."

"What, Willi? Oh, yes, that man has a damned nice set of buns. I'm glad to see you taking an interest in the important things in life," Minnie said. "There are some men worth a lot of effort. He might be one of those."

Willi groaned, leaned back and crossed her arms. "You might better exert effort for *your* man, Auntie."

Glaring at Rodrigo, Aunt Minnie nodded. "Damnnab right."

"You've come collecting books this late at night? How very dedicated you are." Rodrigo's voice invited Hortense to explain the armload she placed on the table.

"*Gal-lhant* as always, but no, Rodrigo. After the ordeal of the trip back today—it was *so* exhausting—I wanted a quiet place to eat where I wouldn't encounter *gargoylish* talk about the unfortunate accidents."

"There's a corner booth right over there." Aunt Minnie pointed. "That'll probably be less gargle . . . uh, garyo . . . nicer for you."

"No, no, Minnie, darling, we cannot let Miss Horsenettle sit by herself."

The librarian pushed up her red-rimmed glasses. "Hortense, Rodrigo, *Hortense*."

Glancing at Hortense's stack of books, Willi asked, "Why are you reading *Satanic Cults* and *Beware the Wiccans*?"

Hortense paused in her flirtations long enough to answer. "They're new acquisitions for the library. I try to read as many as I can as they come in. Unfortunately, these are rather gargoylish in nature, but I must do my duty."

"What are wiccans?" Willi, tapping the book, raised an eyebrow and ignored her urge to say something nasty about Hortense's word of the day, like *Stuff it where the Texas sun doesn't shine.*

"*Wiccan* is a name for satanic followers—witches or warlocks—I guess. I've not read that book, yet."

"Preposterous," said Aunt Minnie. "Those are bugaboos on late-night TV, but right here at this table there is a *witch* or is that *bi*—?"

"Pass the salad dressing, Auntie."

"What? Oh, why? Willi, the waiter took your salad away. Now, where was I?" She patted at the arrangement of rosebuds in her hair, wound a finger around one ribbon and pulled. When she released it, it sprang back into her white curls.

"Bugaboos, you were saying, dearest." Rodrigo smiled. "Unfortunately, not so, my darling. Satanic cults are like street gangs. They attract the young and give them a place to be accepted. *Muy peligroso,* very dangerous."

"In that case, *my* El Cid," Minnie said, "you must stay close and protect me."

"Humph." Hortense fluttered her lashes. She removed her glasses. "Adult cultists make children feel part of a family. But then, it's absolutely gar—"

"We know," Willi said, "horrible."

"—uh, yes. And then those very leaders demand payment."

Willi nodded. "Now, I remember. First, kids are sent to steal small items. Then they work up to more serious crimes."

"More serious crimes than stealing?" Aunt Minnie

clucked her tongue and leaned her head on Rodrigo's shoulder.

"Absolutely," said Hortense. She stretched her legs out to the side, crossed them and with a quick flick of her wrist pulled her skirt up. "Prostitution comes into their lives and drugs, then drug dealing."

"Something should be done about these . . . these dens of iniquity and the leaders," Aunt Minnie said. Stressing the word *iniquity,* she stared pointedly at Hortense.

"Leaders, my hind foot," said Willi. "Makes me mad when professionals like lawyers do this, and in Fort Worth last week the police arrested a doctor for administering drug-doctored stickers to kindergarten kids." Her blue-green eyes sparkled, minute rockets of anger illuminating them. "You know, the kids lick those stickers and get drugs in their system?"

"Not only in the big cities," Rodrigo said. "*Sí,* the lure of the money brought in by the vices is evidently a great temptation in small towns."

"And," Hortense said as she patted the books, "we should be informed about the problem, watch for activity and report it."

"Yes, Hortense, *sí,* you are right." Rodrigo inclined his head in her direction and drew his hand away from Aunt Minnie, who directed a mutinous look at him.

Loosening his collar, he smiled and waved at someone across the room. "Ah, there is an old *amigo.* I will take a moment to speak with him."

Willi couldn't blame him for retreating from what threatened to become a major cat fight.

Hortense took his absence as a chance to freshen her powder and lipstick. Picking a stray hair off her shoulder, she pocketed it.

Willi grinned, but didn't say a word.

"Okay, I know." Hortense patted the pocket holding the

hair. "I told you I'd been reading too much on this subject, not that I take any of the gargoylish rituals to heart, other than as information to help with students. I'll go powder my nose."

When the librarian was out of earshot, Minnie huffed. "If you ask me, she's the wicked Wiccan in Nickleberry. She has that gleam in her eye that says she's after my El Cid."

"Auntie, what gleam?"

"Don't look at me that way. I know what I'm talking about. I've seen that hungry glance many times."

"Where?"

"In my mirror, honey, in my mirror."

THE next morning willi grinned and handed Mama Feather her third cup of Celestial Tea, her fifth lemon drop and a fluffy pillow. The old lady called this room where she stayed during the day the parlor. Around the base of each Victorian chair, overpowering ferns and ivy plants crawled and writhed together in an uneasy coexistence. Wrinkling her nose, Willi punched a finger into moist potting soil which sent forth a cloying odor.

Ten-foot-high ceilings boasted intricate designs which were worn and grimy. A huge spiderweb decorated one corner, but the occupant must have been wandering around in the foliage. Willi shivered and kept a wary eye open for the big creature. Had to be a gigantic brute to build that monstrous web.

What in heaven or Hades had possessed her to volunteer for this duty she had no idea. Her mother would have said her *curiosity*. No way. Mama Feather wasn't the one to come to for information. The old lady never got outside except for Sunday services. Her mind wandered from decade to decade faster than a salesman traveled between

New York City and Fort Worth. Faced with the fact that she had been suckered into one of those chores she hated because she didn't want to say no, Willi grinned again at Mama Feather. It wasn't the poor invalid's fault.

Willi sighed for the umpteenth time, peered up at the web and shook her head. Blast. What she *should* be doing was gathering information about the girls, Adela and D'Dee. Rubbing the back of her neck with both hands, she squirmed on her chair and eyed the occupant of the brass daybed in the middle of the room.

Mama Feather, toothless, sucked away with the happy smacking of a four-month-old. "Sweet, you're sweet to visit with an old lady. Caprithia hated to ask you even for an hour, but she had to take the sitter to the dentist."

The word *dentist* came out like *benish,* and *sitter* sounded like one of those words Willi sent mud-mouthed kids to Detention Hall for saying, but by now she understood the mutterings, so she nodded.

Mama Feather's mind could flutter from the roaring twenties through Watergate and back to the Great Depression. At least the gnomelike lady seemed to be in the *present* for the moment.

In an attempt to keep her in the here and now Willi said, "You must miss Caprithia when she's at school."

"I miss her more on the evenings she has to go out."

"For meetings?"

"Uh-humm. She's such a busy girl. Like you, Wilhelmina."

Well, hell. The old woman remembered the name Willi had worked so hard to make everyone forget. She positioned her lips into a concrete smile. *Girl?* She called Willi *girl* at thirty-two? And Caprithia had to be what? In her fifties at least.

"Another drop?" Large protruding eyes blinked behind their rheumy glaze.

"Drop?" Willi asked. "Lemon or tea?"

"Silly old me. Tea, please."

With misgiving Willi eyed the adult diaper box in the corner. *Hurry up, Caprithia.* Prudently, she poured only a half cup of tea.

While Mama Feather sipped, making the slurping sounds that toothless folks make, Willi surveyed the room again. The walls, covered in burgundy flock, smothered any feeling of lightness brought in by the circle window placed close to the ceiling. Running a finger through dust embedded on the sill, she squinted.

Be a perfect place for that gross, hair-legged creature to roam.

"Mama Feather? Caprithia doesn't go out in the evenings. She stays with you."

"Well, Elvis died, you know. That might have hit her hard. Was he kin to Elliot Ness?"

"Never mind," Willi said, shaking her head.

She touched the brass lamps and silver picture frames. Good grief, with books to read, places to go, people to see, somebody took hours to polish such things.

Mama Feather piped up, startling her. "We used to go to church twice a week when Hiram was alive, you know. He wouldn't put up with her foolishness, I can tell you."

Poor old lady. Willi nodded and only paid attention from time to time.

"She was a wayward girl, Hiram said, and had to be brought into the everlasting and loving arms of the lamb. Of course, one didn't disagree with one's husband back then. Not like now. Divorce, you know."

"Divorce?" asked Willi, feeling guilty for not keeping up her end of the conversation.

"Just read the other day where the Windsors, the duke and duchess, you know, had to deal with her divorce, so

they could get married. Makes much more sense to be
happy for the short time you have in this world, don't you
think so, Wilhelmina?"

"Yes, Mama Feather." She wasn't about to ruin the old
lady's reminiscences by telling her that both the lady and
her duke were dead.

"Guess you've heard about Betty Norris's folks, recently divorced?" Mama Feather made a fast trip back to
the twenty-first century.

Her interest piqued, Willi said, "That's hard on a child.
How do you know about Betty?"

"Well, Willi sweetie, wasn't she a friend of the girls
who were killed in Galveston?"

"Killed?"

Mama Feather covered her mouth with her frail fingers.
"Did I say that? Girls ought to stay put. You *really* should.
Before your folks died in that Licorice Lane accident your
mother, bless her, often told me how you always got into
trouble, were at places you weren't supposed to be. Curiosity killed the cat, you know, Wilhelmina sweetie."

"Yes, Mama always said that." She'd considered her
mother's words as kindly meant, but coming from Mama
Feather's mouth, they seemed like a snide twist aimed to
hurt.

"So," the old lady insisted again, "girls ought to stay
put."

Uh-huh, sure. Pregnant and barefoot and standing over
a stove. Willi bit her bottom lip. She *would not* say anything. She held Mama Feather's hand with the birdlike
bones in her own tanned fingers. "The Galveston authorities think the girls had accidents, horrible accidents." She
didn't believe what the sheriff said, but that was no reason
to upset Mama Feather.

"Hiram would never hear of his daughter gallivanting

around a strange city. I told her before she went, he'd be angry. A lemon drop, please." She opened her mouth like a baby bird and Willi cringed. Grabbing hold of Mama Feather's hand again, she placed the drop in her palm and closed her fingers around it.

The tiny fingers opened, and the candy spilled out on the floor. "Caprithia puts it in for me when I'm tired."

"Right. Okay." Taking another lemon drop from the bowl and closing one eye as if that would lessen the distaste of the task, she plopped the candy in Mama Feather's nestling mouth.

No breeze wafted through the close room, and the scent of lemon hung in a miasma. No wonder Caprithia had been excited about her trip to Galveston. How awful that her one vacation had ended so tragically.

"Mama Feather, Caprithia is some fifteen, twenty years older than me. About fifty-six or -seven, right? Your husband, even if he were alive, would probably not be telling her what to do, where to go." Willi tried to say the words gently in case Mama Feather's mind was circling around events of three decades past.

The old woman's eyes snapped fire and her fingers twitched on top of the lace sheet. "Old goat. I'll kill him someday. Folks tried to assassinate Winston Churchill, you know." The light in her eyes diminished and she smacked on the candy. "John Kennedy is a handsome man. Think he'll get in the White House? Hiram wouldn't like a Catholic as president."

Willi opened her mouth to answer, decided it was a moot point and giggled.

Mama Feather yawned. With her head back against the pillows and her eyes half closed, she snored. The unfinished lemon drop hung in the corner of her mouth. Yellow drool dribbled down her wrinkled chin.

Oh, good grief. She couldn't let the old lady choke in her sleep. With tentative movements and using a paper napkin, Willi reached out and grabbed the morsel. "Uck."

She collected the teacups and candy bowl and went into the kitchen to wash the dishes.

A black cat, mismatched eyes blinking, reposed on the kitchen counter. "Hello, kitty." When she set the cups down, the cat sprang, hissed at her and scraped razor-sharp claws across her hand.

"Ouch!" Droplets of blood oozed from the cut. Blast that damned cat to Hades. Willi pulled her hand back and rubbed the wound. Dang, that burned. Yeah, she could hear her mother now. *Willi is always where she shouldn't be and so accident-prone.*

The mouser bolted through a ripped place in the screen door.

Quickly, she turned on the water. After washing the cut underneath the antique spigot, she finished the dishes and set them on the cracked tiles of the cabinet.

The kitchen window on the right side of the house faced an alley, and the building across the way, an abandoned house, offered nothing in the way of a view. That cursed cat sat atop an overflowing trash can. The black tom snarled and spat. In the cat's eyes, she saw something unaccountably frightening. She dropped a sliver of an Ivory bar.

Something clanged in the alley. With a heavy thud, the tom bounded onto the roof. He bent over, touching his whiskers to the window screen. Viewed upside down, he didn't seem *quite* so frightening. She narrowed her eyes and stood on tiptoe to see more clearly out the window. Someone was sneaking along the outside wall. A trash can toppled over, sending forth a stench of rancid meat and rotting cabbage. At the same moment, the cat, hissing and spitting, jumped and snapped its claws onto the window screen.

Willi screamed, stepped back, slipped on the Ivory soap and crashed to the floor.

CHAPTER
7

GRADUALLY, a painful throbbing brought her to. She sat up and felt the knot on her head. For a moment, she remained on the cold linoleum and figured her folks had been right. Her overactive imagination had conjured up something frightening, and her reactions had been less than graceful. Scrambling to her feet, she shook her head. What had scared her? The figure in the alley and that damned cat.

She peered across the floor and out the screen door. No cat, no figure.

Behind her, the kitchen door squeaked on its hinges. A shiver ran up her spine. She twirled around.

"Dear, dear, dear," Caprithia said, entering. "You look like you've seen a ghost."

"Yeah, well. Someone was prowling in your alley."

"No, no, dear, no. Not possible in the daylight. I often have to call 911 at night because kids seem to want to get into the Robertsons' old place next door, but never during the day. You probably heard Sweetpea, that naughty tom."

"Sweetpea?"

"Mama Feather named him before we knew he wasn't sweet or female."

"We could look around."

Caprithia grabbed her by the elbow. "Nonsense. Wouldn't hear of you doing that. The patrolman watches the place closely, really."

"Okay."

"Are you sure you're all right?"

Willi touched the back of her head. "Fine." She picked up the Ivory soap and replaced it. An idea blossomed and she snapped her fingers. "Your mother was so helpful."

"Oh, my, my, my. You're so kind. I'm sure you listened to nonsensical ramblings all morning. She probably talked about me as if I were all of thirteen. What did she say?"

"Just reminded me about a friend of Adela's I should have talked with earlier." Willi grabbed her purse. That lead was worth the geriatric feeding time. "I should have thought of Betty Norris. She was with Adela moments before she fell from the window. I've been so frustrated and tired the thinking cells stopped functioning, I guess."

"Willi, you should really leave this matter to the Galveston authorities, the professionals. They said the girls' deaths were accidents. We all cared, Willi, but take it from another professional—we all have to turn loose, let them go."

"You're right, Caprithia, you're right." Willi placed her fingers over her lips. Well, another white lie, but there was no reason to embroil Caprithia Feather in what the counselor obviously believed to be a wild-goose chase.

Stopping at Betty's house, Willi was disappointed to learn that the girl would be out all day. She walked back to her car, sighed and stretched her arms. She needed a place to sit and think. Driving east toward Ozzie's Barbecue and Emporium, she tried to ignore the thought that she was again embroiled in someone else's problems, a murder—two murders, no less. Maybe she ought not to stick her nose into this problem anymore. Perhaps Caprithia was right and the matter should be cleared up by the law, not her.

Peering in the rearview mirror, she whispered, "And Texas doesn't have the Two-Step, black-eyed peas or Dallas Cowboys."

OZZIE Oxhandler seated her in a corner booth, further secluded with jars of pickled beets and native cacti plants surrounding the headliner. He served her a guacamole salad and boomed, "Enjoy that, now hear?" Stifling the urge to stick her fingers in her ears, she smiled and nodded.

Munching on the salad, she mulled over what she had learned about the deaths of Adela and D'Dee. Bits and pieces that might amount to some sense if she got her gray cells fed so her brain could function a little faster. The girls—well, Adela—had wanted to talk to her about something stupid they'd done. Maybe killed two small animals? Obviously, that incident rankled and grew sickening to them. Even D'Dee had agreed to talk when everyone returned from the ferry ride.

Only D'Dee hadn't returned. Someone had shoved her off the ferry to a horrible mutilation.

Willi shut her eyes for a moment. That person had used the same method to rid themselves of one talkative Adela Zeta. Adela had not jumped from that hotel window. She'd been pushed to the pilings below.

Willi looked up to find Quannah Lassiter peering between the pickled beets and cacti.

Eyes shadowed by his black Stetson, he said, "I've looked everywhere for you. Where have you been?"

"Gathering clues. I think I'm on to something."

"*Clues?* You've gathered clues? Uh-huh."

Infuriating man. She shouldn't have blurted it out like that. "Forget it. Why were you looking for me, Lassiter?"

He removed his hat and laid it on the table as he slid onto the seat facing her. "Two things. I've got a message for you. Also, you might help me on an . . . uh . . . investigation."

"Right. You want my help—a woman's help. Okay. Sure, and I'm believing every word you say, oh you so strong and more intelligent sex of the species."

"Doesn't take much to get you into a high-and-mighty fit, does it?"

"You, Lassiter, are the one that walked out of the Blue-bonnet Restaurant after getting me there under the pretense that we'd talk about the case."

"Guilty. I did have an ulterior motive. I wanted to see you eat and not look so gray and worried." He chuckled, signaled Ozzie for a glass of tea and winked.

"Don't do that."

"What?"

"Wink. You're always winking."

"Hell, you silly woman, it's body language. Means I'm mostly kidding you."

Ozzie shoved one of the oversized Mason tea jars in front of Quannah. He drank and said nothing more until he finished the tea.

She swore not to break the silence, and that she would not be the one to leave. It was her booth first, by dang, and Lassiter and his ponytail could go take a jump off Maple Leaf Bridge. He'd have to say what he came for soon. He didn't; he just sat there and smiled once, then got a serious set to his jaw and that look in his eyes that unnerved her, but she would not give him the satisfaction of knowing it bothered her. And why in Hades did it bother her?

Because you're vulnerable with him in some way.

Certainly not.

Because you don't want a repeat mistake like Dan Oxhandler.

She wouldn't break the silence, by damn. She wouldn't. Well, hell, maybe just to get rid of him. "Oh . . . what?"

"What?"

"You said you had a message, too."

"Yes, ma'am, I do, but I've been pondering how to break this to you, because I don't quite understand what Uncle Brigham said, either." He reached toward her as if to take hold of her hand.

Frowning, she jerked away. He could get her in a foul mood faster than anyone she knew, including Frankie Buzader in her fifth period class. "Let me guess. You're leading up to one of your nasty remarks by sneaking in sideways, right? Let's see, now what could it be? You've discovered research proving that females have less muscle per square inch and therefore are inferior?"

"Now, wait a minute."

She waggled a finger in his face. "Well, let me tell you, Lassiter, we have more gray cells working upstairs than men, no matter what other biological facts you want to bring into the argument."

"Hold it, you silly woman, I didn't—"

"Call me silly woman again and you're going to need a shin splint." Hell, her temples throbbed, and she could barely catch her breath. Worse, much worse, she didn't know what they were arguing about. She felt like a fool for letting her mouth outrun her brain and damn everything to Hades, she was embarrassed for acting like one of her students.

"*Winyan,* I was trying to figure how best to break the news that Uncle Brigham sent, you silly—"

She kicked his shin, got out of the booth and said, "I warned you, Lassiter."

"*Hiya!*" He glared, reaching for his hat.

She stood transfixed. Oh my gosh, she'd gone too far. What the hell was the matter with her?

He slammed his Stetson on his head, got up and grabbed her wrist. "Put it on the tab, Ozzie. We're in a hurry."

"Lassiter, stop this minute. What do you think—?"

Pulling her out the door, he answered with a growl. "If you had closed your mouth for two minutes, I could have been nice. I tried. You remember that, Gallagher, okay?" He stood with arms akimbo until she got in his Rover. Getting in on the driver's side, he winced and rubbed his shin. He mumbled and growled as he started the engine.

She caught only snatches.

"Damn . . . busybody . . . vicious . . . can't make sense . . . mouthy *Winyan* . . . be locked up."

Revving the motor, he roared out of the parking lot.

Her head crashed back against the headrest. Stars exploded. Sitting upright, she rubbed her head and said, "Lassiter, you're the one who should be locked up."

He whipped the truck to the left and careened around the corner on two wheels. When he straightened the Land Rover, he smiled. "I feel better. How about you?"

She swung a shaky hand to slap his face, but he grabbed her wrist as if the act were no more trouble than brushing away a fly. "You don't *ever* want to do that." His eyes narrowed, but he smiled.

"Your silver star and six-gun came out of a Cracker Jack box, right?" She folded her arms in front of her. "I don't know why I kicked you. It was infantile, and I've never—" Sighing, she swallowed and pushed one word past tightened lips. "Sorry."

"What was that?"

"I didn't stutter, Quannah Parker."

"Lassiter."

She rubbed her temples and nodded. "Freudian slip."

Driving at a sane speed, he said, "Now that's what I would expect from an intelligent and well-informed teacher. If you're in the listening mode, Gallagher, this is important, really. That's why I was trying to figure out how best to tell you."

"If the Great Chief of the Road cares to give it, yes, I'm listening." What the hey. The sun on her face made everything better with the world, and she couldn't keep her anger at a red-hot pitch, especially when she didn't know what in blazes she was angry about, except that she was afraid of allowing him to get too close to . . . the *real* her.

He pulled to a stop at the Nickleberry Hospital and grinned, an action that softened his features.

She sat stiffly and waited for him to open the door. Finally, she faced him. He covered her hand with his own, but this time she didn't pull away. Something in the way he tilted his head, or maybe the way his dark eyes telegraphed seriousness, made her heartbeat quicken. The message, whatever it was, didn't bode any good.

"What was the message? Why are we at the hospital? Who?"

"Why? A stroke. A mild one the doctor said."

"Sheriff Tucker?"

He shook his head, patted her hand and got out. "Come on. What's keeping you?"

"The door, Lassiter. In civilized societies, the man—"

From his side, he pointed. "Pull that thingamajig right there. The handle."

"Yes, I know, Lassiter." She wasn't about to tell him how all the thingamajigs in life confused her. She couldn't count the times she'd been stymied by some blasted whatchamacallit that was so easy for everyone else to manipulate. On her third try, she got it open.

"Is it a student? Another of the honors students? Hah,

that ought to prove something to Sheriff Tucker."

"*Hiya,* woman. No, not a student."

He took large strides toward the hospital's entryway. She rushed out of the vehicle, slammed the door and said, "Wait up, Lassiter. Who?"

"A Mrs. Truffle. A special friend of yours?"

Her heart skipped a beat and then began a frantic cha-cha-cha against her ribs. "No. Auntie. How?"

"Sorry, Gallagher, I didn't know. She the feisty old lady who sat with us in the restaurant?"

Absently, she nodded and repeated, "How?"

Taking a hold on her elbow, he hustled her into the elevator. "Happened about three hours ago."

He grabbed her hands, and she was thankful for the warmth. All the sun's heat had drained from her.

"She's okay, Gallagher. Uncle Brigham said so, but she's worried and wants you to find Charlie Brown."

"Charlie Brown? Who in blue thunder is Charlie Brown?"

"You got me. Here we are. This room."

She rushed inside, halted at the sight of the fragile woman barely making a bulge under the crisp sheet. Unbidden tears sprang to her eyes. She approached the bed. With one finger, she touched Minnie's hand.

"Oh, Willi, you're safe," whispered Aunt Minnie around a tube which stuck out of her nose. "Worried about . . . Charlie Brown."

"Don't try to talk."

"He's helpless. India . . . kill him. Oh, there's . . . something . . . else. Have to warn . . . you."

"Warn me? Nonsense. They've got you so medicated, you don't know what you're talking about."

"She's drifted off," Quannah said. "You're as white as she is. Sit down on the bed." The phone rang. Continuing to hold his hand palm outward to quiet her, he answered.

"Yeah, I got her here, Uncle Brigham. *Han?* Oh, really?" He lowered his hand and turned his back to her.

What was going on? He had no right to keep anything from her. She glared at his broad back and the thong-tied ponytail. She'd like to cut the damned thing off. Who did he think he was to order her around, tell her what to do when Auntie, the dearest and—? She blinked against burning tears and wiped moisture away from the corner of one eye.

Quannah leaned back and rocked on his boot heels. "Yeah, is that so?" He glared over his shoulder at her.

What the heck had she done?

Hanging up the phone, he marched up to her.

"I want to know."

He held up a palm and narrowed his eyes. "Sit down and—"

"But—"

"—*and* I'll explain."

She sat, crossing her ankles and drawing her feet as far back as possible while her heart fishtailed against her ribs.

"That's better. Uncle Brigham sent me to find you not because your aunt had her mild stroke, but why. First, she got an ugly phone call." He raised an eyebrow. "That's your fault."

"My fault?"

"Don't prattle on," he said, "I'll tell you."

"Maybe sometime today?"

Shaking his head as if remonstrating a child, he said, "You've been sticking your nose in where it's not wanted, asking questions you've no right to ask. Uncle Brigham says that's a habit of yours. Pity."

He tightened his lips and breathed deeply. "Some jerk calls your aunt, tells her to stop you or he will. I believe"—he paused and studied the ceiling—"the caller told her some of the rather violent ways he might halt your activities."

"Oh, Auntie." She placed trembling fingers on her aunt's arm below where the IV was taped. "I'm so sorry."

"That wasn't all," Quannah said. He stood in front of her and folded his arms in his Big Chief stance. "Poor little lady walked outside her apartment. A rooster, hanging head down and with its throat cut, was strung onto the doorknob. Picture the blood draining out all over her walkway. Nasty, real nasty, Gallagher. You'd think you'd have more respect for an old lady like that."

"I didn't do anything."

Palm outward again, he shook his head. "No, but you're the cause. Stop meddling where a woman shouldn't meddle."

She jumped off the bed. "You insufferable red-faced—"

"Willi?" Minnie lifted her fingers in a pleading gesture.

"Now, look what you've done, you . . . you . . . savage. She's upset."

"I did not jolt the bed when jumping off," he said with the fingers of both hands spread across his chest. He pointed a finger at her and raised an eyebrow.

"Willi, see Charlie Brown, won't you?"

"Of course, but who is he, and where will I find him?"

"India Lou . . ." Minnie slowly closed her eyelids, but finally spoke again. "Mr. Investigator, she's the only near kin I've got."

"Well, now, ma'am, I can't do anything with—"

"Yes, you can. Please." Opening her eyes, she grasped his strong hand. "She gets into so much trouble, and she's—" A yawn interrupted the flow of words.

Gently, Quannah eased her tiny hand underneath the sheet and backed away.

Smacking dry lips, Minnie said, "—accident-prone. Her curiosity, you know."

Willi smiled and kissed her aunt's cheek. "Rambling about who knows what. Don't pay any attention, Lassiter. It's nothing that concerns you."

Caprithia Feather knocked on the door frame and entered. "You were kind, kind, kind to step in this morning," she said to Willi, "and I've come to return the favor." She deftly straightened Minnie's pillow and positioned her IV arm more comfortably.

She smiled at Quannah. "You're Brigham Tucker's nephew, aren't you? We're so very, very, very proud of Sheriff Tucker. Well, of course, guess you and your uncle talk shop all the time. You're that special investigator with the Texas Rangers. Exciting, exciting. Guess you're on vacation? You don't have your pistol or badge or anything."

"No, ma'am. In fact, Galla—Ms. Gallagher and I need some R and R right now. We have to look up Charlie."

Caprithia tilted her head. "Charlie Henderson? He's down at the barber shop. I know him really well."

"No, ma'am. A different Charlie."

Diving into her enormous bag, Caprithia came up with glitter in her hair and a stickum note on one finger. She shook it loose into the trash can. "Oh, guess you mean Charlie Odom over to the Nickleberry Feed and Seed. Now, he's such a sweet, sweet, really sweet fellow, and he gave me some free fertilizer the other day. Don't know why. I was in the store talking to him for maybe half an hour, not any more. Carried it right out to the car. We would have talked longer, but he had another customer. A phone customer waiting, he said, but I never heard the phone ring. Is he the Charlie you want?"

First peering at his watch, then up at the ceiling and finally toward Willi, Quannah locked glances with her.

She sighed and took pity. "No, not him either, Caprithia, but we do have to hurry, and since the doctor said Auntie was fine, and if you don't mind staying—"

"Be on your way. I know how to make a body comfortable. Been doing this for years. No, no, go on with you. The sitter is with Mama Feather until ten tonight. When you return, Willi, bring some of your auntie's dusting powder and gowns, house shoes and such. A body is always more comfortable in their own clothes."

Willi kissed Minnie's cushionlike cheek. Only a flutter of eyelashes responded to her gesture. She followed Quannah outside after opening the door he'd allowed to swish back in her face.

"I can get to India Lou on my own steam, thank you anyway, Lassiter."

"She lives near the hospital?" His smile could only be classified as a smirk.

He was up to some foolishness, but she wasn't sure what. Blast, she had to mentally stay on her toes every minute with him.

He repeated, "Near the hospital?"

"No." She threw the word at him and tilted her nose in the air. "Take me back to Ozzie's Restaurant for my car."

"Say *pilamaya ye*." Winking, he held his hands behind his back and leaned toward her.

"I don't want a pile of Mayas, thank you, and—"

"Exactly. That's what it means."

"Lassiter, no word games."

He waggled a finger in front of her nose. "*Pilamaya ye* means 'thank you.' "

"Oh, you will take me back to Ozzie's Restaurant. Well, thanks, uh . . . *pilamaya ye*." She paused to breathe deeply. She had to lighten up. He was being nice, and he'd already warned her that his wink was to kid her back into a good humor. Besides that, he might know what

Sheriff Tucker really thought about the girls' deaths. Smiling, she repeated, "*Pilamaya ye.* I'm ready to get my car now."

"Nope. Waste of minutes to gallivant back and forth for another vehicle. You've got to learn to make better use of your time. Besides, Uncle Brigham had one of your students who works as janitor for the jail hot-wire your car and drive it to your farm. We'll find this Charlie Brown together.

"Who is he?"

CHAPTER 8

"WHO knows?" willi said. "Auntie might have ditched Rodrigo last night after his gallantries with Hortense. Charlie might be an old flame, a new flame, a boozer, a clown or a banker. You can't ever tell with Auntie. Only Charlie Brown I know is the one in the song."

Quannah scratched his head under his hat. *"He's a clown, that Charlie Brown?"*

"That's the one."

She reached for the Rover's door handle, but he pulled her hand away, saluted her by touching two fingers to his hat brim and opened the door for her. Settled in the seat, she studied him. His skin tones evoked a pleasant response and she smiled, but quickly hid her reaction behind her hand. Damn one Quannah Lassiter. She didn't want to like anything about him. She would not get involved with anyone else for a long time after what she'd been through with Dan, and she sure didn't want someone who kept her at sixes and sevens all the time. One minute chauvinistic, the next the most supportive of men. Which was the real Lassiter? No matter.

When he looked at her, sunlight twinkled in the depths of his dark eyes.

Still peeking from beneath her lashes and reaching for the radio, she asked, "You like golden oldies?"

"I found my thrill on Blueberry Hill, went walking after midnight and shook, rattled and rolled with the best of them. As an aside, reservations produce the best drummers and foot stompers this side of the Missouri."

She grinned and gave directions to turn left as he drove out of the hospital parking lot. Minutes later, they arrived at her aunt's apartment complex. Lassiter got out and locked his door, which gave her a moment to study him as he walked around the Rover. She liked that he could laugh at himself, not just her, and best of all she hadn't had that unnerving feeling he was reading her mind. Be that as it may, he wasn't going to get the better of her again. On the second try she opened the truck door and hopped down the high step.

About to grasp the handle, Quannah withdrew his hand, raised an eyebrow and nodded. When she strode purposefully in front of him to reach the apartment, India Lou Aiken opened the door before Willi could knock.

India Lou's ebony skin was covered in a layer of perspiration, and she scowled.

"What is the matter?" Willi asked, staggering back a step.

"I ain't a-gonna put up with that lowdown scum no more. Don't care what your auntie says. I'm a-gonna kill that Charlie Brown. Bottom line, I'm a-gonna kill the sucker."

"That's why Auntie wanted me to hurry."

India Lou smiled and nodded at Quannah. "Didn't know you had your boyfriend with you."

"He's not. We're—we're working together."

India Lou's sigh could have been felt all the way down

Licorice Lane. "Too bad," she said, patting Willi's arm. "Someday, someday." She turned her six-foot-plus frame around and walked inside. Over her shoulder she said, "You all comes right on in here. Wish I hadn't been over visiting next door when that old rooster was left hanging on the door. I'd a-done somebody some harm, yes, ma'am, if I'd a-caught them. I talked with your auntie 'bout two hour ago. How she be getting along now?" India Lou had Willi and Quannah seated on a pink velvet sofa with glasses of frosty tea in hand before Willi answered.

"She's going to be fine. The stroke was so minor it can barely be termed as that. She'll be fine." She whispered the last affirmation to convince herself.

"You be here for that lowlife."

"Uh—lowlife?"

"Charlie Brown." India Lou heaved her bulk out of a chair. She reached one long muscled arm around and rubbed her back. "This here is why I can't do that high school work no more and can't take care of Charlie Brown." Her black face lit up with a toothy grin—a smile that had won Willi over many years ago. "I likes a-working *with* a quality lady like your auntie. She onliest has this little kitchen what needs mopping." Frowning, she scratched her head. " 'Course, needs more mopping with the *three* of us here, but she lets me cook, and I love to make vittles for a 'preciative audience. Got a bedroom here, too. Bottom line, we's company for each other." She stretched and said, "But, I ain't a-gonna put up with the likes of Charlie Brown." She took long strides down the hall, opened the bathroom door and returned. A black streak of fur flew between her feet. "Here he be."

Charlie Brown woofed once in Quannah's direction, then ran toward Willi and bounded into her lap. "Ah, good puppy, down, doggie."

Quannah reached over and rubbed behind the dachshund's ears. *"Sunka kin cistila."*

Quirking up one side of her mouth, Willi waited.

"Small dog." Quannah leaned back to study Charlie Brown. "Not much there for the stew pot."

"You don't really eat—?" Willi sighed and petted the dachshund. Little fellow was the softest sensation, like stroking velvet come to warm life. The pup nuzzled her hand with his pointed nose and blinked long lashes over big doe eyes, mocha brown and moist, ready-to-cry-or-laugh eyes.

"This is Charlie Brown?"

"Yes, ma'am, that's him all right. Your auntie wanted to have him house-trained before your birthday."

"My birthday?"

"Bottom line, he's an early birthday gift. With you a-getting so old like and not seeming to make any headway with that Oxhandler fellow, your auntie thought some companionship was better than none, 'specially considering how you be always getting in the broadside of trouble." India Lou patted her on the shoulder. "Ain't it your thirty-third coming up?"

Grinding out each word, Willi said, "We'll discuss this later, India Lou." Willi imagined a mirror reflecting her at age ninety-nine. She rubbed her temples while she managed one of those smiles that she hoped said Please-for-God's-sake-and-Budda's-shut-your-ever-loving-mouth.

Seemingly undaunted by her pained expression, India Lou said, "Maybe thirty-four?"

"Four? Thirty-thr—? . . . uh, I'm thirty-something, and my birthday isn't until, well, later."

"December," Quannah chimed in and poked Charlie Brown's side. "That pup wouldn't even make good baby-back ribs."

Willi's face grew hot. How did he know her birth month?

"You'll be," said Quannah, squinting and then whistling as if approaching an outrageous sum, "*wicemna yamni sam nunpa* years old. I can translate that if you'd like."

He had an uncanny way of being right on the mark and probably had thirty-two years in mind.

She said, "No, thank you."

Waggling his finger in front of her nose again, he said, "Can you say that in Lakota?"

I don't want to say any—"

"Maybe India Lou's right. Might be *wicemna yamni sam topa* or thirty and—"

"All right, thank you, no . . . uh . . . a pile of Mayas."

"*Pilamaya ye*. Gallagher, *pilamaya ye*."

The phone rang and India Lou picked it up and said, "How do?" She frowned. "Who this be? Don't talk that stuff to me." Her mouth stayed open.

Willi jumped up, placed Charlie Brown on the carpet and took the receiver out of India Lou's hand. Raspy breathing came over the line. This was probably the sick jerk who frightened Auntie. Her own breath quickened and a thin coat of perspiration made the phone slippery.

Quannah grabbed around her hand on the receiver and tilted the phone so he could hear, too.

"Don't snoop," said the dry voice. "Tell Ms. Gallagher to mind her own business. I'll make her bleed. Tell her. Like the rooster. Tell her."

"But I haven't done anything," Willi said. "Who the hell is this?"

Brows knit together, Quannah grabbed the phone from her hand and pulled a finger across his neck. Even she understood that sign language. She tried to move out of range, but backed into the lamp table.

He slammed the receiver down. "Damn you, Gallagher. He hung up."

"Wasn't like you had a trace on the line, for heaven's sake."

"Actually, we did."

"We? We who? What's going on here, Lassiter? You tell me right now, or—"

"Or what, *Winyan,* or what?"

She eased away from the table and walked back to the couch. Blast, she'd done it to herself again. Opened her mouth before she thought the consequences out. Or what? Very good question. At last, she snapped her fingers. "Or I won't cooperate and tell you what I know."

"You have only what I told you at the hospital," he said, placing his Stetson on his head. He tapped the brim of his hat and grinned at Charlie Brown. "Get your pitiful little *sunka.* I'll take you home, *Winyan.*"

That word again. What in heck did it mean? She glanced up at him.

Eyes sparkling and with arms akimbo, he rocked on his boot heels like a kid daring someone to take a swipe at his jutting chin. She wouldn't ask. He was probably dying to tell her it meant something like *weasel* or *buttinsky.* Nodding, she picked up Charlie Brown. What in the world would she do with the pooch? She held him at arm's length.

"He be a registered miniature dachshund," India Lou said. "Don't hold that baby that a-way. No. Gots to watch out for them long-slung backsides. They can get unhitched or something."

"I thought you were going to kill the lowlife."

India Lou sniffed and drew back. "Only when I mops the kitchen floor fifteen times a day." She handed Willi a stack of papers. "These here's special instructions and his fancy papers. Silly little pup has a last name, Von Munch-kin."

Frowning, Willi stuffed the papers in her purse.

"Your auntie thought he be good protection."

"He's not a foot off the ground. What possible protec-tion—?" At the stern expression crossing India Lou's face, Willi sighed, ending with, "I'm sure he'll grow into a strong brute."

Quannah filled the Land Rover with Charlie Brown's pine-needle-filled pillow, a wicker basket, various meat-flavored toys and his potty patrol box, then stalked back for a second load.

Warm and soft, Charlie Brown nestled in her arms. She felt the sudden urge to cry and knew the pup would un-derstand. This wasn't like her, but she was so damned tired. No rest before the trip to Galveston, then the girls' deaths. Now, poor Aunt Minnie. A tear cascaded down her cheek, and she drew the puppy close, hugging him against her wet face, which she turned away from Quan-nah.

He heaved a bag of Purina puppy chow and a box of liners for the potty patrol box into the back, jumped in and said, "That *sunka kin cistila* is going to be trouble with a capital T. Trouble. Hey, what's the matter? Sure, he'll be trouble, but—" Reaching his arm across, he touched a fingertip to her chin, pulled her around to look at him and with his knuckle wiped a teardrop from the corner of her eye. "—but, he's not worth crying about, Gallagher."

"Don't be silly, Lassiter." She sniffed and cleared her throat. Well, at least she knew he couldn't read every thought in her head. "I'm probably allergic to something in your truck, that's all. Maybe those rocks on your dash-board or that stuff."

She pointed to some dried weeds tied to his mirror. Her

nose twitched with curiosity, but she wasn't going to ask him simply because he expected her to do so.

Leaning back and smiling, he peered at her once, twice and once again. "Okay, *Winyan,* suit yourself, suit yourself."

"What the heck does—?"

"Yes?" His grin changed to one of those crocodile smirks.

Narrowing her eyes, she frowned, turned away from him and stroked Charlie Brown until the puppy fell asleep in the soft curve of her neck. Damn Lassiter if he'd thought she'd ask much less cared about those dumb rocks or silly weeds or what the hell some stupid Lakota word meant. Humph. Probably peyote. She'd read about those ceremonies.

The highway sights blurred and in her mind's eye she saw another world, *an encampment around glowing fires where a warrior with his back to her sang in a lusty voice about something called Wanka Tanka. His bronze muscled torso was coated with more than perspiration. Smoke swirled around his figure as he turned to face her. His direct gaze bore into her mind, took her breath away with its intensity, made her heart jitter up to her throat, and she screamed out, a word: "Heyokah."*

Only when the bluebonnet field came into view did she realize she'd said it aloud, and she glanced toward Quannah.

He grinned and winked at her. "Heyokah, huh? The Trickster, the Clown."

She faced forward. He's winking, so the word wasn't anything serious like that *winyan* word. Devil's eyes, not only could he get into her mind and draw out her thoughts, he could—she blinked and swallowed—he could put thoughts into her mind. Nope. She shook her head. Another explanation was needed here, a simple one.

She was tired, confused and frustrated. Because of that she couldn't quite remember when he'd said that word, but she must have unconsciously picked up on it. That was it. Simple. Still, something told her he'd never used that word in her presence. So, where in Hades did she get that message? She peered at Quannah from underneath her lashes.

"Heyokah, the Trickster, has many ways to teach lessons. If a message is from him, best be ready for things happening that aren't very dignified. In other words, you're about to be made a fool of in some way, or perhaps get into some deep trouble. The up side is that if you survive whatever Heyokah brings, it will be a valuable lesson for you. And, generally, his lessons are tinged with some humor. Just remember that some days, Gallagher, you're the top dog, and some days you're the fire hydrant."

Moaning, she leaned against the cool windowpane.

She had herself under control by the time Quannah drove the Rover into the driveway at the farmhouse, a rambling but comfortable home on acreage she leased out to men who baled hay and ran calves on the Sudan grass.

Elba, in a rocking chair, conversed with Rose Pig, a two-hundred-pound pink mound that served as an almost constant companion and, at the moment, as a footrest for the short-legged Elba.

"Her and me are contemplating what to do next," Elba said by way of explanation for not being inside cleaning. "We could weed the herb garden or we could do the laundry or we could enjoy the sunshine."

Willi wanted her to do the washing, but Elba would do exactly what she wanted in the order she wanted so Willi refrained from commenting except to say, "You've one more chore. Watching out for Charlie Brown." She placed the soft bundle in Elba's outstretched hands.

"This sweetie is soft as down, as sweet as molasses, as wet as—gosh almighty tarnation!" Charlie Brown looked thoroughly ashamed, wagged his tail and tried to hide underneath Elba's arm. "Okay, no big problem, right, Rose Pig? We just do the laundry first." Rose Pig grunted agreement and blinked.

"How do, mister," Elba said and nodded. She waddled off the porch and Rose Pig followed with a stately swaying stride that matched the old woman's.

"I don't think Charlie Brown's going to be anything but help with a capital H. Help," said Willi.

"Well, whatever. I'll see you later." He tapped his hat brim and climbed into his truck.

"Wait a minute. I thought you said my car would be here waiting."

"Kid probably stopped for a Coke or something. Don't panic, *Winyan*."

Leaning her arms on the open window of the passenger side, she opened her mouth wide, but the question stuck in her throat. "Nothing." She tapped the door, ducked her head and looked at the ground. "See you later, and uh . . . *pilamaya ye*."

"Anytime, Gallagher, anytime." When he drove away, gravel spewed up from underneath the Rover's tires.

No sooner had the Rover disappeared than she raced inside. Elba had a pink stickum message on top of the phone for her. Great. Her car had sputtered and died, but the kid had managed to baby it along and take it into Rick's Service, her regular place. They'd bring it back tomorrow.

Well, that wasn't going to stop her. She jabbed in the numbers of Dan Oxhandler's phone. What she wouldn't give to lay her head down on a pillow for just a half hour, but she could sleep later, maybe work a nap in while she ate or something. She tapped her foot against the hard-wood floor, waited and mumbled.

"Think you have all the answers, Lassiter, don't you? Think again. I know folks around here. They'll talk to me, you ponytailed renegade. *Winyan,* my grandmother's red garters. *Weasel,* huh? Maybe it means *crazy* like *loca* in Spanish. I'll show you who's crazy, crazy enough to come up with answers. If you suppose I'm gonna sit around and wait for that kook to leave me hanging like a headless rooster, you've got—"

"Huh?" Dan said from the other end of the line.

Jolted by his Oxhandler volume, she held the receiver away from her ear. "Sorry, Dan. Verbally getting off a little steam. Uh . . . I was just curious—"

"Tell me something I don't know."

"When you get here."

She bided her time by giving Elba a rundown on Auntie and by putting on her own brand of warpaint—Elizabeth Taylor's Passion perfume and Lush Roses lipstick. She'd leave Quannah Lassiter and his hat in the dust.

"Call me a *winyan,* will you?"

She lifted the top off the cookie jar. Bless Elba's heart. Placing a doily on a paper plate, she set three dozen Ranger cookies on top and used a colored see-through plastic to wrap them. "Perfect excuse to see Adela's folks."

Ten minutes later, she climbed into the passenger seat beside Dan Oxhandler. He said, "Good thing you speak pretty fluent Spanish, although I don't know what made you want to learn that language. And I don't know why these folk won't just learn English like they're supposed to. This is the U.S. of A."

"Dan—have you ever, for one moment, considered—"

"Huh?"

"Have you ever thought that maybe your attitude smacks of bigotry and prejudice?"

"No way. There are a lot of my brown *amigos* I like to sip Dos Equis beer with, but I prefer they speak American."

A mile down the twisting Licorice Lane, she stole a glance at him, and wondered for the umpteenth time what she had ever seen in him. She had learned the language because she was drawn to its beauty and to its people and their music. She was also pragmatic enough to realize the language's usefulness anywhere in Texas. For the next five minutes she tuned him out. He guided his beat-up Oldsmobile past a sun-dappled valley of bluebonnets.

"We've got to talk."

Peering over her shoulder, she frowned. "Did you see a blue Rover behind us at that last curve?"

"No. Pay attention, Willi, for five minutes."

Twisting around in the seat, she sat on one leg and leaned on the seat back. "I'm sure I just saw movement on the other side of that fence row in those bushes. See?"

"Huh? I don't see anything." Dan rubbed his forehead.

"Sorry, really." She looked at him with what she hoped was a compassionate expression.

He sighed and said, "Fine. Like I said, I hope we can be friends."

"Of course, Dan Oxhandler, we'll be friends." She tapped the top of his hand. "Now, what did you really want to talk about?"

"What did I—? *Us. That* is what I—" He studied his hands grasping the steering wheel so tightly the knuckles whitened. "You haven't heard one word, have you?"

She took the moment to search the area outside the rear window. Something glinted in the copse of trees, like sunlight winking against a piece of tinfoil. Shoot, now it was gone. "Uh, Dan," she prompted, "what is it?"

He sighed. "Will you help me find out what happened to D'Dee and Adela?"

"Of course. I've already begun. That's what we're doing now. Let me tell you. First, you've got to trust me that the conversation in the library was a discussion of whatever or whoever the girls were involved with."

"Okay, so?"

"They were both afraid. Oh, sure, D'Dee gave it the typical Oxhandler try of convincing Adela all would be great, but she was afraid, too."

"Who were they scared of?"

"That I don't know, but D'Dee did . . . or thought she did. She was ready to blow the whistle on the leader of this group."

As Dan drove the car over a rough part of Licorice Lane, the Olds bounced into a hole bigger than the Grand Canyon. She caught a glint of something again and tried to study each tree and bush.

"Slow down, Dan. You have to crawl on this section. You're rattling my teeth loose on each chug hole."

"Willi, if D'Dee knew who this creep was, then—"

"Exactly. She let it be known and someone didn't want that identity revealed."

"And Adela?"

"Well, Dan, the girls were best friends. The killer wouldn't have been safe leaving either one alive."

He snapped his fingers. "So who else overheard them?"

"What?"

"In the library that morning."

"I was the only one really close enough to hear all of the conversation."

He grimaced. "D'Dee is . . . was . . . an Oxhandler. Think I don't realize others think we're as loud as—"

"Okay. Others might have heard snatches. Let's see. Hortense, of course. Paul Undel was grading papers in the corner. The counselor's aide, Toni Benton, was testing some kid for the Specially Challenged class. Oh yeah, Jerald Stanley sat reading the newspaper. Couple of other kids doing reports like Lance and Betty. Even the principal came in to post the honor roll list. Dan, it really wouldn't make any difference. It wouldn't necessarily have to be one of those. Anyone could have simply mentioned some part of that conversation to the wrong person, and that's all it would have taken. Or D'Dee could have already approached the jerk sometime before the ferry ride. That could have been here at home or on the way to Galveston."

"Yep, you're right. Did you see that?" Dan pointed by tipping his hat brim.

"What?"

"Coyote or something over there in the woods."

Coyote?

Hairs on the back of her neck bristled, and her scalp crawled. She recalled the night she'd seen a man highlighted by moonlight in the woods beside the school, a man who had haunted her thoughts, a man who somehow knew the next words out of her mouth, maybe even put words in her mouth. Damn him. Well, she hoped he got this message loud and clear. Squinting, she glared at the woods bordered by bluebonnets, caught movement and a flash of brown among the leaves which made her think of bronze skin and said, "May your peace pipe choke you to death."

"Huh?"

"Nothing, Dan. Just wondering about *winyan* and Heyokah."

"Never heard of it. Japanese food, maybe. Why do you always have to be thinking, Willi? Don't you ever get tired of the brain going?"

Without answering, she touched her nose to the cold

windowpane. Yep, that was typical Dan Oxhandler, all right. He wanted a woman dead from the waist up and lusty down south. Near the high school, she pointed out the Zetas' street. "To the left."

Holding the plate of Ranger cookies, she punched the doorbell.

Adela's parents weren't home, but Trujillo, Adela's older brother, invited them inside. "Nice of you, Mr. Oxhandler, Ms. Gallagher." Trujillo's eyes, muddy and sunken, slid away from her glance. He took the cookies to the kitchen counter fronting the living area. "*Gracias,* Ms. Gallagher." No dining area existed. A few TV trays scattered about gave testimony to the Zetas' eating arrangements.

"The funeral. It's tomorrow." His shoulders slumped, and again his glance slithered into a corner of the room, to the floor, the ceiling, anywhere but at her or Dan.

"We know," said Dan. "Trujillo, do you think your sister jumped from the hotel?"

She could have kicked Dan. Subtlety was never his strong point. "Trujillo, if you don't feel like talking, we'll wait, but the longer we do, the harder it will be to find out the truth."

He backed away from her outstretched arms, but smiled at her and made eye contact for a moment. "It's okay. I can talk." Stuffing his hands in his jeans' pockets, he spoke to the thin gray carpet. "No, she don't do something stupid like that."

Biting her lip to keep from correcting his grammar, Willi leaned forward. He tried in class, had worked his way to Honors the hard way from two levels down. His agitation simply took precedence over grammar.

He freed one hand from his pocket, bit on his knuckles and cleared his throat. "She don't jump. If she woulda been thinking that way, hey, she woulda done something crazy long time ago." He clenched and unclenched his hand, finally stuffing it back into his pocket. He had that hangdog look, worn and dusty, gray and hopeless.

Willi spent the few minutes soaking up atmosphere and wondering what tack to take with him. The house, though a small structure, was sparkling clean, but an odor hung over the rented TV with the tag still attached, surrounded the one picture on the wall and permeated the covers hiding the old furniture. Probably incense.

Dan's thoughts had evidently followed the same road, and in typical Oxhandler loudness, he asked, "You all Catholic, huh?"

Trujillo's glance shifted from the dingy carpet, and he stared out the window. "I am Catholic. Only me. Want to see Adela's room? Sometimes it's easier to say good-bye when you can be near something of the person."

"Have you said your good-byes, Trujillo?" Trying not to stare directly at him, she peeked while pretending a great interest in the *TV Guide* on top of the television.

He frowned. "No, I have one last thing to do. Then I say *Vaya con Dios* to my little sister, if *Dios* will have her." Swallowing hard and sniffling once, he pointed down the hallway. "I'll wait outside." The screen door closed after him.

She wanted to reach out, hold him, comfort him in some way, but couldn't. His hurt was too deep to touch, the pain too raw.

She walked down the barren hall and stood in the doorway of the last room. The cleanliness hadn't invaded Adela Zeta's ten-by-ten cubicle painted bloodred.

She blinked against the blazing color and shivered. Everything else was candy pink: the bedspread, curtains, chair cover and picture frames. A sequined vest and a pair of faded jeans were strewn on the floor. Two pairs of panty hose lay crumpled on the dresser. To get to a pile of books, she shoved aside a plate covered with hardened egg and bits of bacon, grimaced at a glass with week-old milk crusting the sides and gulped when she uncovered a fork stuck into a half-eaten frankfurter. Ants had gathered on it for a feast. Papers and notebooks littered the floor, the dresser and an old cardboard box. The padded cloth picture frames contained depictions cut from magazines of heavy metal singers such as Rock Killer and Go Damn Low. Willi straightened a picture frame. Half dressed in cut-out pants where their bare buttocks sported tattoos of inverted crosses and skulls, the bodies were frozen as if each had just reached an orgasm to the accompaniment of a cataclysmic chord.

Dan opened every drawer, but found nothing. When he bent to look under the bed, Willi said, "Watch out. Anything could slither out from under there." Immediately, she wished she hadn't voiced the thought.

Dan lifted the corner of the bedspread.

"No," Willi yelped, "I mean it. Something—oh, be careful."

"Take it easy. Better go see about some hormone shots, Willi."

"Fine. Get your damned nose bit off by a rabid rat. I'd like to see a snake bite your smart lip. Go ahead. No reason to take care. Knock yourself out."

He whistled low and signaled for her to kneel. "Look. What do you think of that, huh?" He shook his head.

Her heart skittered so fast, she pulled one of Auntie's maneuvers and placed a hand over her chest. She didn't want to see what was there.

"My God," Dan whispered in his Oxhandler boom.

CHAPTER 9

" 'MY Lord satan' would be more appropriate," Willi said. A five-foot wooden cross lay beneath the bed. Like those on the singers' rear ends, the cross was inverted—the arm section was at the foot of the bed. Standing up, she bumped against one of the pink gingham frames on the wall. It fell with a muffled thud onto the carpet. When she knelt to retrieve it, she frowned. She shook the picture frame, and paper fluttered to the floor.

"Hey, what's that?" he asked.

Picking up the sheet, she spread it open; crackling, it resembled parchment. One sentence careened across the page in perfect calligraphy.

"Blessed be the bearer."

In a more childish hand as if slashed there in anger so hard that the paper tore, was a message:

"No, no, NOT ME!"

The red walls seemed to pulse and push closer and closer. Willi shut her eyes.

Dan waved dismissively. "Probably a special pass to get into a rock concert. I've seen all kinds like that. Line from some song, you know."

"Maybe." She shivered, opened her eyes and slid the crinkly paper in a side pocket of her purse.

On the way out, she stopped to say good-bye to Trujillo.

Dan shoved her aside and blurted, "What do you know about the cross under your sister's bed? Prop for a school play, huh?"

Trujillo blanched but didn't answer.

With hands on her hips, Willi glared at Dan and moved between him and the boy. Touching Trujillo's arm, she tried to soften her own words. This time he did not draw back, but he flinched as if she were going to strike rather than comfort.

"Trujillo," she said, "you've got to tell us what you know. Take your time. We're in no hurry." *Yes we are. Someone else could be in danger.*

She repeated, "We're in no hurry."

Dan opened his mouth to protest, but with one quick shake of a finger she silenced him and asked, "Adela was involved, wasn't she?"

"I can't tell you *nada*."

"Don't you want to find out what happened to your sister?"

"I know."

"Oh?" Dan said. "What do you know? You weren't in Galveston."

"She don't jump from no window, man. Okay? So, somebody pushed her. I know someone did. Adela don't jump."

He ran into the house and slammed the door, but he jerked it open again and with tears streaming, he yelled in Dan's face, "D'Dee, your *loca* cousin."

He gasped and stabbed the air with an accusing finger. "Always. She's always doing stupid stunts, man. You wanna know answers, man? She thought it was funny to scare Adela with these stories about *bearers*."

"Bearers?" Willi asked.

"*Yo no sé.* Don't know what it means, Ms. Gallagher, but D'Dee herself told me that—whatever *bearer* was about—that part, it wasn't true. She just got a kick out of scaring someone." He glared at Dan. "She killed my sister with her devil stuff. *She* murdered my sister, your . . . *family*." The last word ended on a screech and a choke. Shaking, Trujillo withdrew and slammed the door with such rage that it splintered on one side.

An eerie silence surrounded Willi. Her own fingers, trembling and unsure, reached to comfort Dan, but he abruptly stepped away.

In a true whisper, and because of that, so pathetic for an Oxhandler, Dan said, "No, no, no." His face reddened, and he stomped toward the Oldsmobile.

"Just shows how we've lowered our standards by letting *those* people in Honors classes," he blared out. "Lying little Mexican. My niece wasn't into satanism, nor any other cultism, okay? Her friends wouldn't be involved, either. My family has never and will never be involved in that sicko stuff. We have certain standards to uphold in Nickleberry. Granddaddy started the first bank and the First Baptist Church, right there side by side where they are today. Why my daddy was a winning coach of the—"

"—I know, Dan. Right." There it was, his damned closed mind. Thank Granny's garters she'd found out about him before committing for life. "Right, Dan. We'll just ignore the inverted cross. No problem."

Holding her hand over her mouth, she managed to suppress the ugly words, words that would say she might believe Trujillo. Cutting words to shock Dan into awareness that everything wasn't apple pie in Nickleberry, Texas, and there were cultures other than beer-guzzling, barbecue-burping Oxhandlers. Back inside the car, she stared at his bent head.

Shoving his cap low with one hand, with the other he pulled out a set of stapled papers. "See what you think of these." His usual booming voice hadn't returned full force, nor had his blotched face resumed its normal complexion.

She straightened out the sheets. "A history test."

"Yeah."

"From Adela's room?"

He nodded curtly. "Uh-huh."

"Why did you filch a history test?"

"Speaking of stealing, look at the date."

She did and frowned at the implications. "Dated for the week *after* spring break. How did she—?"

Dan just raised his eyebrows. He gunned the motor and drove away from the Zetas', the tract houses and the accusations against the Nickleberry Oxhandlers.

She said, "I wonder if the test has any connection to—?"

"No, Willi. A connection between D'Dee's mangled body under the ferry, Adela's high dive from the hotel . . . with . . . with a stolen test? No way."

Damned man interrupted her all the time. She blinked, but gave him the answer he desired. "You're probably right, Dan."

" 'Course I am. There's a bigger reason than that."

"Uh-humm." Clenching her teeth, she managed a tight smile and tucked the test into her purse with the parchment. She snapped her fingers.

"What?" Dan asked.

"Oh—nothing, nothing." She remembered something said at the Bluebonnet Restaurant about covens and their strange crosses, maybe some tidbit from one of Hortense's books on witchcraft. She absently tapped the end of her nose. That nervous nose-tapping was a sure sign things were about to happen. And that sense of foreboding crept in. Someone else was in danger. Auntie? Lassiter? Herself? Maybe this wasn't the day to be top dog, but rather the fire hydrant. Perhaps Heyoka, the trickster and clown, had something worse in store for her today than miserable time spent in the company of one Oxhandler. Maybe Heyoka had one of those lessons to teach—now, how did Lassiter put it?—through opposites, in a reversed manner. Sounded about as appealing as backed-up plumbing.

"Step on it, Dan. We've got things to do. Lassiter would have taken that last turn doing fifty."

"Is that so?" Dan slowed the Olds to a crawl. "Well, I *ain't* some stupid Lakota Indian named Lassiter."

Willi bridled not only at the purposefully thrown out *ain't,* which he knew she disliked, but at the word *stupid* applied to Lassiter. She clamped her mouth shut, but couldn't tamp down the next thought. "Lakota is the language. He's lived with Comanche and Sioux. Got the language from the Sioux, I think."

"Sure, we all talked about the Indian kid who came to visit Sheriff Tucker every summer. Tucker's half sister's brat. Couldn't believe she'd prefer to live on reservation land when she could have stayed in Nickleberry. Tucker offered to take her and the kid in a number of times. I remember Aunt Verna being real upset by that." He scratched under his cap. "Folks didn't know Tucker had Indian relatives back when. If they had, he'd never have been sheriff."

This time, Willi sighed and kept her lips in a thin line. Men were absolutely the most hardheaded, self-centered oafs this side of Tasmanian devils. Truth to tell, she didn't need either one of them, certainly not Dan. Each narrow-thinking layer he revealed disgusted her more than the last.

When they drove past the picture window fronting the drugstore, Willi did a double take. There sat Betty Norris chugging down a drink. Not an opportunity Willi could afford to miss. She asked, "How about dropping me at the next block?"

"What for?"

"Uh . . . shopping. I've got to do some shopping."

"How're you going to get home?"

"I'll call Elba. Your family is all at the funeral home, anyway, and they'll be expecting you to help. I suppose Ozzie's Rattlesnake Roundup is off for now?"

"Postponed for two weeks."

"Drop me here." She grabbed her purse, and when he wheeled over in front of the sheriff's office, she got out. *"Pilamaya ye."*

"Huh?"

Smiling her most innocent smile, she waved and headed in a brisk stride for The Apothecary Shoppe, a down-home pharmacy, malt shop and teen gathering hole. A faint scent of cough syrup permeated the place.

She jostled her way to the old-fashioned soda bar, seated herself on the stool beside Betty and ordered a cherry Coke. She'd just gotten the first sip and was enjoying the bubbles tickling her nose when Quannah appeared beside her, tapped the brim of his Stetson and sauntered over to the fragile scrollwork bench on Betty's other side. He placed his hat on the counter. A puff of dirt rose where he flopped it down.

Willi, looking over Betty's head, complained, "Mind moving that dusty eyesore? And where did you come from?"

He thumbed to indicate the back room filled with video games, TVs and local teens.

"You want to trade places, Ms. Gallagher?" Betty asked. "I'd be glad to change."

"No, thanks, Betty. I'd much rather talk with you."

Betty sucked noisily at the remains in the bottom of her glass, shoved it back and scrabbled in her purse for change. "Maybe later, okay?"

"You're not leaving?" Willi grabbed her arm.

Quannah winked at the girl and said, "Don't rush away on our account, Betty. Want another? My treat."

"Well, I don't know you."

Damn the man. He was going to be a constant stone around her neck on this case, horn in on her sources and be a general bother, but she couldn't be out-and-out rude to the sheriff's nephew. After all, for Sheriff Tucker's sake she had defended his kin only moments ago. Making curt introductions, she then ignored him and directed her questions to Betty. "How about a lemonade or cherry Coke?"

"Thanks, Ms. Gallagher, Mr. Lassiter. Lemonade."

Willi said, "I've been wanting to speak to you. I'm curious, especially after visiting the Zetas' home."

"Oh?" Quannah drew the word out, narrowed his eyes and asked, "You did?"

Feeling heat rise in her face, she was going to answer him, but Betty interrupted.

In a breathy rush, she asked, "Honest to God? You went there? Were her parents at home? Oh, my gosh. What did they say?"

Betty's eyes opened wide, and she splayed her fingers on the counter as if to steady herself. "Did you say anything about me? I mean . . . no reason to mention me, right?"

Frowning, Willi shook her head. "I'll answer *your* questions, if you'll answer some of ours, I mean, *mine*." Shoot, he was a difficult man to ignore. Willing herself to forget Lassiter's presence, she sipped her cherry cola until she could return her full attention to Betty. "What do you remember about the accidents in Galveston?"

Considering her answer, Betty drew patterns on her frosty lemonade glass. "I rode the ferry like you did, but honest to God, I didn't see what happened to D'Dee."

"I didn't really expect that, but I wondered what D'Dee was thinking that day. Did she mention any problem with anyone?"

"Everyone has problems." Betty pulled out her ever-present bubble gum, unwrapped two pink pieces and popped them into her mouth. She slurred around the glob, "Problem with one of the teachers about a test. I'm not sure, but maybe she'd been accused of cheating." Blowing a big bubble, she stuck her finger in the end to pop it, pulled the pink wad out of her mouth and poked it back inside. "D'Dee was afraid she'd lose her Honors position."

Now that was interesting. Willi smiled and touched the corner of the history test sticking out of her purse. Maybe she should show Lassiter. He *was* the law. Shrugging that ridiculous thought aside, she frowned at Quannah, who had his head bent to his own drink, obviously ignoring them both. Yeah, that act really fooled her. Perhaps now was the time to get an explanation from Betty and show one Lakota-speaking Comanche investigator she knew what she was doing. Pushing her unfinished cola away, she placed a comforting hand on Betty's shoulder and squeezed. Just enough pressure to signify concern, and then she turned loose.

"Betty, why would Adela have a Crows' Foot cross beneath her bed?"

She couldn't have said what she'd really expected to accomplish with the outlandish question, but certainly not what happened. Betty, with a strangled cry, ran out the door.

Quannah sat very still and said in that quiet voice she'd learned to respect, almost fear, "What the hell have you been doing? You may have just warned off our killer, you—" His eyes glazed over. He bit his bottom lip as if he were trying to control some fury eating at him.

"Me?" Willi asked. "How could I—?"

He held his palm toward her. "You do try a man's patience."

Fine. She'd shut up. She didn't have to take silly histrionics from some ponytailed investigator who thought he knew these hometown folks. Fool that he was. Even by biting her tongue she couldn't keep back one comment. Insolently, she looked him over from head to foot and said, "What patience?"

"Perhaps your yelling out the Trickster's name was a warning to me. You're going to get someone hurt."

"You said there was no case. Your uncle said so, too. Why then are you hounding my every step? If you two faced facts and did something constructive maybe no one would be in danger, but I do agree with you, Lassiter, on that one point. Somebody *is* in very . . . real . . . danger."

"Your inner knowing I will not question." He slammed his Stetson on his head and folded his arms across his chest. "If, and I say *if* this were a case, how under Great Eagle's wings could you manage to screw up an investigation in less than half a day? Damn you, Gallagher. Damn you, *Winyan*. Your name ought to be *Zuzeca*."

CHAPTER
10

WITH a flush rising, willi left a dollar on the counter, seized her purse and fled from Quannah's accusations about Betty and herself. Sure, she could confront him, but she didn't have the option of Detention Hall or Off-Campus Discipline, so not much would come of another encounter. One overbearing cop could cool his cowboy heels. Stopping and sucking in air, she grimaced. To find Betty was first on her list. Lassiter stood somewhere about number seventy-nine. Shoot, he couldn't interrogate holy nuns without getting their rosaries tangled. Straightening her shoulders, she opened The Apothecary Shoppe's door. Folks in Nickleberry had to be approached in a roundabout way.

She found Betty sitting on a bench in front of the drugstore staring into the spring's cumulus clouds while she chomped on fresh bubble gum, five or six pieces from the wrappers littered around her. Willi bent, picked up the wrappers and read one of the jokes inside. "Knock, knock."

Betty raised an eyebrow.

Good, good. The absurd, the opposite of what was expected, worked. "Knock, knock," she repeated.

With both cheeks packed with bubble gum, Betty garbled her answer. "Who's there?"

"Orange."

"Orange who?"

"Orange you glad I'm not the mean cop?"

"Ms. Gallagher, sometimes you're a little nutty. No offense. He wasn't mean to *me*."

Willi frowned. "You call me nutty. What about that cross at Adela's?"

Betty pulled her sweater down over her bulge, got up and spat the wad of gum in the trash bin. Unwrapping another two pieces, she shoved the fresh gum in and worked the gobs like a squirrel storing nuts on one side of its jaw.

"No reason to be nervous, Betty. We're just talking, not having an interrogation." Well, hell, here came Quannah. Maybe it would turn into another tongue-lashing. She persisted. "Is the satanic stuff cool? The in thing?"

"Honest to God, those phrases are outdated, Ms. Gallagher, like you know, those archaic ones you tell us about in literature."

Quannah narrowed his eyes, grasped hold of the chains attaching the trash bin to a large oak and shook them. "They should have more respect for this Old One."

Betty asked, "Old One? You say it like the tree was a person."

"He's not a Two-legged like us. This Old Oak is a Standing Person. He has offered his gifts and talents for many years to those sitting in his shade, those needing a momentary place to lean, those that admire the animals and birds nestled in his branches. When you touch his bark, he gives a special comfort, a definite spiritual healing." He placed his palms on the trunk, calmed and finally turned to face Betty.

"They really shouldn't chain him, then, should they?" she asked.

"I knew you would understand." Quannah looked up at the sky. "Do you remember who the teacher was?" Even though the question came from out of left field, he uttered it in a comforting, confiding way.

Betty tilted her head. She got up and sat back down with one leg folded underneath her. She reached behind the bench to touch the roughened oak's trunk. "Will the chains really harm the tree?"

"If left on long enough, yes." Quannah knelt on one knee and plucked a grass stem. "Now, young lady, tell me about the teacher who thought D'Dee was cheating on her tests."

"Don't know, really. Mr. Undel or Mr. Stanley."

"Betty, you were friends with Adela and D'Dee," Willi said. "You must want answers. Help us out here. Why would Adela have a Crows' Foot, a satanic cross, beneath her bed?"

"Weird. Never heard of such a thing."

An obvious lie. If she needed proof it was in the high color of Betty's cheeks and the fact the girl looked at the oak, the trash can, the blue jay and hummingbird—anywhere other than at her. Scrabbling in her handbag, Betty brought out a half-eaten Baby Ruth bar, unwrapped it and stuffed the chocolate and nuts into her mouth.

"I've seen you reading a book about witchcraft, Betty. I know you're hiding something." Willi placed a hand on Betty's shoulder. "I'm worried about your involvement."

"I've only read a book or two."

"What you read affects your thinking," Quannah said, pushing his hat back on his head. Chewing on the grass stem, he stared at Betty and then at Willi. "Ms. Gallagher is right to be concerned. Young lady, *you* decide what you believe before looking into things others want you to believe."

Blinking, Betty tightened her lips for a moment. She searched in her bag, but evidently found the mobile cupboard bare. "Honest to God, how do you know what to think, like you know, how? Unless you look into things, huh?"

Willi grinned. Good question. *Now, let's see Big Chief give the kid a worthy answer*.

Quannah tapped his chest. "Here. In here you have an inner knowing if something is right or wrong. All the answers are within yourself."

Willi nodded. "He's right, Betty. You don't really want to be entangled with this Satan worship, do you?"

Betty folded her arms across her round tummy, and pressed her lips into a thin line. Creases between her brows grew more pronounced.

"Can you tell me *anything* that might help?" she asked Betty.

"Maybe you better talk to the person who checked the book out before me," Betty said. "He was on the ferry when D'Dee got mangled, on the same floor of the hotel when Adela fell out the window."

Willi leaned forward, touched Betty's arm and sat down beside the girl.

"Like don't have a cow, Ms. Gallagher."

Willi bent her fingers toward herself in that give-me-more signal.

Nodding, Betty said, "He marked sections with those little yellow stickum sheets. You know, things about animal sacrifices. The name on the slip was J. Stanley, the guy who teaches across the hall from you, Ms. Gallagher."

* * *

"**SO** suppose we try your method of investigation?" Quannah said, with one hand under Willi's elbow.

She glanced up warily from underneath her lashes. "What do you mean?"

"You know these folks. They talk to you more easily than they do to me. You just proved that to me."

Willi blinked and tore her gaze from his intense eyes. "I guess we could see if Jerald Stanley is at the high school before calling it a day." Perhaps if she conceded this small thing, she might learn more important details he might have kept from her. In the Rover on their way to the high school, Willi said she didn't think they'd gotten a lot from Betty.

Quannah narrowed his eyes against the sun on the horizon. "That J. Stanley's name came up twice. What's the *J* stand for?"

"Jerald. In his defense," offered Willi, "Hortense, our librarian, has been urging the faculty to learn about the occult. He may have gotten the jump on finding out about the kids' problems. We can't fault him for that. Right?"

Quannah said nothing, perhaps because he was lost in his own thoughts. She studied his profile of aquiline nose, high cheekbones and the proud, almost overbearing tilt of his head. Why had she thought she might get information from him? Nope, the two of them were not going to be able to *share* details. Seemed as if he held back when she was ready and vice versa. She sighed, and one of Elba's pithy sayings came to mind. *A woman's got to do what a woman's got to do.* She had to get one Quannah Lassiter out of her way, so *she* could go talk to folks. Time was a wasting.

"I won't keep you much longer," he said, grinning.

Infuriating man. She'd wished he wouldn't do that mind thing, but she smiled sweetly in his direction. Damned if he'd ever know it bothered her. Maybe he didn't even realize he pulled words from her mind. If so, she wasn't going to be the one to inform him.

"How would you describe D'Dee's home life?" he asked.

"Sad. Her mother, Verna, is a devout churchwoman and active on every civic committee she can work into her schedule, but D'Dee existed outside that realm Verna calls 'my civic duty.' "

Quannah drove into the high school parking lot and stopped. Turning off the motor, he twisted around to face her and tilted his Stetson back. "Go on."

"I'm not saying Verna doesn't . . . didn't love D'Dee. She did. She just expected her to grow up like a plant— an occasional watering and dusting."

"How about the girl's father?"

"Lester Oxhandler always said he wanted to go to every play, recital, picnic or anything else D'Dee planned. But, he's a farmer." She paused as if that explained everything, knowing it didn't. Not by a long shot. An ache grew and filled her. She should have done more to be a friend to D'Dee, but she was too late, far too late to help the girl who had been enmeshed in chains for a while below the Galveston Ferry.

Quannah placed his hand on her wrist and squeezed. "And?"

"Could be weeks when D'Dee and her dad might not get to speak. He'd be up and plowing before D'Dee left for school and not get in until she was asleep. She'd leave little notes for him on the refrigerator and Lester would show up like Verna about every fifth occasion." The desolation of that picture was too much, the pain in her chest had burst, making her want to cry. She bit her bottom lip. Not in front of Lassiter, by damn. No telling what he'd be calling her if she bawled. She opened the door and placed a foot on the newly laid asphalt parking lot. A pungent odor engulfed her. Wrinkling her nose, she shaded her eyes with one hand.

Paul Undel and Jerald Stanley came down the high school's steps.

"Okay, okay." Jerald yelled in the direction of the double doors before they slammed. He brushed a hand through his white hair, which turned silver in the sun's glare.

"What's up?" she asked.

Jerald turned to speak, but Paul Undel beat him to it. "Painting walls and waxing floors." His nasal twang grated. "You all can't go in." He strode out to his classic Corvette, and Jerald headed for the ten-speed he favored in the spring and summer.

Quannah narrowed his eyes. "Which one is Stanley?"

"The one with the white hair. Premature, I might add."

"Got him."

"Got him?"

"I won't forget his face." Quannah tapped his head. "He's forever up here."

"Okay. Now what?" asked Willi. "We can't get into the test bank. Guess you'd better drop me by the house."

"We might discover something in D'Dee Oxhandler's bedroom."

"Lassiter, you don't have the right—We can't just walk in."

"Sure we can. They keep the key on the bell rope in back. All the cousins use the thing."

"Oh?"

"Uncle Brigham is sending me officially with the permission of the family. Actually, at their request. Her folks can't seem to accept the idea of an accident. They want all options covered."

"So, there is a ca—"

"No. Uncle Brigham made that clear. This is just a reassurance call—one he doesn't at the moment have time for."

"But, we'll be *searching*."

"Yeah, like you and that Oxhandler fellow searched the Zeta girl's room. Obviously upset the boy."

Heat burned her cheeks. She'd been right. Lassiter had followed her and Dan. The fact that she'd sensed his presence didn't comfort her one bit.

Quannah gunned the motor, hit the highway doing fifty-five and didn't bother to slow down for the first corner out of town. Some of the rocks on the dashboard shifted and one toppled over.

Quannah said, "Sorry, Tunkasila." He picked up the stone, patted it and returned it to a position between some shiny rocks, quartz maybe, and a beautiful piece of turquoise, her birthstone.

"Tunkasila? What kind of rock is that?"

"A Stone Person, Gallagher. This one is special, a teacher and a protector. It's bornite from the Black Hills." He took another sharp turn.

"Does he protect passengers, too?" She tightened her hold on the door handle.

"You must find your own, or . . ."

"Or?"

"Someone must give you a protective stone as a gift."

"I see, sort of, I think."

With a twinkle in his eye, he said, "*You* probably need more than one. They can be very strong Medicine."

"I'll take Geritol when I'm fifty."

Smiling, he let the steering wheel skitter through his palms, but said nothing more.

She peered out the window. "Why are you helping Sheriff Tucker? Thought you were on vacation. Don't you need to go back to the reservation for a Pow-Wow or something?"

"*Hiya, hiya.* No, I don't think so, and I've already done the Sun Dance."

"You're evading the question, Lassiter, and the Sun Dance was outlawed years ago. There's something more than a vacation with your uncle keeping you here. You said Auntie's phone was tapped, remember?"

"Did I? Maybe you assumed that. Either way, loose lips sink ships, *Winyan*." He glared. "And the Sun Dance has been revived." He ground out, "Now, is it the farm or with me?"

Shoot fire, if she didn't go with him, she wouldn't know whether or not he found anything useful. "I'll go see D'Dee's room." She took a deep breath. "Sorry about the comments. That ritual is obviously important to you. What do you mean it's been revived?"

"For your mental files, the Sun Dance is now recognized as a part of native religion and no longer on the books as illegal. *Sacred* would be a more appropriate word than important." After that tidbit, he kept silent. Damned closemouthed Indian. She'd like to yank that ponytail out hair by hair.

The approach to D'Dee's home was down a rutted drive. The stone house nestled underneath live oaks and cottonwoods. Wild onions and tomatoes grew next to the house and surrounded the area with a raw, fresh scent.

A collie, blind in one eye, greeted them by way of wagging his tail, but refused to budge from the cool dirt of his freshly dug hole beneath the cottonwood stand.

Willi followed Quannah, who got the key off the old bell rope, passed through the cluttered kitchen, the woodsy den and down the hall to D'Dee's room.

What a contrast to Adela's room. Smiling, Willi stepped on white carpet and trailed her fingers along sky blue walls. A quilt of blue and pink triangles lay across the bed. Tilting her head, she pulled out a book here and

there from the shelf above the bed. Typical reading fare
greeted her search: Harlequin teen romances, *Franken-
stein*, and *Dr. Jekyll and Mr. Hyde* shared space with car-
toon versions of *Beauty and the Beast*. Not having
realized until that moment that she'd been holding her
breath, she let it out. "Refreshing. She's . . . she was a
typically romantic teen."

Quannah rolled up his sleeves and went through the
drawers of the white French provincial furniture. "Interesting." He perused a paper in his hand.

She peeked around his broad back. "The same exam."

"What do you mean?" Quannah raised one eyebrow,
drew close to her and stared deeply into her eyes.

His intensity frightened her and she blinked. Well, this
was one time he couldn't grasp her thoughts. Good. She
shook her head.

"Loose lips sink ships, *Lassiter*."

She fluttered her lashes, smiled sweetly and walked
away with that little extra "oomph" in her hip sway before
she glanced over her shoulder.

His piercing gaze raked over her; he bared his teeth in
a grimace while breathing in slowly, so slowly, she knew
he was calming himself, not reacting with the first emotion of irritation. He slapped the exam on his open palm.

She would not give in. Absolutely not. Stiffening her
back, she thumbed through old yearbooks.

He said, "D'Dee *was* cheating, right? I gather that from
the date. That's why you wanted me to drop you at the
high school."

Her conscience prickled her as she said with a straight
face, "I believe in *sharing* information, don't you, Investigator Lassiter?"

He inclined his head like a shaggy buffalo about to
charge, sighed deeply and gazed out the window before
considering her. "Stubborn, very stubborn."

"I prefer to call it tenacity."

"So be it." Shaking one finger in her face, he said, "One thing only. I'm not at liberty to say more, now. I'm not exactly on vacation, and I'm not exactly on duty. There may be a related case to these girls' deaths *if,* and that's another big if, these deaths are homicides."

"I knew it. I knew there was something else. Now, tell me, just a hint about the case. Does it have to do with students at another school? Or is it the method of death? Oh, oh, what do you guys call it?" Snapping her fingers, she said, "Modus operandi?"

He waggled the test paper.

"Oh, yes, sharing," she said. "Okay. The students can't get into those computer test banks. Only the instructors."

"A more important question might be, why? D'Dee was an intelligent girl—an Honors student, on the honor roll every six weeks since she started school."

Willi nodded and folded the paper, adding the exam to the growing collection in her purse. She paused a moment and showed him the matching test from Adela's room and the parchment with calligraphy.

He held on to the parchment while he shoved aside perfume bottles on the dresser, and was absently folding it when Willi held out her hand.

"Is it important?"

"Huh? Oh, no." Quannah handed it back to her. "But, keep tabs on those papers. Can't tell when they *might* be important." Changing tack, he said, "Somebody would have to make getting the tests so easy the girls couldn't resist the few extra points. But who and how? We'll have to ask Undel and Stanley if they caught either girl cheating." He coughed. "I need a cold glass of water. Be back in a minute."

Alone in the room, Willi shivered. The sunlight shone through the white curtains, dappling the room in muted light, but suddenly the blue walls didn't appear so heavenly. In fact, they wavered back and forth between red, black and blue.

Conscience bothering her? Okay, so she didn't tell him everything. She'd bet he hadn't *shared* every tidbit either. She took a deep breath. She'd resisted the urge while Quannah was present, but now she got down on her knees and lifted the quilt edge to peer beneath the bed. She sighed with relief. An old perfume bottle, an algebra textbook and a stuffed dog lay there, but no Crows' Foot cross.

"*Zuzeca* might suit you, after all." Quannah's voice echoed above her. "Crawling being what they tend to do."

As she rose, she hit her head on the box spring. "Ow." She rubbed her temple and sat down on the bed. "Calling me a worm, right? Well, let me tell you so—"

"I wouldn't call you a worm." He looked offended that she'd thought that. He flicked a dust ball off her crown. "*Zuzeca* is snake. Not at all ladylike or schoolmarmish." Quannah clicked his tongue, but offered her a hand up. "Looking for something in particular? A cross maybe?"

She blushed, but turned away so he couldn't see. After straightening the quilt, she rested on the bed and smoothed out the wrinkles. She slid her hand under the fold of the pillows.

"No." The sun streaming through the pristine curtains seemed to falter a moment. The kaleidoscope of blue, red and black again swam before her. "Oh, Lassiter," she said when he loomed over her.

She drew out her hand and opened her fingers to reveal what she'd discovered beneath the pillows. A small cross, again with the broken bars slanting. Around the wood, strands of hair, stuck into place, stood out at irregular angles. "That's not glue holding the hair, is it?"

"No, *Winyan*, it's blood."

"Like the kitten's and the puppy's? It's just animal blood, isn't it, Lassiter?" She shivered, and even Quannah's arm around her shoulder brought no warmth.

CHAPTER
11

WILLI dropped the cross and closed her eyes so she wouldn't see the blood-matted tufts of hair. "What do you think?" she asked.

"You're seeking my advice, *Winyan*?" Quannah, using a handkerchief, picked up the offensive article, wrapped it and placed it in his shirt pocket.

"Yes, Chief Know-it-All. Does this tie in with anything on your case?"

"As a matter of fact, She-With-Acid-Tongue, sure as hell looks like it. Lab will be able to tell for positive."

"That's all you're sharing?"

"Gallagher," he said, placing a comforting hand on her shoulder and squeezing, "I'm beginning to trust you. Why don't you try that on for size? You don't have to fight the whole world by yourself, you know." Patting the pocket containing the cross, he strode out of the room.

In the hallway he said, "Let's go, *Winyan*. I'll take you back to the hospital before touching base with Uncle Brigham."

"In a minute. I'll catch up."

All of D'Dee's books and notebooks were neatly

stacked between the door and nightstand as if ready to pick up for school on her way out. One notebook was shoved behind the nightstand. Sheets stuck out every which way.

"Humm. I wonder."

Grabbing it, Willi leafed through a few pages. It appeared to be a diary.

The book created a bulge in her purse, but she shoved the bag straps onto her shoulder. When she got in the Rover, she kept her purse on her right side and thought about the Ranger baseball team, the UTA Lady Mustangs, Elba Kackelhoffer's crystal, the mating habits of salamanders, anything and everything but *the notebook*.

Halfway to the hospital, Quannah faced her. "Mustangs are exciting to see on the open range."

"Excuse me?"

"Horses. Don't know why that occurred to me." He eyed her with curiosity.

She smiled, patted her purse and said, "Lots of things are exciting." She took some pleasure in his puzzled expression as they entered the hospital and made their way to Auntie's room.

Willi said, "Auntie, the doctor says you're going to be fine." She patted the frail hand on the blanket.

"I know." Minnie's voice sounded stronger than the day before.

Willi bit her bottom lip and patted her aunt's hand again. "Rest. You'll be going home tomorrow."

Minnie nodded and slipped off into a medicated dreamland—a dreamland Willi feared more than she was willing to admit.

An hour later, after Quannah dropped her off at the Nickleberry City Library to do some "school research," she settled down to reading a magazine article about a cult called the Benjamites who were holed up in south

Texas—a little town called Hallettsville—where their leader claimed he was the Antichrist and today was Armageddon. Strange name for an Antichrist group to take. Thank heavens the mess was cleared up about a week ago. She ran her finger back over the first few sentences. Wait a minute. Smiling, she tapped the paper.

"So, Sheriff Tucker, there aren't any *cults* around, are there?"

Maybe, just maybe there was a connection, some tenuous thread between what had happened in Hallettsville and what had occurred in Galveston to two Nickleberry girls. Feeling the rightness of that supposition, a warm glow enveloped her. She breathed in slowly and out even slower. Yes, Special Investigator Quannah Lassiter had something to do with the case in south Texas. She read the article again, which mentioned FBI, local PD personnel, sheriff's deputies from surrounding counties and the involvement of the Texas Rangers. Now this was definitely getting interesting.

CHAPTER
12

AT one point in her research willi lifted her head and rubbed her eyes. A pimply faced youth tacked up a bright sign on the bulletin board labeled NEW THINGS.

ALARM SYSTEM COMING SOON. NEW LOCKS AND LIGHTS ON TIMED SETUP. SEE SCHEDULE BELOW.

About time the place moved into the twentieth century. In the 100's section she spotted Jerald Stanley browsing. Light glinted off his shock of white hair and his bifocals. Not seeming to find what he wanted, he shrugged and moved to the card catalog, a twenty-case wooden structure bisecting the room. He returned with a small piece of paper to the same area of the library. Ah, so he was searching for the books that she herself had garnered from the shelves.

"Won't be long until we have to herd our own kids back through the halls," he said.

"I'm looking forward to class. This whole spring break has been so . . . unsettling." She felt that was an understatement, but didn't think he'd want to hear a litany of her fears and concerns. Instead she asked, "Won't you be glad to be back in classes?"

"Sure thing. The sooner we get in school, the sooner

we'll be out for summer." His earlier grimace returned and no lightness of voice took the cynicism from his statement. He stroked the edges of one of the books she held.

"Planning on getting through to their minds with sorcery, Willi?"

"Uh . . . no . . . just doing a bit of personal research."

His eyebrows rose in a sardonic twist that made her jump backward. The aspect faded from his features when he gently pried the book from her hands.

"Lot of interest in this subject. Guess you heard about the animal killings—horses and sheep—down in the valley?"

"Yes. That was months ago, though."

"True."

He handed the book back to her. "But more mutilations have occurred. Seems the general direction is toward this area between Hallettsville and Fort Worth. What do you think?"

Willi didn't know why the innocuous question made her heartbeat escalate and her mouth fill with cotton. "I wondered about the kitten and puppy found on the school grounds," she managed to say.

"Does give one something to think about, doesn't it, Willi?"

He excused himself, saying he needed to talk to Paul Undel across the way. The manner in which he stated his intention boded no good for Paul. Willi drew in a deep breath. Jerald climbed the stairs to the second floor labeled 900's, HISTORY AND BIOGRAPHY.

She lost sight of him around the curve of the oak staircase. He might have gone on up to the third floor to the 800's, Fiction. That particular arrangement used to confuse her as a youngster. By age twelve she decided fiction offered the clouds, the stars and the universe. That section deserved to be above all the other mundane subjects—the realities of the world.

She returned to the occult. Wiccans, she discovered, were what early practitioners of the Old Religion labeled themselves. Many of the rituals and symbols came from the belief in the *Wo/Man* idea that the qualities of reproduction presented in woman and the abilities of the hunter presented in the horned woodsman governed all life and all functions of life. Well, that didn't sound so horrifying.

Eyes growing weary, she labored on. She drew her finger along the page. The horned hunter came to represent the present-day view of the devil—Satan. Satanism turned many of the curing rituals of white witchcraft, such as that practiced by Elba and Agatha, into killing and mutilating rituals—rites seeking power from Satan.

Leaning closer to the book, she squinted. That bothersome little inner voice said, *Remember?* Remember what? She sighed, opened her eyes and read the same passage. ". . . killing and mutilating rituals—rites seeking power from Satan." Someone at school had said something about *power,* awesome power, but . . . who?

She couldn't recall anything with the pounding in her head, the dryness in her throat. She'd gather information and ferret out later how it might apply.

A long set of questions circled in her mind.

Who were the bearers—the blessed bearers of the Crow's Foot cross? Or was she even interpreting the note correctly? Did Lassiter know more than he admitted? How the hell could she find out?

She arched her back. When she peered across the room, Paul Undel smiled from a cubicle opposite her. He waved. She returned the salute.

Caprithia Feather strode past with a Harlequin romance and an Agatha Christie mystery tucked under her arm. She never noticed Willi. She probably had to hurry home to

Mama Feather, Sweetpea and her life among the dusty ruins of the creaking old house. She didn't begrudge Caprithia her romance novels and her escape into another realm.

Willi yawned again. Time for a break. She strode down what she and her childhood friend, Francis, had termed the Hall of Horrors, a cavernlike corridor leading to the bathrooms and water fountain. Some misguided architect had erected the eight-foot-wide hall down the middle of the first floor's back area. Founding families insisted that the unusually large and strangely decorated building should be preserved as it was, maybe be made into a museum in the future.

At irregularly spaced intervals, a statue half embedded in the wall protruded outward for two feet or, in some cases, three or four. The local artisan who'd needed work during the Depression had decided the tone of the library would be enhanced with the addition of particular characters from fiction. Hence, soldiers, dragons, waifs and wolves stepped partially from the walls while snakes and slimy extraterrestrial shapes entwined at intervals between. A high vaulted ceiling with one fanlight at the end of the two hundred feet offered scant light. A half-dozen electric bulbs scattered a few of the larger shadows. At the end of the corridor were four doors, two on each side. She and Francis had always held hands as they slowly walked along, fearing some monster would come alive and lunge forward to chase them into the recesses of the storerooms or one of the lavatories. Even now, chills crept down Willi's neck. When she bent toward the water fountain, the chills inched across her back, too. She wished Elba's last card reading hadn't depicted danger around books for Willi.

Not until she was halfway along the corridor on the return trip to the reading room did she sense someone or *something* else in the gloom. She froze, heard a slight shuffling and turned.

"Who's there?"

Jack London's wolf stared coldly at her. Sir Lancelot's sword hung menacingly in the air. Tolkien's flying dragon, whose one great wing swooped from the wall, towered over Frodo beneath him, forever locked with one foot in the wall, unable to escape the great beast above. Only statues. Nothing living. She chastised herself, but admitted that Francis would have been a great comfort right now.

Seated again in an overstuffed library chair, an unaccountable uneasiness settled around her shoulders as if she were impaled on an insect board for study.

Willi squirmed in the chair and rubbed her neck, yet the sensation of being studied persisted. All right, she'd overdone it, maybe she hadn't gotten enough sleep.

She opened the book before her. A picture depicted a bloodred chalice, a goblet, which during certain ceremonies held red wine or animals' blood. Just like Jerald Stanley's glass.

"Yes, yes, here it is."

She trailed a finger across the picture with the caption: "Witch's Foot or Crow's Foot cross often inscribed on the inside bottom of the chalice."

Summoning her favorite librarian's assistant, she asked, "Marilyn, tell me who recently checked this book out."

"We really shouldn't, Willi, because, well . . . because it's . . . policy not to." Marilyn brushed a filmy gray curl out of her eye. Poor lady, she had pinned five brooches to her bosom today. Usually, she only had three. Made it easy for folks to remember her name, though: Marilyn Pinn. "No, not at all . . . the . . . uh . . . policy."

"Oh, that's too bad. I found a very intimate letter, and I know whoever wrote it would want it back."

Marilyn fluttered her hands across the brooches. "Are there . . . are there . . . uh . . . names on the . . . uh . . . intim . . . the letter?"

"Names?" Willi smiled and blinked. "No, no real names. Just Snuggle Bunns and Pookie."

"Snuggle . . . oh, my. Ooh, well, let me go see." Marilyn took forever and a day to get to the checkout area.

Willi frantically wrote gibberish on a sheet of paper and folded it. "Hell's bells, I'm worse than some schoolkid." She reopened it, signed "Pookie" at the bottom with lots of hearts and kisses. She peeked behind her. Quickly, she dabbed on thick lipstick and smacked the paper several times. "Forgive me, Marilyn Pinn."

Marilyn fingered through a file and returned. Giggling and pushing back the curl that kept falling in her eye, she said, "I don't think . . . uh . . . the epistle . . . could belong to either one of the two I found. The book is new, so they are the . . . uh . . . only ones listed."

"Who?"

"Jerald Stanley." She twirled the wayward curl around her finger and it spiraled to the top of her head, bouncing there like a lone antenna. "And Betty Norris."

"No, no, you're right. Guess someone else just randomly chose this to hide a letter in. Maybe the person receiving it will come and pick it up later. I'll just put it back."

"Uh," Marilyn asked, "would you . . . uh . . . like me to . . . uh . . . shelve the volume for you?"

"Thanks, Marilyn."

Holding the book close to her brooch-covered bosom, Marilyn trotted around the corner.

Willi waved, not feeling one bit guilty since she'd gotten the names. She tapped her pencil on top of the next book. Well, if nothing else today, she'd gotten confirmation about Betty's outburst. Stanley *had* checked out the book before the girl. Yeah, there was confirmation for something else, too. Betty knew exactly what the two crosses were. Exactly, and she'd not been totally truthful.

Someone tapped Willi's shoulder and she yelped. Hortense, whose arm stretched toward her, screeched, too.

Marilyn, gray curl drooping on her forehead, and still holding the book, approached. Lights flickered off the brooches pinned to her bosom to make them seem like five great winking eyes.

She said, "Really, ladies, we don't allow yelling in the *city* library. What you do at the high school library may be something else." She stepped around the corner.

Hortense straightened the ruffles of her blouse. "Sorry. We didn't intend a *ghoulish* display. I merely wanted to deliver a message, Willi. Here."

Hortense handed her a "While you were out" slip. Before she could read the note, Hortense said, "Betty Norris called your house and the school. Luckily, being in the audio storage room, I picked up the phone. Something about that girl is so . . . *ghoulish*." Hortense smiled at her own effort to work her adjective into a sentence.

Willi shut her eyes.

"Anyway," Hortense continued, "Betty seemed so upset, I thought she'd feel better if I took the message. Do you know what's wrong?"

"No, well, maybe."

Hortense hee-hawed and shoved the red frames back up her nose. "That tells a person a lot." She laughed again and the hee-haw turned into one of those adenoidal snorts.

Marilyn Pinn glared around the bookshelf and huffed. "Uncalled for, I should think."

"So," Hortense said, "you don't know what the problem is?"

Good grief, was Betty Norris in trouble? Willi looked

at the glint in Hortense's eyes behind the red frames. Willi
shook herself.

"What do *you* think it might be about, Hortense?"

"Boy trouble, what else?"

"Yes, perhaps you're right."

Right? Nothing was right. Not really. Did Betty Norris
know she had talked to Hortense Horsenettle on the
phone? If Hortense had disguised her voice, Betty might
have thought she was talking with one of the secretaries.
If Hortense were guilty and surmised that the girl knew
about her involvement, Betty was in danger. Willi tried
to appear normally alert despite the thickness of the air
pressing against her lungs. Her senses felt stifled by Hortense's proximity.

"How . . . how do you know it's boy trouble?"

"You can tell, can't you?"

"How?"

"Well, Willi, are you blind? It's sure not water reten-
tion. How mindless can girls be to get themselves in trouble in these days and times? There are wonderful condoms
on the market, although I admit many have such ghoulish
names."

"What . . . what are you talking about, now?"

Hortense took her glasses off and waved them before
Willi's face. "The girl is pregnant."

"Pregnant?"

"Yes, you know it happens to a number of high school
girls every year. I feel so sorry for Betty, though."

Willi noted the sincerity of the statement, but her mind
wouldn't quite accept that Hortense wasn't the cultist
who'd killed in the Oleander City.

"I need to get in touch with her," Willi said.

"She said"—Hortense tapped the note with her
glasses—"she'd be at your farmhouse tonight about eight.
I wrote the time on the slip. Take it easy on the child.

Here's the nurse's home phone, too, in case you need some help."

Hortense handed her another slip of paper. "Don't look so defeated, Willi. We should be glad Betty feels she can confide in one of the teachers. Must not be much love in that family. Just ignore that other little note. That's just my adjective for the day, uh—"

Willi glanced at the paper. Hortense's handwriting was as neat and clear as her attire, sleek—but just short of elegant. A *P* and a *U* was in the corner in lower case. What did that mean? Something Betty had told her and Hortense hadn't written all the way out?

Hortense walked toward the next room over, and Willi flipped open the tome before her with the end of her pencil. Pages fluttered past, until she stuck the eraser end near the spine and held the pages in place. Finally, a symbol she recognized.

"Yes, and I remember where." A goat's head in gold on black stared from the page. Tapping it, she whispered, "Caprithia Feather had one." Like a million others whose birthdays fell in December under the sign of Capricorn. Like Willi herself.

The feeling of being under a microscope before dozens of eyes haunted her. She surveyed the room, which seemed deserted. How long had she been reading? Maybe if she read something more wholesome, the sensation of gloom and doom would evaporate. She would explore the innocuous fiction shelves. The lights blinked, warning patrons that ten minutes remained before closing time. For some unexplained reason, Willi felt she had to find something to read, something pleasant and lulling, a good murder mystery, an adventure story, anything that didn't have to do with Satan worship.

Yet, every book her hand touched seemed destined to taunt her: *Rape of the Witch, Ghostland, Haunting of*

Georgia High, Wiccans Walk. Her breathing grew labored, almost forced. As the dark shelving closed around her, her heartbeat quickened. Someone *was* watching her.

The lights blinked again. The head librarian called out an obligatory, "Is everyone out?" and doused them.

The great oak doors crashed closed. Willi cringed and yelped. What kind of warning was that? Ten minutes could not possibly have passed since she got up to look for something light to read. Scuttling sounds behind her, then to the side, echoed. She crouched down.

Damn. She was locked inside *with* someone.

Willi crawled to the end of the shelving and headed toward the only source of illumination, the minute skylight in the long corridor. With her breathing nearly normal and the first flutter of panic under control, she pushed against the wall and stood. She was in the Hall of Horrors. Iciness clutched frozen fingers around her heart and squeezed. The misshapen creatures leapt from the walls and in the faint illumination from the skylight they seemed more alive.

One of them breathed.

Standing near the wolf's mouth, she gingerly touched its muzzle. She'd not have been surprised if she had caressed warm fur instead of frigid stone. Her legs betrayed her with their noodle consistency, what years ago her friend Francis would have called scaredy-cat legs.

One footfall echoed. Another. Shuffling. Rustling. The maze of partially formed creatures closed around her, suffocating her, cutting off her breath. Light-headed, she tried to pierce the shadows for movement. She searched her childhood memory banks to recall which critter of literature came next. Tolkein's grouping of Wizard Gandalf and Hobbit Frodo reassured her.

She almost had herself convinced that nothing more menacing than a heavy-footed mouse roamed the building, but the sound of slithering and a raspy breath sent chills skittering down her spine. Again, she reverted to all fours and moved inch by inch down the long corridor. If she couldn't see her pursuer, then neither could she be seen. Fine, no reason to panic again. Everything was under control. She made good progress until she bumped her nose against a knee. Her heartbeat mimicked an Olympic footracer's going uphill.

Not daring to move, praying that whoever she'd run into hadn't felt the small bump, she closed her eyes. No movement, not a sound. Lifting one hand from the floor, she touched the knee, a stone appendage of Alexandre Dumas's man in the iron mask. Heat suffused her face. She yelped, stifled the sound quickly and stood.

With eyes widened, she bit her bottom lip. If someone were nearby, he couldn't have helped hearing that screech.

No sooner had the thought formed than a voice, distinct yet grating, rose in an eerie wail to chant a strange incantation.

> *Blood and magick*
> *Origins of power*
> *I will bend thee to my will*
> *Blood and magick*
> *Origins of power*

An evil laugh echoed down the corridor to find a resting place—a hidden pocket of primeval and ancient fear of unbidden horrors—deep within her being. She clung to the Masked Man as if he were protective flesh and blood beneath her trembling grasp. Her heart did a somersault up her throat and back down.

When a feather-light touch suggested itself in the air before her face, Willi, like the savage of yore who ran from lightning and fire, raced down the hall and crashed

into the Dragon's outstretched wing. Behind her, sounds—
a swish of robes, heavy footsteps, the men's room door
slamming with its characteristic squeak—rose and echoed
in the empty building. She held her breath.

Quiet. *Too* quiet.

Precious seconds were wasted as she took steadying
breaths. Okay, nothing supernatural had invaded her
world. Probably a kid playing a prank. He'd be escaping
through the men's room window.

She entered the two-stall room. Sure enough, the window would have been an easy escape route since the sill
rested only a scant foot above the ancient flooring. She
peered around and with the help of the outside lights and
moonlight could make out some shapes in the room. She
could also see that the window was locked.

"Blast."

This Hall of Horrors escapade had been planned. No
one might believe her intuitive knowledge of the fact, but
that was neither here nor there.

She knew.

She smiled and envisioned Quannah, knees bent while
he plucked a grass stem with one hand and tapped his
chest with the other. *The knowing is within you. No one
can take that away from you.*

The sicko who had accosted her in the library believed
magic of the occult and bloodletting equaled the ability
to control.

An awesome power.

Hoping the attacker had provided for two possible escape routes, she stumbled into the ladies' room. The
window was closed there, also. Sighing, she studied it. If
the alarm was set in this area and if she opened the window, warning blasts would blare, maybe alert the law.
Just wonderful. Sheriff Brigham Tucker and his nephew,
Investigator Big-Chief-I-Told-You-Not-To-Get-Involved-

Quannah Lassiter would be at the door to arrest her. Or scalp her.

She had no choices left. With trembling fingers, she reached toward the window. Rough hands grabbed her and swung her around. Before she could respond, she was struck on the head. Great nauseating pain catapulted her toward a chasm—a fissure between a sudden explosion of light and darkness. Silk rustling against her cold skin sent a shiver of pure terror through her before that fissure closed over her head.

WAVES of nausea engulfed her and pain somewhere close to her left ear undulated through her body when she began to see a light—no, a grayness—around her. Hell's bells and blast. She couldn't move. Her hands were bound behind her. Elba said she had a hard head, but enough was enough. A golf ball wouldn't get knocked this hard on a round of play.

She swallowed against a gosh-awful taste in her mouth like gray, fuzzy mold. As she tried to sit up, she screamed, but no sound escaped the gag. Her head touched what smelled like a wet mop. Her neck ached from the rag tied around her mouth. She must be in one of the storage closets by the bathrooms. She'd never again doubt Elba's cards, palms or whatever else foretold danger. Damn.

She had to get someone's attention. Hortense? Paul Undel? Jerald Stanley and Caprithia had both been here, too. One of them would return for her . . . for . . . what purpose? She refused to dwell on that.

When she tried again to scramble upward, she discovered her feet were also bound. She lay on her side and crab-crawled toward the faint light showing under the storage room door. Turning over, she scooted into position, pulled her legs to her chest and thrust her feet forward. Luckily, her tennis shoes beating on the door created a booming loud enough to wake the creatures in the hall. She shook that vision from her mind immediately and swore off reading any Dean Koontz for the next few weeks.

Every time she raised her legs and hit out with her feet, a new shaft of sickening pain traveled the length of her body to find a lodging place at the base of her neck, but she continued to hit the door. She couldn't bear the thought of being locked in all night, gagged and bound and waiting . . . waiting . . . for the one who believed in *blood and magick.*

As she bent her knees for another assault, the door swung open and one of the janitorial staff with flashlight in hand bent over her. Norton Pinn, Marilyn's brother, said, "Golly, I figured some dang kid was up to no good, 'cause not all the lights are supposed to go off, none of these back here."

Willi tried to scream at him through the gag. He shoved his cap back. "Was just going to check the fuse box, and heard some gosh-awful banging. Guess that was you, huh? Golly, Ms. Gallagher, golly."

TWO witches bent over willi. A light from somewhere behind them silhouetted a stout short figure and an angular form. The phrase *double trouble* entered her mind and stayed there as a chant. She wanted it to go away, but couldn't push herself awake enough to silence the litany.

"She's as white as a sheet, as white as a ghost, as white as new gym socks fresh out of the package."

"Yes, Sister," said the taller form. "Quite pale."

Recognition gave Willi blessed peace. Elba and Agatha would take care of the pain in her throat, the pounding in her head. The cloud that shrouded her prevented movement. She couldn't reach out to them, but their words came through, as if muffled by cotton.

"If that don't beat all, I don't know what does. We get to take the aunt home from the hospital and find Willi has to stay the night. Good thing that Romeo, what her aunt calls her El Cid, come on around to help India Lou."

"Love is wonderful at any age," said Agatha.

Elba snorted.

"You get along home, now," continued Agatha. "I'll take care of her the rest of the day. You, after all, stayed the night with Minnie."

A roughened hand glided gently through Willi's hair, and a departing grunt came through the miasma before Elba's round figure disappeared.

Willi turned her head on the pillow, focused her eyes, and frowned. "What's that?" The words came out in a hoarse whisper.

Agatha gave her a sip of 7 UP that tickled her nose and lips, but was so cool. "I'll get you some ice water if that burns going down. Dr. Burleson said you were fortunate not to be killed with the germs covering that rag in your mouth, never mind the dang knock on the noggin." Agatha smoothed hair back from Willi's forehead. "That investigator fellow came by and left these wildflowers and a rock." Agatha moved the two items on the side table closer.

"Rock?"

"Here," Agatha said, placing the stone in her hand and closing her fingers around it. "He said you'd know what to do with it in time, whatever that meant. For some reason, he thought this would make you feel better."

"Really?"

"Don't worry, I'll throw the ugly thing away if you want."

"No, no . . . I want to keep it."

"Okay, suit yourself. I'll get a vase and water for the flowers."

Willi narrowed her eyes and stared at the huge bouquet of cowslips, squaw-weed, and purple snake-herb. She squinted. Yeah, a couple of stickers tucked in with one lone bluebonnet. Some lawman he was, picking the state flower. She raised the stone before her eyes.

Tunkasila.

He shouldn't have given a rock that meant something that special—a representation of the Black Hills—the Grandfather of . . . ? Now, what in Hades did it mean? Without finding an answer, she drifted to sleep.

At five the next evening, she emerged from the medicinal hiatus to eat a bland, soft menu of Jell-O, rice and pudding. Assuring her she would be okay with rest at home, Dr. Burleson dismissed her.

She stood on the lighted steps outside the hospital doors.

"Wait," Agatha said, "I'll go see where Elba parked and come back for you. No use both of us wearing out shoe leather."

Willi glanced behind her after moving down a few of the steps and onto the grassy picnic area. She crossed the grass and reached the sidewalk. A light breeze caressed her, lifting the fine hairs on her arms. Maybe she should have waited in the lighted area at the top. Reflections from an old pickup's lights cut across the curve of the parking area. Ah, Elba and Agatha.

A hand clasped over Willi's mouth and dragged her down. She hit out blindly, but the attacker slunk away as quickly as he'd come. Such strong hands. Brakes screeched. A door slammed.

Elba and Agatha pulled her from the bushes. "Mercy, what happened? Did you stumble?"

"No." She recounted what happened.

"Yep. These is sorry times when a body can't go out past dark without some drugged-up jerk trying to rob them."

"You're right, Sister," Agatha said. "Guess your headlights frightened him away."

Elba put her hand underneath Willi's elbow. "Was it a *him*?"

"Well, he was awfully strong."

"Strong like one of them Derby skaters on TV? Strong as an Outback aborigine? Strong like one of them Amazon women?"

"Well, I'd say it was a male."

"What'd he say?"

"Nothing. Guess there was no reason to after you arrived."

"Maybe we ought to tell Sheriff Tucker," Agatha suggested.

Willi rubbed her neck. "I'll let him know in the morning. More than likely it was some druggie. They're always hanging out near clinics and such, trying to get their hands on anything they can." She edged toward the vehicle.

Eyes stared back at her from the bed of the rusted rattletrap Elba called transportation. "Oh, my Lord." She clutched at Elba's arm to pull her to safety.

A soft oink calmed her.

"You brought Rose Pig."

"Sure, she's my familiar, Rose Pig is. Not a better two-hundred-pound sow around. But she does seem upset."

Heart slowing to a more normal pace, Willi approached the pickup bed.

The sow's pink snout, somewhat resembling Elba's own turned-up appendage, nuzzled Willi's face. They were old friends. She rubbed the rough hide and opened

the door of the pickup by reaching inside and snapping
the half-broken lever. The door swung open, and Willi
gasped. Staring back at her from the seat, right beside one
exposed spring, lay a poppet, a satanic cloth image with
braided hair, a small bell around the neck and a tiny book
titled in scrawled calligraphy *Shakespeare*. Definitely a
representation of her. Her hands trembled. For a few moments things blurred. She blinked rapidly.

"Something wrong?" asked Elba, coming around to the
driver's side and opening the door. "Now, isn't that ugly?
No offense, Willi, but that's as downright low as a snake's
snout, a worm's belly or a termite's bed, come to think
on it."

"Sister, hush." With great care, Agatha lifted the poppet. Light careened across the figure.

"What in the world?" asked Willi.

A knitting needle protruded from the heart. Fresh blood
drizzled down the needle and onto the ugly likeness.

In unaccustomed silence the three got into the pickup
with Elba on the passenger side, the better to comfort
Rose Pig in the pickup bed, and Willi in the middle.

Agatha, behind the wheel, asked, "What exactly did
you take from D'Dee's or Adela's room, Willi, that would
have made someone retaliate with . . . with this?"

Willi looked sheepish and drew out the parchment paper showing the calligraphy from her purse: "Blessed be
the bearer."

Agatha screeched to a stop in the fast lane; two cars,
horns blaring, whizzed around her, barely missing the rear
bumper. Slowly, as if nothing had happened to cause
Willi's heart to start an erratic cha-cha-cha, Agatha ac-
celerated and moved over to the slower lane of traffic.

"The way some people drive is enough to make a body
crazy," she said.

Willi loosened her death grip on the dashboard, swallowed painfully and turned toward Agatha's angular profile.

"What do you know about 'Blessed be the bearer'?"

Agatha squirmed and adjusted her satin skirt against her long legs beneath the wheel. "Some things about white witchcraft differ greatly from satanism or black witchcraft. I'm probably wrong in my thinking, so until Elba and I talk about it I'd hate to say." A frown creased her usually happy face. "I'd hate to say."

CHAPTER
13

ELBA'S herbal tea, orange pekoe, relaxed Willi as she reclined in the Herculon and stroked Charlie Brown's smooth coat. The dachshund blinked his big eyes. He occasionally nibbled at a tea-flavored finger she offered. Willi patted the pile of texts and her notes. Bless Miss Pinn. She'd dropped off everything Willi had left at the library.

Squinting one eye and snorting, Elba peered out the window. "Wind sure is picking up. Gonna be a nasty Texas spring storm, and not the kind of weather I cotton to driving through. Glad, too, that Agatha went along home. She was worried about Clyde, that fool cat of hers."

A sharp blast of wind howled, and the ancient oak's branches scraped against the windowpane. Willi's scalp prickled. She shivered and pulled her collar up.

On the lamp table, propped against the bookstand, stood the poppet. She kept her sight on the abomination. The braided hair flowed over the shoulders. The simple white dress offered a glaring contrast to the blood, dried now. Lamplight glinted off the tiny bell.

"Maybe you shouldn't have removed the knitting needle," she said to Elba.

"Had to. Didn't want you to have a heart attack or anything. Me and Agatha practice white witchcraft, not the black arts, but that don't mean that malice don't work on weak minds or—"

Willi glared at the old woman.

"—or confused hearts. Seems to me you've been stumbling around heartwise. Now, take the young Oxhandler fellow. He and you did real well for a while, and—"

"Elba, please, I'm tired, so—"

Shaking her head, Elba crossed her arms under her bosom to better wiggle her ample form into position. "Well, then, let me get on with my thoughts. Interrupting me can be more dangerous than derailing a train, than inflight diarrhea, than—"

"Elba, for heaven's sake, what about Dan?"

"He's one of them pretty fellows what's real stuck on hisself. Fine for a kiss in the moonlight, a cuddle in the backseat, a roll in the—"

Willi rubbed her temples. "Please."

"What I'm saying is, heart trouble comes in all kinds of ways. India Lou was talking to me and Agatha the other day whiles we were in Kroger's."

"About me?"

"Yep, you and the strawberries. You need someone interested in more than your body and weekend beach trips."

"Just you three talking, right?"

"Well, Mrs. Lyle, the preacher's wife, stopped by a minute. She showed an interest in your welfare, too. Wanted to know all about the weekends on the beach."

"Oh, God."

"Exactly what she said. Here, let me freshen that tea for you, but I'll have my say first. Anyway, we all believe you need a man what's interested in loving you even though you're always in trouble. Maybe a real strong man what could calm you down some, and just might be you need someone who stimulates ... uh ... how did India Lou put that ... a man who stimulates your"—Elba snapped her fingers—"brain. A feller who's downright smart, and one who can make you laugh now and again. You don't laugh much. A woman nearing forty—"

"I'll be thirty-two, damn it."

Charlie Brown woofed and sat up.

"Whatever. Close enough as to make no nevermind. Now, about Sheriff Tucker's nephew. He's turned out right—"

"Enough." Narrowing her eyes, Willi concentrated on loosening her strained neck muscles. "To ... change the subject for a moment, Elba." Frantically, she searched for a topic. Her glance fell on the effigy of herself, and she pointed. "Is this a special kind of doll, figurine, whatever?"

"Poppet. A warning poppet, just a dangnab warning."

"Warning. You did call and check on Auntie?" Willi intoned, staring at the rough doll.

"Done told you she's fine. India Lou ain't gonna leave her side no ways."

Elba ambled toward the kitchen, returned and handed her a steaming cup of tea. The old woman plopped herself down on the love seat opposite Willi. "Them that's using the poppet this way ain't up to no good, Willi."

"What way are they normally used?"

"We white witches use them for healing. Only the evil devil satanists use them to cause harm. 'Course I seen other cults like those Benjamites down in Hallettsville what does strange things with dolls, too. Makes me sad to think there might be that kind in Nickleberry. I'll make you a protective one."

The wind whistled and whined. Branches scraped sharply like chalk on a board. Goose bumps rose on

Willi's arms. Shivering, she peered out the window. Lightning careened across the sky, arced like a Crow's Foot cross with the arms angled upward, down another flash seared through a roiling cloud and a boom sounded in the distance.

She gasped and pushed Charlie Brown out of her lap.

"Bet Orlando's Dairy lost a tree," Elba said.

Swallowing the unreasonable panic that welled inside her, she said, "Back up. Did you say Hallettsville?"

"Yep. Been in the news since you left for Galveston. Guess you hadn't had a chance to sit down with a paper or the TV, though. Anyway, there's a compound down there. FBI and whatall has the place surrounded. News says police and the feds went in 'cause somebody in the cult is responsible for some deaths—satanic killings—down that way. Ain't folks plumb crazy?"

"I read that Texas Rangers were involved in a case in Hallettsville."

"Yep, same thing. Them Benjamites' special sign is what we call a Crow's Foot cross."

"You don't say." Willi tapped the end of her nose. "Well, that explains why Agatha wanted to talk with you first and why Chief Know-It-All pocketed the cross from D'Dee's room. There's some connection."

The phone rang, startling Charlie Brown. He barked. Elba waddled to the instrument and picked up the receiver.

Willi shut her eyes, but when she did the lightning in the shape of the Crow's Foot cross blazed across her eyelids. Damn. Sitting up, she looked out the window, cringed when skeletal hands reached from her fertile imagination to strangle her; she mentally kicked herself. Nope, this was no time to go off into a daydream or a nightmare, either. Gulping the warm tea soothed her to some extent, but she couldn't completely relax. What the hell was bothering her? Ah, of course, the poppet. She hid it with a napkin.

Elba, covering the telephone with one hand, said, "Out of sight, out of mind, you think?"

"Maybe." Willi held the curtain back with one finger. Was some crazed being out there watching her, wanting to push her underneath a ferry, down onto steel rods in the sea . . . kill her? Visions flashed haphazardly through her mind like a fast slide show. Animal blood. The puppy and kitten. Seagulls screaming overhead, ferry pistons shrieking, two figures at the far end of the ferry. A thong-tied ponytail whipping in the breeze. Heyokah, the Trickster, slithering through the tall grass. A decapitated rooster, blood dripping, hanging on the doorknob.

Willi shivered and covered her eyes. Then came the Crow's Foot cross and now the poppet. Somehow, all of this had a tie-in with the Hallettsville mess. That's why one special investigator for the Texas Rangers was in town. But what was the connection?

"Girl by the name of Betty Norris said she's gonna come by," Elba said, setting the receiver back in its cradle. "What a night to come visiting. Fool child."

"Good. She was supposed to come last night. Her parents have recently divorced." Willi didn't mention the teen's pregnancy. Just because Hortense said it was a fact didn't make it so.

"Be that as it may, you got your own heart problems what need looking into. Maybe you ought not spend so much time putting out the fires for other folks. Remember what we all said—Agatha, India Lou and me."

"No more, Elba."

"Okay, okay. By the by, for some reason the reverend's wife, Mrs. Lyle, put you on her prayer list."

Willi grinned, leaned back on the recliner and napped. **When Betty arrived, Charlie Brown woofed once and** seemed satisfied the girl wasn't a monster, but he wouldn't settle down again. He wandered around the room, poking his nose in one bookshelf after another.

Elba said, "Raining hard enough to drown the fish. Shoot fire, raining strong enough to soak Jonah and that whale, maybe even bad enough to scuttle the blessed ark. Here. I'll take your raincoat to dry in the kitchen. Could you do with a cup of hot chocolate?"

Nodding, Betty sank onto the love seat. Her breathing was labored and raindrops beaded on her face or perhaps it was perspiration. Pallid around her mouth, she closed her eyes for a minute.

"Betty, are you all right?"

"Sure. I rode my bicycle, you know. I'd forgotten how far out you lived. Even on my ten-speed I needed forty-five minutes. When I left town, there wasn't any rain at all."

Charlie Brown slapped a paw on the rug near her foot, but Betty seemed to take no notice.

"Sorry you had to wait so long."

"Don't worry about that. I'll drive you back home. You're not riding in this storm again tonight."

Holding a tray of corn bread and hot sirloin stew redolent with onions, big slabs of lemon meringue pie and mugs frothing on the top with cream, Elba entered and cleared away a space on the lamp table.

"Wow. Thanks. Honest to God, you didn't have to go to all this trouble."

"Bicycle riding can give you an appetite," Willi said. "Elba thought you sounded anxious on the phone."

Wind pierced the air with a sound as shrill as a five-o'clock factory whistle. Charlie Brown leaned his head back and howled.

Betty's eyes widened, but she swallowed and didn't utter a peep. She grabbed a fork and the lemon meringue pie. Between munches, she said, "I wanted to share some

things, but they may not be really important, and you
didn't hear any of this from me, you know, Ms. Gallagher?"

"Not a word."

"You were right."

"About what, Betty?"

Thunder rumbled overhead, and the lights flickered.

"Old lady dropped her sack of 'taters. That's what my
Granddaddy used to say." Elba, gathering up the tray,
grinned. "Better get the candles. It's about time lightning
hit the transformer. Never fails. As dependable as diaper
rash on a baby, as reliable as mucking time in the barn,
as sure as farts in church service. Never fails."

"Elba, go."

"I said I was." She ambled off, hips swaying much like
Rose Pig's.

"Now, Betty, what was I right about?"

"D'Dee and Adela. The coven."

A dozen questions crowded Willi's mind, but she stilled
her tongue.

Betty chewed the last bite of crust. "They had an initiation or something, you know, before the Galveston
trip." Lowering her glance and her voice, she whispered,
"The initiation had something to do with the cat and dog
found on the school grounds."

Wind reached a roaring crescendo, and thunder clapped
like gigantic cymbals through loudspeakers. Lights went
out, came back on and flickered.

"How do you know D'Dee and Adela had something
to do with the animals' deaths?" Willi asked.

"I heard them talking." Her glance shifted around the
room.

"Are you, too, in this coven?"

"No . . . well . . ." She swallowed, seemed to come to a
decision and sighed. "That's not exactly, you know, the

truth, Ms. Gallagher. I guess I am, but I seldom go any-more. I have a boyfriend, and I spend a lot of time with him. You and that Indian guy were right. Only kids who don't have any love elsewhere get involved. But, once in the group, they don't want you to get out. I tried to warn Adela and D'Dee. Part of the initiation is having one of those crosses beneath your bed from one full moon to the next. Too weird, but it couldn't hurt you." She repeated, "I tried to warn them."

The phone jangled. Holding up one finger, Willi crossed the room to answer. "Sorry for all the interruptions, Betty. Don't lose your train of thought."

She picked up the receiver. "Nothing but static." She frowned.

Betty held the napkin that had covered the poppet. Her mouth worked like a fish out of water, and she raised one hand to her temple. "They're everywhere. They knew I was coming. I trusted you. I was about to—"

"Betty, what are you talking about? Are you all right? Don't let that scare you. It was a warning to—"

"They'll kill me if I tell."

"Well, the poppet was left for me, not you, as a warning."

The little color in Betty's cheeks drained away. "I didn't tell you anything, if anyone asks. Ms. Gallagher, please?" The last word was a drawn-out wail that mixed with the wind's protests.

Willi tried to grab her as she ran past and out the door, but the girl evaded her, jumped on the ten-speed and headed into the inky void illuminated by lightning flashes. "Wait!" If Hortense was right about the girl's pregnancy, she shouldn't go off in the storm alone.

The screech of car brakes sent a rivulet of fear coursing through her.

"Betty!"

The word was flung back with an icy blast of rain. She
ran down the steps and into Sheriff Tucker, who tromped
onto the porch.

"Thought you had sense enough to get in out of the
rain. Shoot fire, everyone's crazy. Like to have run over
some child on a bike."

Pushing her inside, he wiped his face with a red bandanna. "Lord, kids are crazy. If I weren't shaking so, I'd
give the darn fool a ticket for not having reflectors.
Damn." He stuffed the handkerchief back in his jacket
pocket, where three more peeked out, all different colors.

"She was upset, Sheriff."

Slapping his hat on his knee, which sent a shower over
the hall floor, he said, "One of your understatements, mayhap?" After hooking the Stetson on the coatrack, he drew
out a blue bandanna and again wiped rain from his face
and neck.

She went into her home library nook. In his excited
welcome, Charlie Brown almost tripped Tucker. The pup
took an intense interest in the sheriff's shoes, as if they
had been to far-off places—exciting places like dusty
streets, barnyards and new car lots.

With one of his own massive paws, Sheriff Tucker
picked up the wiggling bundle.

His actions, similar to Quannah's, made her smile.

"Cute little feller, ain't he? Heard your auntie gave him
to you for company, seeing as how you can't seem to find
the right feller."

"Guess you discussed that while pinching the strawberries, too, huh?"

"Beg pardon?"

"Nothing, Sheriff, nothing. Nickleberry's still a small
town, that's all. I want to show you a doll."

"A doll?"

"There on the table. It's called a poppet. Would you care to sit?"

"Mayhap you best tell me what this here is all about."

He shook his head and pulled at one ear. He handed Charlie Brown to her and took the doll. Studying the hole left by the knitting needle, he pursed his lips and raised his bushy brows.

Setting Charlie Brown down and pushing him toward the far corner, she pointed at the knitting needle on the lamp table.

"What's going on, Sheriff Tucker?" She folded her arms together. "Your nephew isn't here just for a visit, is he?"

"Mayhap you better ask him that question."

"This poppet was one of many surprises the evening held for me, Sheriff, when I got out of the hospital. I guess your deputy reported what happened in the city library?"

"In the Hall of Horrors? Yes, ma'am. Can't say as I cotton to walking down that dark corridor full of half-formed creatures. That there place would give anyone the heebie-jeebies. I'm sure glad you inherited your daddy's hard head. But what were you doing there at that time of night?"

"Doing?" Willi strove to find a plausible reason other than her delving into a closed case, but she only repeated, "Doing? Uh, doing?"

"Three times hasn't changed the question. Yes, ma'am." He set the poppet down and took the inevitable box of cough drops from his shirt pocket. As always, he courteously offered her one.

Stalling for time, she accepted, popped the drop in and smiled.

"Could this research in the library have anything at all to do with the wild accusations made by Mrs. Zeta? She called me and said you were in her house unasked."

"No. I mean yes." Willi answered. "I mean that we were asked. Dan and I were invited in by Adela's brother, Trujillo. He practically said to go into her room."

"Now, how come you think he wanted you all to do that? Maybe he hoped you'd find something?"

"Uh . . . well, that's a possibility." Willi hated to keep back information from Sheriff Tucker, but she didn't want to incriminate Dan in anything, either. "I might have found something interesting, Sheriff."

"Okay, Miss Willi, I see what you're heading toward. Fine by me. *You* found something. How about letting me in on this, and I might just have something interesting to tell you about the Zetas."

"You think that I'm right, that the girls' deaths weren't acci—"

"Whoa, hold the horses right there, hold 'em right there. The case is closed. *Closed.* Officially closed."

"Yes, Sheriff Tucker, I see what you're *heading* toward. We're two friends doing nothing more than gossiping."

His face brightened. "Now you're talking, Miss Willi, now you're talking."

And she did. Long into the night she told the sheriff about visiting Adela's room and finding the note in calligraphy, the illegal tests, the Crow's Foot cross. She discussed what little she'd gleaned from Betty Norris outside The Apothecary Shoppe, too. "I hope she got back home safely."

Charlie Brown stretched, yawned and padded to the kitchen. His rustling among his pillows and blankets finally quieted. She turned her attention to the sheriff. "What do you know about the Zetas?"

"Not pleasant facts. Downright mean, nasty things, I learned." He pulled out his blue bandanna. "I remembered the bruises on the Zeta girl's arms the night we discovered the dog and cat on the school grounds. Mayhap you recall?"

"Yes, the night before we left for Galveston. Her mother tore an earring out of one ear."

Rubbing his nose back and forth with the huge handkerchief, he shook his head. "Don't rightly recall that, but anyways, I run a check the other day—"

"Uhmm?" Willi smirked.

"Yep, even though the case was officially closed. I run the check out of . . ." In a dismissive manner, he waved his hand in front of his face.

"Out of curiosity?"

As if repeated action would erase that feminine quality from himself, he waved his hand again.

"Anyways and anyhow, the Zetas have been in Nickleberry only two years. They was brought up on charges in Dallas about eight years ago, two or three times. Then they up and moved to Fort Worth. Had charges brought against them there." Tucking his thumb against his palm to emphasize his words, he said, "Four times."

"What kind of charges?"

"Child abuse."

"Both parents charged?"

"Yep."

"Well, why are they still free?"

"That's the dang blame kicker that sticks in my craw, too. Charges was dropped every single time. No convictions." Disbelief must have shown on her face, since he continued, "That ain't all. Folks that bailed them out and prepared the defense were big-name lawyers, no penny-ante attorneys. Don't that seem strange considering the financial status of the Zetas?"

Sheriff Tucker continued. "And, don't know whether this is important or not, but those children were adopted by the Zetas. Now why adopt kids and treat them like dirt?"

Willi added another to her list of unanswered questions. Did any of this child abuse have a tie-in with the Satan worship and have anything at all to do with the girls' deaths? She sighed. Not once had Sheriff Tucker mentioned Hallettsville and the Benjamites, nor had he brought up the subject of his nephew's involvement.

She peered out at the storm, at the oak's branches, whose swaying leaves mesmerized her. She shivered as the coldness touched her as if she were outside, *skulking along the ground, but it wasn't her snaking a path through the wet grass.*

No, it was a bronze-skinned Indian buck, naked to the waist, where his breechcloth was tied. Carrying a knife in his teeth, he snuck up to a ridge overlooking the Hallettsville compound. His ponytail lifted in the strong wind. A look of shock spread across his face, and he froze. There, tied to stakes in the middle of the compound, was a dark-haired woman. She was reciting something. A few words lifted and the wind carried them toward the ridge. "Ghastly grim and ancient Raven wandering from the nightly shore—"

He raised up on his elbows. "No, couldn't be, couldn't be."

The woman's voice grew stronger. "—Quoth the Raven, 'Nevermore.'"

He groaned, laid his head on his folded arms and said, "Damn you, Winyan, damn you. Be aware. Be aware."

Fingers snapping in front of her nose made her blink.

"One more item, Miss Willi."

She brushed the bothersome fingers away. She couldn't see if that dang Indian was going to save the woman or not.

"Miss Willi, mayhap you could pay mind to this?"

Blast. "What? I mean, I am paying attention."

"Since I did a background check on the Zetas, I felt mighty inclined to carry through with all those concerned with the girls at home or on the trip to Galveston."

Still not quite back out of the scene, she asked, "Do you know what the Lakota word *Winyan* means?

Shaking his head, Sheriff Tucker said, "Mayhap you could ask Quannah later. Your daddy, old Phidias Gallagher, told me he worried about you, the way your mind would be hundreds of miles away, about how many times you were a—"

"I know, Sheriff, a trial to him. Go ahead, I'm listening, really. What about the girls?"

"Another feller didn't come out lily-white on the files."

"Who?"

"Jerald Stanley, one of them teachers who went to Galveston. The feller who teaches history."

Her scalp prickled. Three times his name had come up in conversations about the girls' deaths. Clearly before her mind's eye, a crystal glass—a bloodred goblet—appeared with Jerald's name etched on the bottom.

CHAPTER
14

"TELL me the whole story. Jerald Stanley's name has appeared too many times for there not to be a fire somewhere," Willi said.

"You ain't gonna like what I've got." He sneezed into the bandanna. He told the facts straight out.

When he finished, she plopped down in the Herculon, jumped back up, offered Sheriff Tucker a hot drink and went to get him a cup of strong coffee. She had to have something to do with her hands, her mind and her suspicions for a few minutes. The routine clattering of coffeepot and spoons did the trick. Coming back to the library nook, she said, "You're telling me simply because of suspicions and innuendoes, he left his last job." She handed him the mug of coffee, but took the hot chocolate for herself. "Furthermore, he left because of involvement with a female student?"

"No, ma'am. According to the records, he left for other reasons, but it's my thinking what says mayhap the real *problemo* was him and this senior girl. Now, all this is so much piecing together from when I talked to his sister, Tasmania. Ain't that a handle for you?"

"Better than Chippewa Dakota."

"A chip of what?"

"Tasmania and Jerald's brother. Their mother had a penchant toward the eclectic."

Sheriff Tucker pulled at his ear and shook his head. "Miss Willi, sometimes you use big words that don't make no sense. *Pitch hit* I might take a guess at, but that other one, no way." Folding the bandanna, he replaced it in his back pocket.

"Jerald's mother was interested in looking into a variety of subjects, studied about everything." Willi grinned at him. "Bet you have a worse time understanding your own nephew with words like *pilamaya ye, Winyan* and *Heyo-kah,* don't you?"

"True, but I admire the boy for staying true to his Sacred Path learning. I denied my racial ties for so many years, I sure regret it, I do. But even this old man picks up a little bit from him, being as he's got a lot of Wolf Medicine. That there means he's a teacher of the tribe. You got that Medicine, too."

"What do you mean?"

"You're a teacher, so you got some of that there Wolf Medicine. You two got that in common." Sheriff Tucker worried his left ear. "Now with the case closed and all, I want you to take especial care not to get any more involved. You hear me?" He gulped down the last dregs of his coffee, wiped his lips with the back of his hand and headed for the front door. Clamping his Stetson on his head, he faced her while folding his arms across his chest.

Uncle and nephew were definitely alike in some ways. She stifled a laugh.

"You best leave this up to Quannah. He knows what he's about and why, and he don't like women in his way."

"Oh, really?"

"Can't blame him. Last partner he had was female.

Damn fine officer from what he said. Before he come over to the Texas Rangers. When he worked drug enforcement for the DEA."

"What happened? She leave him and get a human partner who could speak in plain English, not riddles, someone who didn't jump down her throat without provocation? Can't imagine what would make a *female* do that." She folded her own arms and glared at Tucker.

"Nope. She done got herself killed. He don't work with nobody no more if he can help it."

Blushing, Willi backed and turned away. "That must have been awful."

"He sure enough won't take to working with an amateur snoop, especially you. Now, don't get your feminine dander up, Miss Willi."

"Certainly not."

"See, you done gone and got all cold-like. I know you can snoop out all sorts of things I couldn't get close to. But the case is closed, no matter what I've found in the dang files. Nothing you nor me can do except keep our eyes open. Nothing else, hear?"

Smiling, she said every word with saccharine sweetness. "Why little ol' me, southern belle of the new millennium, wouldn't dare cross you big brave men. Now, don't you all go worrying your little ol' heads about me. I'll just keep myself to home and cookin'." She shut the door. Home was where the heart was, and the best cooking came from a microwave. A Stepford wife, she wasn't, much less a southern belle. She leaned against the thick wood door but heard Sheriff Tucker grumbling.

"She's gonna be trouble again. I know it sure as God made hopping frogs. She's trouble. Quannah ain't gonna like it, neither."

* * *

THE next morning she opted for a turtleneck sweater along with a matching cardigan and left. When she reached the Bluebonnet Apartments, the rain fell only intermittently, but her cardigan was damp, so she took a minute to hang it over the back of a chair. She glanced in her aunt's bedroom mirror.

Finally, she perched on the edge of a pink chair and leaned across the boxes of candy, gift wrappings, hand lotions and roses and kissed her aunt. Rodrigo, holding Minnie's hand, stood on the other side of the antique bed.

Aunt Minnie said, "Haven't I raked in a haul? I ought to get sick more often. The recuperation is so much fun!" Her cotton-ball curls bounced, and she fluttered her lashes in Rodrigo's direction. "El Cid, dearest, will you remove some boxes, and we'll have a good chat?"

India Lou brushed past before Rodrigo could comply. She cleared the silk comforter and the nightstand, found a red velvet chair for Rodrigo and served them all cups of peppermint mocha.

Minnie's white curls bobbed as she chirped out, "We have to share the good news. Rodrigo is thinking about getting a transfer from Tyler to Nickleberry."

"That's wonderful. I'm happy for you both. You'll get to share so much more now," Willi said.

"We already are. These"—Minnie patted some romance novels—"we're reading together." She wiggled her eyebrows in a suggestive manner. "Danielle Steele's *The Ghost* is wonderful. Shows that whether you love in modern-day times or in France of years ago, the story is still as sweet."

Rodrigo hugged her. "I could not leave her. Impossible. *El sol* for me would never shine again."

Minnie leaned aside and whispered to Willi, "That horsey-faced woman went too far. She grabbed and kissed him, right out in the parking lot. I saw from my window.

A man like Rodrigo likes to think he's making all the moves." She winked at Willi. "You remember that, girl."

A few minutes passed with the obligatory pleasantries of weather, state politics and candidates for governor—a subject that set Minnie into a righteous dither.

"How that fool man thinks he'll ever get elected by telling women that rape is no worse than a mosquito bite is beyond me."

"Don't get me on that nasty subject," Willi said and sipped the mocha.

"Rape or the politician, hon?"

"Men."

"They can be exciting, if you find the right one." Looking up at the ceiling and fluttering her lashes in an exaggerated way, Minnie said, "Exciting even if not the right one, sometimes. Any problem in particular we can help you with? Perhaps with that interesting investigator, what's his name?"

"Big-Chief-Who-Hates-Women. No, thanks, I don't want help with that, but with this."

She held up D'Dee's diary. For a moment, she hesitated, remembering what an unpleasant encounter with a headless rooster and threatening calls had done to her aunt.

"And what, Willi, is this?" Rodrigo reached for the notebook.

"D'Dee Oxhandler's diary. I thought I could read through and see if it contained anything useful for the case, but knowing the girls, I feel like such an intruder." Smiling sheepishly, she straightened her skirt. "Guess even my curiosity has limits. Maybe while recuperating, you might read it, but not if you think it would upset you too much."

"Nonsense." Minnie nodded. "I want to help. Besides, there aren't any threats to us in a girl's diary."

Willi said, "Thanks. Since the emotional coloring wouldn't be there for you, maybe the interpretation might be more objective."

Minnie caressed the top of Rodrigo's hand and grabbed the diary. She thumbed through a few pages. "Lord have mercy. This isn't like diaries we used to keep in my day. Listen to this." She read a selection ending with "girls just want to have fun." "Not that we didn't, but we would never have admitted the fact."

Peeking over the fragile shoulder, Willi grinned. "I think those are the lyrics of a popular song. Go further down."

"Yes, dear. Here we go. 'I told the ass today I wanted no part of the plan. If he keeps bothering me, he'll be sorry!' What in the world? Is that from a song?"

"No. Does it say who the *ass* is?"

Minnie handed the diary to Rodrigo. "More tired than I thought. But I could listen to Rodrigo read all day."

When he began, Willi had to concur. Not only did he resemble a shortened and older version of Charlton Heston, but his voice was a facsimile of the actor's.

He intoned, " 'Adela can't handle the group. We gotta get out. The kitty and puppy were like gross . . . bad. Now this BEARER crap they want to talk us into. Something new they want to start within the first decade of the New Millennium. No way, José.' The youth of today have such a base level of communication. She has 'bearer' in caps," Rodrigo said in an aside, "if that means anything?"

Willi closed her eyes. Yes, it might, considering the note found in Adela's room behind the picture frame: "Blessed be the bearer." She only raised an eyebrow in response to his question.

Minnie fluttered her fingers. "Go on, my El Cid. This is intriguing."

"As you wish, my heart." He continued. " 'Bubble Gum

Betty will know first. God, we feel so sorry for her, but what can we do? Just because she let that goofy boyfriend in her panties one time. Still, like get real. There are other options. Letting the coven—well—it doesn't sound right.' A few sentences are scratched out, but afterward she writes, 'Jim Bolder asked me'—*me* is underlined three times—'to the folk dance festival when I return from Galveston. Awesome and good-looking ass on that dude. This is going to be the best spring break ever.' Ah, the language may change from generation to generation, but the emotions, the passion, no. Those, they are the same."

Minnie placed her hand in his. "Yes, my El Cid, they are."

Rodrigo nodded his head, suddenly stared past Willi to the door behind her and smiled. He rose, handing the notebook to her in passing, and held out his hand to Hortense Horsenettle.

"My lady, so nice of you to visit Minnie. Come." He steered her toward the chair he had vacated. "Sit here."

Minnie fluffed her hair and smiled. She reached around to plump up her pillow, but instead pounded it.

Willi sighed. Hell's bells, why did Hortense have to show up? The visit would probably end in a fatal stroke.

Hortense adjusted her red-rimmed glasses on her sloping nose—the better to see her victim—and asked, "What were you all reading? Sounded like a young girl's ramblings." Her eyes remained on Rodrigo Vivar.

Minnie answered. "Research. Willi's doing research, and *my* El Cid and I are helping."

"Oh. I see. Silly me. I thought I heard the name Jim Bolder, a student at school." Hortense glared pointedly at Willi and the book.

Willi swiftly slid the diary in her bag. She'd have to drop by later and give it back when *Horsey* wasn't snooping. Why in Hades was she so curious anyway? Well, that was unfair. The librarian was one of the chaperones, after all, and naturally wanted answers about that horrible Galveston trip.

"He was D'Dee Oxhandler's boyfriend, wasn't he?" Hortense pushed the red rims higher up her nose. "Does he know anything about the murd—the deaths?"

Willi pictured Hortense thirty years down the road. She'd be like Mama Feather, toothless, but still thriving on every morsel of gossip no matter how ill-gained. "I really don't know."

She bent toward her aunt and kissed her. "I've got to run by the high school." She winked. "You look great, Auntie. Don't do anything to change that." She stared meaningfully at her aunt with the hope that she'd get the message not to say what she really wanted to say to Hortense. At last, Willi squeezed her aunt's hand and departed.

As things turned out, the morning was taken up with errands and silly delays here and there. The rain abated. The sun shone boldly, creating an uncomfortable humidity, but at least Quannah Lassiter didn't invade her thoughts. It was almost sundown before she headed for the Nickleberry High School. For a Wednesday of spring break there were a lot of teachers doing overtime—unpaid overtime. At least fifteen cars shimmered before her eyes in the humid heat wafting up from the asphalt. Her shoes stuck with each step in the same way her mind boggled at each new clue presented about the girls' deaths.

Bubble Gum Betty will know first. The girl had been on an emotional slide since the deaths.

Okay, so Betty Norris wasn't upset over just the rift between her and her mother. Her reaction to the poppet indicated a firsthand knowledge about the local coven, cult, whatever in hell it was. She'd even admitted being involved with the group, and now, according to D'Dee's scribblings, was making some arrangement with the coven to rear her baby after birth.

Willi pressed her knuckles to her temples. Betty was smart enough to know her child would be raised in a brainwashed, controlled environment. If she herself was afraid of the group, how could she give up her baby to such a nasty crew? As soon as the question formed, Willi answered it. Betty was running scared, had no parent with whom she felt she could discuss the issue and like most folks—teens or otherwise—she wanted the road of least resistance. Obviously, the group had offered her anonymity, perhaps even a chance to help raise the baby without the need to claim the child. There was the possibility of an abortion. Remembering the rounded tummy, Willi amended that idea. Too late probably for that choice.

Great, just great. Willi's mental ramblings had given her a headache, and she found herself no closer to a solution. Scrambling in her purse, she shook her head. "Well, wouldn't you know, not one aspirin tablet."

She stuck her hand in her skirt pocket, smiled and touched stone. She had forgotten about the gift. She rubbed Tunkasila.

"If you can help get rid of a headache, now would be the perfect time to let the force be with you or whatever."

She trudged doggedly up to the computer lab, walked in and found one screen lit up but unattended. On the monitor was a grammar test for Honors English II. It was one for the next six weeks. Looking around the room and then out the door, she cocked her head. No one. She walked across the hall and into the lounge where the floor-to-ceiling picture window was. Not a teacher in sight.

Glancing out the window, she grinned. Well, Auntie must have gotten tough. With an armload of books, Hortense slammed her car door by shoving it closed with one hip and trotted to the front steps.

Not believing the stupidity of a teacher leaving the test on the screen unattended, Willi returned to the computer lab room. She was tempted to switch the monitor off. Oh, it didn't really matter, considering that no students were in the building during spring break, and probably the instructor had run downstairs to grab a Coke before completing a printer run.

She rubbed the Stone Person again, sat down at a monitor in the corner with her back to the door and sent to Bin B-7 the past six weeks' grades for period five, English IV. Hortense's bray echoed down the hall. Willi couldn't tell who answered.

Halfway through the checking of period six grades, she rubbed her neck. No headache, not even a twinge of pain remained, but something niggled. She glanced up. "I didn't see you come in, Paul."

"How you all doing, your aunt and you?"

"She's recuperating."

"Heard you had a spell at the library."

"Yes, but I'm fine." She had no intention of giving out the details of that encounter, nor of the poppet incident.

He sat in front of the monitor with the test on the screen.

She opened her mouth to tell him not to bother with it.

He struck a combination of keys, obviously the printer command since the ancient Panasonic KX-P1191 whirred to life. He'd only had time to enter the one command, so he couldn't have changed to another file.

She frowned, punching the keyboard, but eyed him from beneath her lashes. No reason to embarrass the guy. He'd find out when he checked the three printed pages that he'd just run an English teacher's file.

Jabbing a touch-sensitive spot on the front printer panel, he ran through an extra sheet, then tore off all four pages.

She turned her own machine off, checked the computer Paul had used and stared as blankly as the screen before her. Only English teachers had codes to get into the department tests. Math teachers had codes for their exams and not anyone else's. So how did Paul Undel get the English code, and why was he using it?

He said, "If the Nickleberry School Board wouldn't give all of their money to athletics, we all might make use of a color laser printer."

"Not fair, Paul, considering they just bought jackets for all the UIL Literary participants and hosted the Honors students' trip."

"Yeah, well, that's how a lot of you all might see it." With that disgruntled and unexplained comment, he studied each page and nodded. "You all take care." He left after waving the pages at her.

Idiot. He wasn't going to admit he ran off something totally useless to him, an English test. She checked the time. Oh, shoot.

She ran down the steps and into the office, begged some aspirin tablets from the summer aide and realized when she bent over the water fountain that the headache was gone. She placed the aspirin in her purse. Tentatively, she reached in her pocket to feel Tunkasila. Well, just coincidence, like Elba and her Tarot cards being right on occasion. Just coincidence. But the comfortable warmth surrounding her at the contact told her there was more, much more.

Feeling as if a heavy burden had been removed, she easily lifted the purse straps to her shoulder and stopped in midstride. The purse should have been heavier. Oh my gosh, no. She patted her purse and peered inside. No, no way.

Running up the stairs, she searched around her computer console, raced into the lounge, but didn't find anything. With the fingers of her right hand splayed across her neck, she fought the panic. Breathing under control, she pounded one palm with her fist. After she retraced her steps, she closed her eyes. Only three possibilities—Paul Undel in the lab, Hortense out in the hall and whoever talked to Horsey.

Sighing, Willi walked outside. She'd never heard Paul Undel approach, so she couldn't have heard anyone else. She should have turned the notebook over to Quannah. What a fool she'd been. To have lost vital evidence which might have offered a path to the murderer . . . no . . . she'd never be able to face Quannah or Sheriff Tucker with that. The guilt gnawed at her. Slowly forcing one foot in front of the other, she headed outside. Perhaps she could make amends if she found another way, another clue, another trap for the killer.

CHAPTER
15

SHE shivered as she reached her car and glanced around before sliding behind the wheel. Across the street and down half a block, The Apothecary Shoppe's door opened. A customer walked away. The lights went out.

Willi's scalp tingled. She wrapped her hands about her elbows to give herself a comforting hug. Tears, a much-needed pain-letting, coursed down her cheeks as she drove home. She had gone the wrong way, having headed the car west instead of east. Finally, she made a U-turn, waving at Ian Kirby, the officer on duty at the Maple Leaf Bridge.

Sitting sidesaddle on his traffic bike, the lanky officer started to put away a half-eaten hamburger, but he only shook a finger, letting her drive across the railroad track and onto the curving Licorice Lane toward home. The tears abated about the time she drove up to the farm, but exhaustion settled in bone-deep. Elba would have said she needed sleep, come Texas tornadoes, high waters or marching Republicans.

After feeding Charlie Brown, she climbed the thirteen steps. Not for the first time, she wished she had not been drilled with her daddy's superstitions. The number thirteen, black cats crossing a path and walking under ladders were taboo while she was growing up. To forget those and the myriad horrors of her day, she took a long shower, letting the liquid needles of heat slough away the strain from her shoulders and neck. She stepped over to the dresser and tapped Tunkasila before pushing the stone to one side.

She curled her toes in the thick carpeting of her bedroom and walked over and pulled aside a curtain. Something—she knew not what—drew her there. She opened the window and leaned out to meet the cool breeze from the woods as an old and trusted friend. Sitting on the floor, she propped her head on her elbows atop the windowsill to peer out at the night's canopy, now thankfully without sign of menacing clouds. With the oversized towel wrapped around her, she felt at peace.

Earlier in the evening she would have been able to hear the Orlandos' radio two miles away. The uncanny position of her farm sometimes made her think she was in the middle of a stereo system. Sound traveled so far out in the country.

She must have leaned on the windowsill some time. Her long hair, fluffed and dried, tickled her shoulders. Sighing, she rose and reached to close the window, but halted. Lights flickered in the distance. At first, she thought of her mother's place, the cabin where her mother painted, but the lights came on and off farther to the left. Nothing in that direction other than thick woods belonging to one of the Orlando clan, a city boy who never visited his prosperous cousins on the adjoining dairy or the old shack, which had probably fallen down long ago.

Willi combed her fingers through her hair. Maybe folks were having a wiener roast or the kids were camped out. Lights flickered on, then off. Nope, she was not going to

go snooping tonight. Her eyelids were heavier than the
contents of a wet cement bin and about that gritty. The
curtains billowed, floating like her mind, her whole body.
Bed beckoned. She got up, threw her brush down and
knocked Tunkasila off. The stone tumbled underneath the
dresser. Down on her hands and knees, she peered into
the dark recesses.

"Well, I don't need protection from anyone tonight,
anyway." Getting to her knees, she tied the big towel
tighter around her chest.

A wail rose in an eerie cadence.

Human.

That scream had to be human.

Charlie Brown yipped and howled. Goose bumps skittered down her arms. She jumped up, ran out of the bedroom and stumbled down the thirteen steps. Quickly, she
switched on the kitchen lights. Charlie Brown woofed and
scratched at the door.

Someone was there, could see her through the window.

Splaying her fingers above the towel, she gulped. Her
pulse quickened, but she forced her limbs to move.

"Hush, Charlie Brown, hush." She patted his head,
tightened the Turkish towel once again, and sighting the
butcher block holder on the counter, grabbed a knife. She
flicked out the lights. With her heart galloping, she edged
her way to the door. Back to the wall, she willed her pulse
to slow. Keeping a strong hold on the knife, she used her
other hand to open the door. She pushed it wide and
stepped outside into the darkness.

Wind whistled around the house. The three huge cottonwoods crooned a quiet dirge. A coyote howled.

She squinted toward the dairy.

The moon illuminated patches, allowing only the sad
cottonwoods and their shadows to seem menacing.

One dark, masculine shape moved away from the other shadows.

Gasping, she raised the blade.

With little effort, he grabbed her and forced her hand to open.

Dropping the knife, she grasped the towel with both hands. Why wasn't Charlie Brown barking? Dear God. She willed her legs to stop trembling, but they disobeyed.

"Inside," he said, waving the blade. Moonlight glinted off the sharp point. "Inside, now."

Her heart knocked against her ribs. Light-headed, she stepped into the kitchen.

She gazed up into her attacker's eyes. "I should have known all along," Willi said, clutching the towel tighter. "*You.* Horrible things didn't start happening until *you* showed up." She had to stall, had to think. She eyed Charlie Brown, curled up and asleep in his basket. Great watchdog, the kind that couldn't bite a hot biscuit. "The killings were some kind of Indian ritual, right? I did see you in Galveston and—"

"Great Coyote's balls, you do have an imagination. *Winyan,* hush." Quannah laid the butcher knife on the table, plopped his Stetson down beside it and made a half-hearted effort to grin. "You'll be in no danger from me . . . unless . . . you go get on something even *more* comfortable."

"Damn you, Lassiter."

"Many have, Gallagher, many have."

The tiredness in his voice finally got through her ebbing panic. Softening her own words, she said, "Why are you snooping around here?"

"One. Decapitated rooster on your aunt's door. Two. Your attack at the library. Three. Uncle Brigham told me about the poppet doll."

Easing into a Shaker chair, he groaned and rubbed the

back of his neck. "Let's see. Oh, yeah, four. Someone attacked you in front of the hospital." From under strongly arched brows, he squinted. "No telling what else you've been into. Maybe we ought to discuss those things?"

She *would not* think right now about the lost diary or the weird actions of Paul Undel. She'd share when she had something positive. She was not going to look like a fool. She concentrated on the fact that his hair had come loose from the leather thong, the grime his boots had brought onto the kitchen floor—which she didn't give a fig for, but she had to keep her mind on anything other than what he wanted at the moment, her information. The guilt must have shown on her face.

"There is something else, right?" he asked.

"Only coffee." She opened a cupboard, placed coffee and filters on the counter, pointed to the coffeemaker, but didn't offer to brew the beverage. "You take care of this. I'll get dressed."

He eyed her from head to foot and winked. "Wise move."

After she rounded the corner, he said, "That perfume . . . Passion. I like that."

She peeked around the corner to ask him how he knew the name of her perfume, but he was ready with a wink. "I'll never tell you until you share everything with me. Isn't that how it works, Gallagher?"

His voice sounded so ragged. What had he been up to? She grinned and sighed. One for Big Chief. She said, *"Pilamaya ye."*

He raised an eyebrow.

"For the illegal bouquet and for . . . the rock . . . uh . . . Stone Person . . . for Tunkasila."

"Hau. You're welcome. Found him useful yet?"

She pretended she hadn't heard and made her way upstairs while she practiced the new word, *hau.*

The aroma of coffee filtered upstairs along with fried potatoes and onions. *Well, make yourself at home, Lassiter.* She dressed in stonewashed jeans, a soft pink turtleneck and scrounged in the back of the closet for her leather moccasins. "Finally." She pulled them on and zipped them up the back to her ankles. Halfway down the stairs, she halted, turned around and raced back to the bedroom. She reached into the far recesses of a dresser drawer to pull out a bottle of Passion. She grimaced at the reflection of her face surrounded by a black cloud of hair.

"What am I doing?"

Just freshening up, that's all, absolutely all.

She sprayed behind her ears and on her wrists. No, no, that was too strong. She scrubbed most of the scent from her wrists. Her stomach grumbled. Past midnight, but she was starving. For food, she reminded herself sternly, *for food*. She squared her shoulders and headed for the kitchen.

A plate filled with potatoes, onions and buttered toast sat on the table. An empty cup turned over in its saucer rested there, too. Quannah wasn't in sight, but an empty plate, washed and dried, sat on the kitchen counter with fork, knife and cup.

"Well, where the hell?"

Charlie Brown woofed. He licked off a telltale dab of egg yolk from his nose.

"Watchdog, my hind foot. Traitor is more like it. Where did the Great Chief go?"

Charlie Brown got up, stretched his bottom up in the air while extending his paws in front and yawned. Finally, he trotted around the corner and into her library nook.

She followed the pup while swearing under her breath what an ungrateful cur he was turning out to be.

Quannah, snoring, lay back in the Herculon recliner.

His boots rested beside him, socks neatly draped over each one.

Arms akimbo, she smirked. "Uh-huh. We'll talk. We'll find out what's going on. Sure we will, you . . . you . . . Chief-Who-Trembles-The-Earth-Snoring, sure we will." She grabbed a quilt off the sofa in the living room, returned and covered him. As she tucked in his feet, she eyed his boots beside the recliner. Caked mud adhered to one heel.

"What's this? Not something he'd pick up close to the house. Uhmmm." She studied him and then the boot. He must have been out in the woods, perhaps near where she'd heard the wails.

She started to leave, but paused. "What's in the Indian dude's pockets, huh?" she whispered to herself.

No, no, she couldn't do that. What if he woke up and found her searching for tidbits, like a vulture picking over roadkill? *Big Chief won't ever know.*

"I won't do that. I won't."

She stalked out of the library nook and into the kitchen, where she settled Charlie Brown in his bed, but she couldn't eat the cold midnight snack. She sat at the kitchen table and tapped the end of her nose.

Snapping off the kitchen light, she eased back into the library nook and bent over Quannah. Moonlight cascaded through the window. A torn sheet of notebook paper stuck out of his shirt pocket. Squinting, she managed to read one word on the edge, HALLETTSVILLE in block print. His billfold with badge, open on the desk, called to her, too. She reached toward the billfold, then toward his pocket.

Snoring louder than a space shuttle on liftoff, he was no danger.

Her fingers, nevertheless, quivered. She shut her eyes. "Nope. I could, but I won't."

To block out the bright moonlight, she pulled the curtains together before she checked on him one last time.

Reaching out with the intention of tucking the quilt up to his chin, she let her fingers softly caress his jaw. She couldn't seem to pull back. She bent nearer. His warm breath mingled with hers.

Closing her eyes, she brushed her lips against his. The electricity jolted her. What had she done? Acted like a damned silly schoolgirl, that's what.

With heat suffusing her face and lips tingling from that momentary caress, she edged out of the nook and headed up the stairs. She jumped over the first one, just to avoid stepping on thirteen. The last thing she needed was a fall or worse . . . to awaken Lassiter. She climbed slowly, smirked at the pink turtleneck, sniffed the remaining perfume and shook her head. She undressed for the second time that evening, but only tossed and turned in a search for elusive slumber when she got into bed.

She stared at the ceiling.

Counted sheep.

Counted backward.

Counted backward in three languages, and stared at the ceiling again. Her body felt as heavy as a rock.

Rock?

She hopped out of bed, rushed toward the dresser and hit her toe on the Fruitwood hope chest at the foot of the bed. A needle of pain shot all the way up to her knee.

"*Daaamnn.* Damn."

Saying *caramba* didn't help either. Biting her lip against the agony, she reached beneath the dresser and scrabbled around until her fingers closed over Tunkasila.

"This is ridiculous." She hobbled back to bed, placed the Stone Person on the bedside table, punched her pillow and repeated, "This is ridiculous." Snuggling down, she drifted immediately into a sound sleep.

CHAPTER
16

THE next morning, willi pulled her feet back under the covers. The coverlet was tugged aside. Something brushed against the bottom of her foot. "Whaa . . . what?" Twisting onto her back, she pulled the sheet up to her chin and snuggled deeper underneath the covers. When a warm tongue licked gently down one side of her chin, she giggled. She couldn't resist the message in the brown eyes staring at her over the lace-edged sheet, but playfully said, "You . . . you . . . savage, get out of *my* bed."

Charlie Brown woofed and thumped his tail on the comforter.

"Thought you might need help getting wide awake," said Elba, standing in the doorway. "Started to send up the other brown-eyed fellow, but he's sawing logs faster than Paul Bunyan, louder than Popeye without his spinach and longer than Rip Van Winkle."

Willi yawned, and Elba marched out. Those weren't some of Elba's best comparisons, but maybe it was too early in the morning. Could be Elba worked up to three good ones by the end of the day.

"Got taquitos making," Elba yelled.

Sure enough, the mixed aromas of jalapeños, tomatoes, cheese and spices drifted upward. Willi's stomach growled, but she didn't want to face an angry Quannah Lassiter, who might just know she had entertained, even for one moment, an idea about rifling through his pockets. She cuddled into still warm sheets and pulled the pillow over her head. A vision of Lassiter, eyes heavy with something more than sleep, floated in and out, making her blood rush to her head. What would it have been like to awake with his lips . . . ? *Mustn't think that. He might know she'd bent down and . . . Stop it, Gallagher.*

Wiggling, Charlie Brown tugged at the covers and growled. His effort might have been enough to scare a butterfly, maybe. The phone rang once twice and again.

"Elba, please," she whispered.

The two sisters were always fussing at her to put a phone in her bedroom, but she fought the idea of something so intrusive. No one ever called her late at night, and the idea that she might hole up in her room if a burglar entered was ludicrous. She had more spunk than that.

To get her mind off uncomfortable thoughts, she playfully barked.

Charlie Brown rolled onto the floor and cowered beneath the bed. In the safety of shadows and dust balls he sneezed.

"Good place for you while I shower."

On the way downstairs, she grabbed Tunkasila and jammed the stone in her jeans' pocket. She peeked into the library nook. "Uhmm. Maybe he's in the kitchen already."

At the breakfast table, her outlook on the world became much more charitable when Elba placed two lightly browned taquitos before her and poured a generous helping of queso salsa over the egg and sausage concoction.

"Guess Lassiter is washing up?" Willi asked.

Charlie Brown, after receiving a smidgen of the highly spiced meat, sat on top of Willi's sneakered feet. He tugged at her shoelaces, but soon developed a game of flapping the lace ends again and again before he settled down to serious chewing.

As Elba placed the frying pan in a sink of hot suds, she asked, "Can't hear over this noise." She turned the water off. "What's that you asked?"

"Where's Lassiter?"

"That good-looking man you left downstairs all night? The handsome hunk with eyes that'd melt a frozen lake full of frigid women, the man who might melt—?"

"*No*, Elba. Must be a different man."

"Well, Investigator Lassiter hauled himself out of here fast-like. Soon as Sheriff Tucker called him."

"Oh?"

"Yep, hauled his ass right up and out faster than—"

"—but didn't he say anything?"

"Said he appreciated my cooking. I wrapped up a few taquitos."

"That's all?"

"A quart of orange juice."

"Didn't he *say* anything else?"

"Nope, but then we could be talking about two different men. How many did you have stashed in the house last night?"

"Sometimes you are hopeless."

"Not me. I may be old, but I could have done better than cramping him in a chair for the night. You get a tomcat in the cage, you best make use of him. Your mama should have taught you such things. A pretty blouse, perfume, a little come-hither look. You get the idea. Give him a taste of what's to come back for, and—"

"I'm sure the only thing he'd want to come back for is **your cooking. How about another taquito?**"

"Sorry. He looked real hungry. Just got the pan scrapings for the pup, there."

Elba hefted her bosom up by pushing up one side, then the other. She reached into an apron pocket and placed a poppet on the table.

"Got something else you might like, though." The tiny effigy, less than two inches in height, resembled Willi even more than the one discovered in Elba's truck.

"Oh, no, where—? Why?"

Elba bustled around the table and patted her shoulder. "No, don't take on so. This is white witch magic for health and *protection*. Me and Agatha done it up, took it to meeting for special blessing. This ought to take care of any foolishness anyone might have planned with the other one."

"Thanks, Elba. And tell Agatha and the others."

Willi conjured a picture of witches circling a bubbling cauldron. Somehow it was always difficult to picture round Elba and her familiar, Rose Pig, with Agatha and her cat, Clyde, as part of that sight. She was also a bit miffed that she didn't know who the others in Elba's coven were. That had proven one of the few things in life Elba could actually keep secret.

Elba said, "You hold it close by you for the next few days, hear?"

"What?" Willi dusted the mental cobwebs away and smiled. "Right." She didn't believe in the powers of either poppet, but she believed in the kindness prompting the gift.

After helping Elba clear the table, she sat down with a cup of herbal tea. "What do you know about chants?" she asked.

"We done told you we don't share things from the group."

"You never call it a coven."

"Just a group of ladies trying to do good in a way most folks don't approve of, and so less said the better. Folks get real nervous when you use words like *coven*. They get it in their heads only evil comes out of such groups and you can't sway 'em to any other view. Secrets is easy to hear and hard to keep. Know what I mean?" Elba stood, pushed her bosom up again by crossing her arms underneath and pulled her bottom lip in.

"Okay, no more prying." Willi sighed. "If this wasn't something to do *directly* with your coven . . . uh, sorry . . . *group,* could you help me?"

Elba leaned one hand on the table and squinted. "Maybe, maybe."

After relating her adventure in the Hall of Horrors, Willi repeated the chant about blood and magick, passion and power.

Elba pursed her lips, but finally relented. "Typical chant of the high priest or priestess. Probably find that in some book, so I'm not telling nothing out of school. Most probably, in our group, that there kind of chant would be used at the full moon for bringing power so we could do more good."

"Considering the circumstances, though, what do you think?"

"Ain't nobody with *good* in mind."

"Explain, please."

"The chanter was a-calling spirits to give *him* more strengths, not to give a *group* dominion in some area. Alone, weren't he? That calling the power to hisself is bad. Some crazy is out there, Willi. You're going to steer a clear path around such as those folks, right?" Worry lines etched a big crow's foot between Elba's brows.

Crow's Foot. Like the cross. No, she wasn't going to steer clear, but no sense worrying Elba or Agatha. She smiled, trying to keep the innocence in her voice. "I'll leave this up to the authorities this time."

"Can't tell you how glad that makes me. Since I only do a half day, guess I'll be getting busy, okay?" She held up a gnarled finger and shook it at Willi. "First the poppet, then the crazy chanter. Stay away from the Nickleberry City Library, unknown houses, alleys. Anyplace dark and musty."

Willi got up and pulled the dog leash off the wall hook. "I'm going to take Charlie Brown for a jog."

"Fine by me. Of course, I don't think that short-legged critter could walk very far. Stay out of tall grass."

Willi dropped the leash, which Charlie Brown grabbed between his teeth.

"Maybe," Elba said, tapping her head.

"Maybe?"

"Well, when that nice Texas Ranger fellow left this morning, maybe he was referring to your way of getting into trouble."

"So, he *did* say something."

Elba raised a hand to wave the idea away. "Not exactly, but he mumbled about—now, how'd he put that?—having to inspect the premises, maybe see if someone else was keeping an eye on you, snooping on the place? Check on some wailing he thought he heard last night."

"Elba, explain right this minute."

"Can't oblige, much as I'd like. Cross my heart, that's all I heard. He grabbed a note from the pad beside the telephone and skedaddled outside."

When Elba went off for the furniture polish, Willi eyed the protective poppet. Peering around the corner, she searched the small bookstand used for the kitchen telephone. She grabbed the top sheet of a yellow stickum pad, raised it to the sunlight and said, "Aha."

Using a stubby pencil, she shaded lightly over the pad.

Two words showed clearly; another wasn't so distinct. "Hallettsville" and "Horsenettle." What the heck? She twisted the sheet around. Ah, a phone number. She peeked behind her, but Elba, somewhere upstairs, had started the vacuum cleaner. Willi shut the kitchen door. She dialed the number and waited. Three rings. Five. Four more. Blast.

Charlie Brown wagged his tail.

"You keep that going like a helicopter blade, you're just small enough to take off."

He barked, picked up the leash and growled.

"Okay, pooch, we'll go." She opened the screen door, and Charlie Brown raced outside, ran in tight circles around oleander and rosebushes, oaks and cottonwoods. When he lay panting at her feet, she informed him of the day's plans.

"Now, you're too tired for a walk, but"—she glanced over her shoulder—"we're going out to the woods."

She shaded her eyes with one hand. "We can find out about those eerie sounds we heard last night. If one trespassing Indian is where he isn't supposed to be, I'll put my foot down. I can take care of myself. Let's go adventuring, Charlie Brown. I'll get some food together."

She ran back inside, grabbed a knapsack from the laundry room, rushed to the kitchen to snitch cheese, garlic bread, tomatoes, two cans of soda and the sausage scrapings from the bottom of the skillet which Elba had saved for the dog, not for Willi. "Sad case, when a little fellow like you rates higher than the one who pays the bills."

She scooped up Charlie Brown and placed him in the outside pocket of the knapsack where he could rest his front paws and head on her shoulder. A lot of good that leash was.

By the time she'd ambled across the fields of Sudan grass and to the edge of the woods, the pup slept as com-

fortably as any baby in a cradleboard. Indian paintbrush
and bluebonnets waved at each other across the fence
lines bisecting her acreage. The banks of the pond weren't
as steep as they would be when summer winds dried the
water up. Now, grass waved gently, lulling her, and she
breathed deeply, sitting for an hour, perhaps two, thinking
of Quannah's words: *We are Mitakuye Oyasin, a part of
all.*

At last, she reached up and scratched behind Charlie
Brown's ears. "Nothing sinister here." Gently, she deposited the knapsack with its sleeping occupant on the carpet
of spring grass.

She pulled a blade and sucked on the stem. *In here
there is a knowing. Trust yourself.*

"Time to go, Charlie Brown. Wake up. We have to get
into those woods."

No sooner had she unwrapped a piece of cheese then
Charlie Brown snuffled, sneezed and woofed at her as if
she'd forgotten her most important guest. Offering bits of
sausage, she enticed him to amble close long enough to
finish her own snack. His whirling tail should have
warned her he was fully awake and ready to take on any
lions, tigers or bears in the vicinity. He rushed at a promising bush of baby's breath and disappeared. A growl,
deeper than any Willi had heard from the nine-pound pup,
emerged along with a great deal of rustling leaves and
falling blossoms. Moments later, a rabbit darted from the
bush.

"No, Charlie Brown, come back."

Too late. He was in pursuit. Ears flowing back over his
head signaled where he was in the tall grass. The rabbit
hopped around and doubled back as if he knew this mutt
was a novice at the game. Sure enough, before many
minutes passed, Willi caught up to the pup. His tongue

lolled and he yipped, truly happy with his great hunter's prowess.

"Charlie Brown, I don't see anything suggesting people were here last night. My imagination has gotten me in trouble again, I guess."

Rested, he ran further into the woods.

She started to stop him, but the copse of trees had been her goal. Even though her original uneasiness had left, there might be something of interest. Catching sight of his wagging tail or the tips of his ears, she followed. All sense of foreboding dissipated into the hot midday air, leaving her as carefree as a child. He woofed and ran circles around her.

"What, Charlie Brown? What have you found?"

She pushed back a tree branch, scrambled through a hedge and studied the small clearing. After the rains of a few days ago, the earth was moist and loamy, especially beneath the trees' canopy. "The hermit's shack. Uh-oh. We're off my land." She stepped forward and slid on a slick mud hole, but righted herself. She scraped the mud off on a tree trunk. Nearby were fresh prints which looked like Lassiter's boot heels.

"So, Big Chief Investigator, this *is* where you were last night."

The shack, with a lean-to shed attached, listed to the left. One good high wind might tumble it to the ground were it not for the great creepers and vines that held it upright. When she reached the door, Charlie Brown blocked her passage. With muzzle to the ground, haunch in the air, he shook his head and whined.

"Move, you silly cur. Get out of the way."

Every attempt she made only riled the dachshund more. She scooped him up into her arms and started to walk through the open doorway. He nipped her finger, howled and apologetically blinked his limpid eyes. Whatever was beyond the door was one tiger too many. She retreated and deposited him in a grassy cradle between two exposed tree roots.

Taking a moment to soothe him, she said, "That's okay, boy. You took care of the rabbit. I'll see what's inside."

Stepping gingerly inside the doorway, she closed her eyes to give herself a few minutes to adjust to the gloom. When she opened them and surveyed the area, she gasped. If she hadn't done the research in the library, she'd not have known what she stared at now. Slowly, peering at each dusky wall, she circled around the room. No wonder Charlie Brown had refused to enter.

Probably the hieroglyphics—the Seax-Wica Runes, weren't they called?—were etched on the walls with animal blood. The symbols spelling out *power, magick* and *blood* she could decipher. The letter *K* was especially easy since it was the Crow's Cross, the inverted cross with the arms angled downward.

Willi bumped into something hanging from the ceiling. "Oh, damn."

She pushed at the contraption. It spiraled in a slow circle from the hook which held it in place on the ceiling. A witch's cradle. She gasped and covered her mouth. No, such things only existed in dusty tomes in the city library and the Dark Ages, not in days filled with sunlight and bluebonnets, puppies and roses.

She reached out a tentative hand when she realized the contraption didn't hold a body in torment at the moment. Trying to recall details from her library research, she furrowed her brow in concentration. If this were a person, they'd be wrapped in a mummylike shroud of leather or maybe cloth with the arms fastened down in straitjacket fashion. Leather straps held the body in the iron frame while a leather hood shut out sight and sound.

Willi touched an iron band at the top of the instrument. "Ah, yes," she whispered. "This holds the head in place."

The cradle was suspended by a single rope and hook so that it could swing and rotate freely to cause complete disorientation.

Phrases—snatches remembered—drifted through her mind. *Consciousness loosed from physical bondage ... free to roam ... beyond the physical horizon.*

"Looks more like a torture device from the Dark Ages."

Her curiosity getting the better of her, she studied the witch's cradle closely. No one had been recently incarcerated within the leather bindings, if the thick layer of dust could be trusted as an indication.

At last, she turned around and considered the large stone which stood waist-high in the middle of the room. About the length and width of a twin-sized bed, the rock took up most of the shack's meager space. After a closer study, she touched the altar, a slab of marble which rested on hadite blocks grimed with dirt and encrusted with— No, no way—blood. Animal? Human? A shiver tickled her spine.

A sound alerted her, sending her into a crouch. *Calm down.* Probably just Charlie Brown moaning in his sleep. She crept on all fours to the door and shaded her eyes against the glaring light. *Nerves had to be tighter than taut muscles on an Olympic sprinter.*

Nothing out there.

Straining, she frowned. The only sounds were a woodpecker and the skittering of a squirrel. She crawled back into the shadows and bumped into a wall.

No, the marble slab. She trailed her fingers along the cold stone. There were deep grooves, etchings. Standing, she turned her head to see better. Even at an angle, she couldn't see well, so she depended on the sensitivity of her fingertips as they traced the Seax-Wica Runes. The *B,* the first letter, was simple. The next letter felt like an *M.*

"Of course," she said aloud, "that's *E.* The *F*-shaped letter is an *A.*"

Before she reached the end of the word, she shivered. *Bearer.* She touched the protective poppet in one pocket and Tunkasila in the other. In the corner and leaning against the wall was another witch's cradle.

Strange. It should have been hanging. She peered upward. Sure, there was the second hook.

The cradle moved. She blinked and rubbed her eyes. Blasted shadows were playing tricks on her.

"Urgmmmm."

"Oh my gosh, some animal is trapped in there."

Common sense told her to scramble into the sunlight. But . . . but what if no one else came along to free the creature? *Curiosity killed the cat, Wilhelmina.* She cringed at Mama Feather's nasty adage. Considering, she shifted her weight from one foot to the other. Might be a big animal.

"Urgmmm. Mmmrrgu."

She stepped nearer, held out her hand to untie the apparatus and paused. Goose bumps ran the gamut from neck to spine and back again. Surely Sheriff Tucker could do something about this unholy collection of witch's paraphernalia. He would see to the animal.

Might be a skunk or a rabid raccoon.

Or a porcupine or a poor lost dog, or . . . Blast, she had to know. She untied the first leather string at the side.

"Run!"

She screamed. Someone was in there. "I'm getting you out."

"Go . . . mmmrrgu . . . help."

"I *am* helping." She fumbled with the constraints. Suddenly, a sharp pain shot through her neck, down her spine. Her knees buckled. She hit the packed earth floor and spit out moist dirt. A hot trickle of blood leaked from the corner of her mouth.

CHAPTER
17

HER head was circling, circling. Had she fainted? The base of her neck throbbed. An animal attacked her. No, now that wasn't right, either. If she could just hold her head still a moment, stop the motion, the swirling. Something weighed against her chest. She fought for breath and opened her eyes. Blackness, only blackness. Panting quickly, she whimpered.

"Anyone? Help me."

Those words came out more like a garble of nonsense letters. "Enervyhelpprme."

"Stay calm."

Someone spoke from nearby, but she couldn't tell the direction. Friend? Enemy?

Her whole body shifted, floated, circled and turned back on itself. With searing clarity, truth blazed across her mind. She was in that damned contraption, the witch's cradle. Her arms were bound close to her body, her feet rested on something pliable, yet strong. Leather.

"Who's there?" she asked. This time, the words were intelligible. "Get me out of here."

"I warned you."

Oh, no, it was the maniac from the Hall of Horrors, the
. . . murderer. Bending both knees as much as space per-
mitted, she kicked outward. Her prison reeled, knocking
against a hard surface, a wall, perhaps. An ebony miasma
of panic, much worse than the darkness imposed by the
cradle, surrounded and entered her. Hot tears trickled. Enclosed, she couldn't draw in air, but gulped painfully between hiccoughing cries.

"Let . . . me . . . out!"

Kicking again only sent her cage spinning more wildly.
She screamed.

"*Winyan,* hush. I am here."

She sniffled. *Winyan?* "La . . . Lassi . . . Lassiter?"

"Head hurts, huh, Gallagher?"

The sound of his voice immediately comforted her; she
was able to draw air into her strained lungs.

"I . . . don't understand. You . . . you didn't hit me?"

Quannah chuckled. "By Great Eagle's wings, I'll swear
I didn't string you up, but I'd have to be honest and admit
the thought has occurred to me on more than one occasion." He groaned.

"Lassiter, what's the matter? Why aren't you getting
me down?"

"First I must free myself. I'm tied up inside the cradle
against the wall."

"How are you getting loose? Did you see who did this?
Do you know what—?" Her leather prison swirled in
never-ending circles.

"*Winyan.* Shush."

"A knife? You have a knife, right?"

"No good Indian scout would be without one."

Her head hurt like blazes, as if tiny needles kept in-
jecting painful serum right behind her left ear. "Damn, I
wish this thing would stop circling. I'm getting nause-
ated."

"Old shamans use something similar to the witch's cradle to call the spirits. If you calm down, breathe in and out until you find your Sacred Breath and oneness with all, it'll stop gyrating."

"Sure."

"Going to be a while before I cut all of these bindings from the inside out. Wouldn't hurt to try. Unless you prefer to suffer, Gallagher."

"But, the dark. And the smell, like lots of bodies have sweated, suffered, been tortured here."

Her heart beat against her ribs; the panic rose to take her in horrible talons. She'd not live through this. By the time he cut the bindings, she would die from fright, from lack of air.

"I . . . I can't."

"Yes, *Winyan,* you can. Breathe in slowly. Do it now. Let the air out and with it your fear. In and out."

His calm voice interceded between her and the unreasonable fear. Every breath sent a sharp pang through her ribs, too. How did that happen? Maybe when someone lifted her into the cradle.

"Cradleboards, *Winyan,* are a nurturing place to find inner peace, a place to return to childhood's dreams, a place to listen to your inner voice. They have many symbolisms."

Again, she took deep breaths and let them out slowly. Not only did the cradle stop twirling, but her body now seemed suspended of its own volition.

"Close your eyes. See with your inner heart. Relax, *Winyan,* relax."

Panic ebbed and a tender warmth took its place. Light and comfortable, she allowed her mind to drift, and the darkness which now seemed to comfort her, cushioned her.

A breathtakingly beautiful wolf approached her. Nose to nose with the beast, she smiled. Each black hair around its muzzle was distinctly clear on the mystical entity.

In the ebony depths of its eyes were many facets—great wisdom, gentle humor and fierce pride even if it was only a watery reflection.

Willi blinked.

There beside a shimmering lakeside, an Indian warrior lay resting by leaning on one elbow. Dressed in a wolf's skin with the animal's head covering his own, the warrior looked down into the water and smiled at his spirit reflection, the wolf. In undulating lines another animal, a female, came and lay down beside the male. Her eyes were blue-green, a startling contrast to her dark fur. On the bank above, a lovely Indian maiden pushed a long braid over one shoulder, which was partially covered by the wolf skin she wore. She, too, lay down beside the warrior. The pines and oaks whispered in a singsong: Not yet. Someday. Clan of the Wolf. Both are teachers of The People. Not yet. Someday. Not yet. Not yet.

The lake disappeared and Willi was again surrounded by the darkness of her prison, but unafraid, she sighed. This daydream was different, more than a fantasy . . . a vision. Not knowing what it meant, just that it was special, she hugged the details to her and whispered.

"Not yet, but someday."

"I'm hurrying, Gallagher, I'm hurrying."

"I know."

"Ah-yah! *Hiya.* Dropped the knife."

A tinge of fear invaded for a moment. "I . . . I'm sure you'll find it, right?" She pushed the disabling sensation away. He *would* get her out.

"*Han,* yes. There. I've got it."

Quannah was as good as his word and cut her from the cradle in a few moments. After lifting her down from the swinging contraption, he looked closely at her. Even in the dusky glow of the shed, his eyes sparkled. A mirror image of her own eyes shone in the depths of his.

"Ah, you've had a special vision. I wonder if it's one you'll share."

She smiled. "*Not yet.* Someday."

Holding a hand over her aching ribs, she stumbled outside and blinked. What happened to the bright sunshine? "It's almost dusk." She yawned. Lord, she could barely move her limbs. It seemed like her head was stuffed with cotton. She shook it and swallowed to pop her ears, but nothing helped.

Quannah studied the sun's setting rays. "Yes, and time's wasting." She could tell his mind had already taken a quantum leap to the next problem and place down the road. Moving slowly so as not to jolt herself, she searched around the tree where she'd left Charlie Brown. He wasn't there, but her knapsack had a familiar shape to it, and the bag was scooting every which way across the ground. From inside, a few woofs and finally a despondent whimper alerted her.

"Silly pooch."

She straightened the backpack, placed Charlie Brown in the outside pocket after offering him the last crumbs from the bottom of the sack, and tramped toward the farmhouse. Her legs were so heavy. Obviously, full circulation had not returned.

Quannah followed. "Your *sunka kin cistila* hasn't grown much. Still wouldn't be much for the stew pot."

Frowning, she put her hands on her hips. "Indians don't really—"

Palm outward, he nodded. "In Sacred Ceremony only, not for everyday food. The chosen *sunka* is special." He winked, raising his jeans' leg to sheathe his knife. "This little fellow has nothing to worry about."

"Well . . . I suppose that's no worse than eating a turkey at Thanksgiving or cutting up a pig for Christmas hams."

He tenderly parted her hair. His fingers came away with bloodstains. "You get yourself to the emergency room. Your head has had a number of knocks lately. I'll pretend I don't see that stubborn look on your face. Promise me, Gallagher."

"Fine. I promise."

He tightened the leather thong around his ponytail. "My Rover is through those trees. Guess we'll part ways here."

"Wait."

Her mind was a jumble of questions. She calmed herself. This might be the last chance she had to get answers out of him.

"You *were* in Galveston," she said.

"Yes, *Winyan*. Guess after today, there's no reason to deny that fact."

She handed him the scrap of paper on which she'd raised the phone number, Hortense's name and the word *Hallettsville*. "That Benjamite business was finished months ago. What could Hallettsville have to do with two Nickleberry girls' murders in Galveston?"

"Can't leave anything to chance with a snoopy lady around, can I?" He grabbed the stickum sheet and crossed his arms over his chest. "We're not sure about the connection. I helped wrap up some of the last-minute mess on Hallettsville. One tip was that one of the crazy Benjamites, who were satanists, not Christian cultists, was with the group going to Galveston."

"Somebody from Nickleberry?"

He nodded.

"D'Dee or Adela?"

"No, an adult, the one who brought the kids into it."

"Sheriff Tucker knew this all along from the moment the kitten and puppy were found on the school grounds." She stopped to adjust her knapsack. Charlie Brown licked her ear.

"Lucky mongrel," Quannah said, winking. "Lucky to get even a *stolen* kiss."

Outwardly, she ignored the riposte, but inwardly a pleasant glow warmed her. "Why Hortense's name?"

He merely shrugged his broad shoulders. "Loose lips sink ships, Gallagher."

"We've had this discussion before."

He put a hand on her shoulder, waited for her to turn and face him and said, "I've shared much more than I should in the hopes, *Winyan,* that you'll know we're looking into the deaths along with this other matter. Now, you *must* stay out of the investigation. There is a dangerous mind out of control. Uncle Brigham and I will take care of this." He paused before adding, "Please."

She raised an eyebrow and smiled. He must have taken the motion for an affirmative, because he nodded.

He patted Charlie Brown. "You enjoy the sun's last rays and your *sunka kin cistila,* and I'll go hunt bad guys."

"Uh, one more question. You speak Lakota, but you're Comanche, right?"

"Right."

"So, why—?"

"Later, *Winyan,* time's a-wasting."

She was beginning to find some of their abruptly ended conversations irritating. She tromped across the field, walked inside the kitchen and found Agatha there helping Elba. Willi yawned and stumbled in the door. Her legs seemed heavier now than when she had first started her walk back across the fields. Maybe there was some delayed reaction to her experience.

"Lordy mercy," Elba said, with hands on her hips, "you're later than a slow-talking cowboy, more tardy than a towheaded kid coming to hoe and sure as hell too late to keep us two old women from worry."

"Why are you all here? It was to be a half day for you, Elba."

Agatha interrupted. "Don't let her give you a hard time, Willi. We just this minute got back. We went with our ... uh ... ladies' group to Waco and had a wonderful time on the *River Queen* steamboat luncheon cruise down the river. Now, tell us about your day."

Leaving out the encounter with Quannah and the horror of the witch's cradle, she told them about her earlier morning excursions chasing butterflies and rabbits. She hoped neither would notice that she was having a hard time getting her tongue around the words. She could barely hear their responses, the cloud of cotton seeming to thicken with each minute.

"Didn't find that handsome investigator, huh?" Elba asked.

"Did I say I was looking for him?" She frowned. "Anyway, I'm off to talk to Sheriff Tucker."

"Would you mind reminding Brigham about the dance tonight?" Agatha asked, pulling a strand of hair back into her bun. She looked at her wristwatch. "About nine is when the best part will start. He gets so busy, he forgets. I'm making him a butterscotch pie, too."

Grinning, Willi nodded. Long, lanky Agatha was about to reel in one old confirmed bachelor. "I'll be delighted to tell him," she said, and handed over Charlie Brown.

SHERIff Tucker leaned his chair back against the paneled wall, took out two bandannas—one purple, the other green—chose the purple one and worried his nose back and forth. He considered Willi's tale.

"I'm sorry, Miss Willi. Not a thing this old country sheriff can do."

"You can search out at the shack, confiscate those items

in the place—the witch's cradle and the stone slab."

"Nope, Miss Willi, I sure can't. Quannah told me about those items, too, but he knows like me, according to the law, people have a right to gather and worship as they please." He raised his hands in a helpless manner. "Just the same as you and I might go to Sunday church meeting or Quannah and I might attend a Sweat Lodge ceremony. No difference, says the law, if folks want to worship the devil."

"But, Sheriff, I told you what was on the slab and how that word has shown up a number of times in my"—she dared not call what she was doing an investigation—"uh, in this situation."

"And believe me, Miss Willi, the situation, as you call this, riles me more than you know. My hands are tied." He frowned and folded his bandanna. His massive paw rubbed his nose, then spread across his face, rubbing up and down as if that action might produce an answer or at least provide some relief from the problem. "I could see my way to check around about who owns the land and if the folks know anything about the rites going on in the shack," he offered. "Nothing much else can be done as of now."

He picked up the phone and, grinning at her, informed the hospital receptionist on the other end of the line to expect within the next quarter hour one Willi Gallagher who had a knock on her noggin. "Quannah told me you might be inclined to forget a certain promise to take care of yourself instead of everyone else."

Willi smiled ruefully. "Thanks, Sheriff Tucker, and by the way, Agatha asked me to remind you about the covered-dish social and dance tonight. She's bringing butterscotch pie."

His nose turned a bright pink and he brought out his green bandanna, but Willi wasn't fooled. He eyed her over the cloth. Shaking his leonine head, like that tick was again in his ear, he said, "You a-going with that Dan Oxhandler feller?"

"No, Sheriff Tucker. I'm no longer seeing Dan."

"Didn't think that particular boy would last." He winked at her. "Nothing against Dan, mind now, but there's some mighty different feller out there meant for you. He'll be along directly. Someone special." He cleared his throat, got brave enough to replace the handkerchief and said, "Special like my Agatha."

"I appreciate the lecture on my love life. Thanks. Maybe you, Agatha and Elba—oh, yes, don't forget the minister's wife—could have a study group about the problem. Perhaps when the new shipment of cantaloupes comes in?"

"Now, there you go getting your dander up."

She headed out the door, had a problem locating the doorknob and even more trouble trying to turn it, as if suddenly she had boxing gloves on her hands. Maybe she did need to go see a doctor.

He shouted after her. "Them kind like my Agatha is worth the waiting for."

As Willi walked to her car, she agreed somewhat, but hoped she wouldn't have to wait quite as long as the sheriff and Agatha before finding true love. Time to check on Auntie. She left the car window down, the radio off and enjoyed the trill of mockingbirds on her way to the Bluebonnet Apartments. But as she drove into the parking area, she saw Hortense standing within the glow of the porch light, knocking on her aunt's door.

What in Hades did Hortense think she was doing? The damned cheekiness of visiting so much and making such a play for Rodrigo. Wait a minute. Maybe she had another motive. She had been awfully curious about the diary and the discussion between Auntie, Rodrigo and Willi. Perhaps Hortense was trying to get more information. Made sense if she were the murderer. She'd been in the high school outside the computer lab, too, just before the diary was taken.

Willi screeched out of the parking lot, misjudged a turn and almost hit a light pole. Her heart skittered. Something was definitely not right. She finally drove, slowly and carefully, to the hospital, was admitted and had to wait for hours for blood tests and results. Why they always needed those for every cut and bruise, she would never understand, but she figured it had something to do with insurance. An elevator located right outside her room almost drove her to the floor for the mentally deranged. Every time the elevator stopped, it beeped like the Road Runner. Installing a machine with such a sound in a hospital should have been against the law. Elba stepped out from those mechanical doors.

"What are you doing here?" Willi asked.

"Just one of them feelings that wouldn't let a body rest. Agatha had the same feeling, but there was no sense in us both leaving the dance, so I come to check on you, especially after Tucker caught us up on what all really happened today."

"Sorry."

"Ought to be. But we figured you was trying to spare us worry."

"True. Am I forgiven?"

"Only if you live. I'll wait upstairs and check back in a few minutes."

Willi managed one word around the lump in her throat. "Thanks." At times like these, she felt very blessed to have two irascible white witches in her life.

At last, a lab technician arrived with the results. Taller than your average pine tree, he had to stoop to get through the doorway. His identification tag had DAVID BLACK-

BOURNE, M.D. on it. She amended lab tech to doctor.

"Yeah-yep." He spoke to the wall above Willi's head, his Adam's apple bouncing and vibrating with the syllable.

"So," she prompted, "what did you find?"

"Something. We wouldn't have worked on this so fast if Sheriff Tucker hadn't insisted."

She waited, tapping her foot.

He studied the clipboard, tilted his head back again and said, "Something not good."

"Yes?" She tightened her jaw. "Well, what in damnation is it?" Pushing his hand away, she stood.

"Not too bad, though." He peered at her as if she were a fairly interesting specimen under his microscope. "You'll hurt yourself jumping up that way."

Managing not to grab his immaculate white lapels by the simple expedient of clasping her hands behind her back, she glowered. "What is not good but not too bad?"

"You shouldn't drive under the influence." He released his hold and forestalled her denial with a wave of his gaunt fingers. "Influence of something stronger than cough syrup, like one of those all-night kinds that let you rest through the night. To have this much show up in the tests, you probably received a triple or quadruple dose. You are groggy, are you not?"

She nodded, but refused to sit in Blackbourne's presence. "How'd they do that? I was out cold until I felt myself strung up inside the cradle."

"Might have forced it down your throat. It can be done." He stood when the elevator outside the room beeped before halting. Elba's comforting figure ambled out.

With a cold finger underneath Willi's chin, Blackbourne tilted her face.

She peered up not at his Adam's apple, but at a cadaverous mouth full of teeth. Stuffing one hand in her pocket, she clasped Tunkasila, breathed in and out but couldn't seem to calm the anger permeating her.

"Want to?" he asked, raising a brushy eyebrow.

"Want to what?"

"Tomorrow night. You. Me. Bottle of Chablis. My place."

"You insufferable, cold, calculating, self-centered bastard—you—you—sorry excuse for a human."

"No, huh? It happens now and then. Not often, though." He studied her as if she'd mutated into a bothersome germ that might spread contagious diseases throughout the county.

She grudgingly gave Elba her due in the sensitivity department. The old woman didn't utter one *I told you so* or anything about *You might consider him for a boyfriend seeing as how you can't seem to snare that investigator*. Not until Willi's head hit the pillow after eleven that night did she remember something important. And that memory was hazy, having to do with needing to see Betty. She would reschedule with the girl tomorrow. Willi drifted off into deep sleep, one where no nightmares disturbed her through the night.

CHAPTER
18

IN fact, nothing disturbed willi's sleep, not noctur-
nal noises, Charlie Brown or jolting dreams until the shrill
insistence of the phone made her groan. She opened one
eye to look at the illuminated clock face.

"It's 3:30 A.M. What now?"

She groped for her bathrobe, remembered she hadn't
put one out and yawned. The phone jangled again. She
had to get a phone line upstairs or one of those wireless
ones. She added that to her list of one hundred and one
things to do. Charlie Brown, in the kitchen, barked
sharply.

"Okay, okay, I'm coming."

Blinking, she stumbled downstairs and grabbed the
kitchen phone, but her voice refused to cooperate, and her
first words merely rumbled somewhere in the back of her
throat. A distant mumbling reached her ears.

"Willi? Willi Gallagher? Are you there?"

After only two tries, she managed to get the correct end
of the receiver to her ear.

"Uhm—more or less. Who—?"

"Hortense."

"It's late, Hortense."

"Later than you think."

Willi closed her one opened eye. "Please, Hortense. Explain. Be quick and clear."

"Certainly. Normally, I wouldn't have called this late. I thought you'd like to know."

Willi yawned but paid closer attention. Hortense hadn't used one adjective, a sign boding no good at any time.

Hortense said, "I was up reading and listening with an ear to the scanner when I heard an ambulance called to the library—the Nickleberry Public, not the high school's. Well, I was curious."

Gossipy Horsey *would* have a scanner.

"Marilyn Pinn have a heart attack? What?"

"When I called Nickleberry County General, all the call nurse could tell me was that it was a student. They found an ID card. The nurse didn't even stay on long enough to tell me male or female." Hortense paused. "But in the background I could have sworn I heard the name Zeta. But I'm not sure. Is there a Zeta child other than Adela?"

"Trujillo, her brother."

Oh no. Trujillo's fear had been real. Willi just hadn't focused on it correctly when she and Dan visited. The sheriff had indicated that the Zetas, one or both at different times, had been brought up on child abuse charges.

Tentatively, Hortense asked, "Willi, is this number three? What's happening? Why are our students ending up in hospitals with injuries or dying?"

Since she didn't have an adequate answer for that question, she thanked Hortense and hung up. She pulled on jeans and a T-shirt. Grabbing her purse and car keys, she headed for NC General.

* * *

THE automatic doors of the hospital whizzed open. Antiseptic smells drifted toward her. In the lower foyer of muted grays and pinks, tastefully accented with burgundy chairs beneath upturned and fluted standing lights, a faint scent of powder and disinfectant permeated the thick carpeting. A bank of curved arches, small niches for secretaries and clerks, efficiently separated nervous visitors from the lone woman staffing the area.

Willi approached, thinking she might have been wiser to have entered through the Emergency room, until she recognized the young lady behind the archway.

"Ms. Gallagher, it is so good to see you again, you know."

Pippa Rodriguez, one of last year's graduates and office aides, smiled charmingly.

"Good to see you, too, Pippa. I've a favor to ask, if you don't mind?"

"Anything, Ms. Gallagher. I never forgot your kindness, you know, in introducing me to so many people when I entered so late in the year. You made it possible for me to enjoy my senior year."

"In a way, Pippa, this has to do with the school, too. Someone was brought in tonight, a student. Male? Female? I don't know. Is there some way you can find out who it was and what the problem is?"

"Just you wait right here."

She patted Willi's arm, turned and picked up a phone with enough buttons to serve all the armed forces in case of war. Deftly, she manipulated them until she contacted someone in Emergency. She talked for a few moments.

Eyes widened, she turned to Willi and announced, "The patient is someone I don't know, and I can't give out the information since the next of kin hasn't been notified." She squirmed uncomfortably and spread her hands. "Oh, and I wanted to be of help."

Willi sighed. Damn. So close. She knew she could push Pippa, and she'd divulge the name, but that might get her into trouble on the job.

"Is there anyone you could suggest I ask for in Emergency who might give me more information?"

Pippa nodded happily. "He didn't say I couldn't give *his* name, you know." She leaned through the archway and whispered, although not another person sat in the cavernous waiting lounge. "Dr. D.—Dr. *Diablo*, we call him—is on duty tonight. He's a devil with pretty women."

"Seems you have a number of that type around."

"You know, this is true. It's office number 607."

"Emergency is on the first floor, isn't it?"

"Yes, ma'am, but first you meet Dr. D. He sleeps in his office between calls."

With the memo sheet in her hand, Willi traversed the quiet lobby to the bank of elevators and stepped in one of the maws of metal and lights. She always felt like Jonah in the belly of the whale when she used an elevator, the hum of machinery depicting the digestive rumblings of the great mammal. After beeping, it spit her out on floor 6. Here, no carpet softened the slick sound of her tennis shoes, but the lighting, still muted and hidden in recesses against the ceiling, warned her that quiet was expected. She practically tiptoed to a beveled glass door with an embossed strip of chrome on the right side of the door frame, proclaiming this was 607. She knocked.

"Come," a sepulchral voice intoned.

She entered. A tall swivel chair turned away from her.

"Uh . . . Doctor, I was told you might help me get information about the student brought in. I'm Willi Gallagher, English teacher at the high school." She held out her hand in anticipation of him swiveling around toward her.

"Gallagher?"

Why did that grating voice sound familiar?

The chair whipped around and a lanky frame unraveled itself from the leather confines.

"You changed your mind. The Chablis did it, right?"

Blackbourne. No, not twice in one night. She abandoned the idea of retreat as unworthy. The fear gnawing at her innards for Trujillo was stronger than her disgust for Blackbourne.

"I'm here to see about one of our students. This has to do with the case Sheriff Tucker is pursuing and may have something to do with why I was drugged last night."

Not surprisingly, he proffered nothing. That game again. *Okay,* she admonished herself, *don't get angry; get the information you want and get even later.*

"Dr. Blackbourne, I'm not requesting information out of idle curiosity."

He stood with a quickness that cut off her breath, turned sharply away and looked out his long arrow-shaped window. "I know. Sheriff Tucker said earlier I was to cooperate with you, Ms. Gallagher. He also mentioned who your father was—Phidias Gallagher."

Wheeling around and marching back toward her, he towered above, making Willi wonder how long it would take her to race down the hall to the safety of the whale's belly.

"So, what does my father have to do with—?"

"I went to a church school as a kid, not the Nickleberry Independent here in town, so our paths—yours and mine—didn't cross."

"You've lost me."

"Tucker and your father kept me from having to go to the Waco Orphanage when my dad killed Mom. Good men that they are, they kept the horror of that night from the front pages. Your father paid for my education."

"I had no idea." But the fact didn't surprise her. Her

folks were always behind the scenes doing good for everyone. Another shared philosophy of Lassiter's surfaced: "If you're doing good for the whole, the whole is doing good for you."

"Come."

He opened the door and allowed her to follow. He ignored the bank of public elevators and headed instead to the stairway and the service elevators. Punching the button labeled EMERGENCY/MORGUE with a cadaverous finger, he surveyed Willi and said, "My apologies for . . . for earlier. My Chablis comment back there was my way of kidding." He looked her in the eyes, and she grudgingly nodded. He said, "Sheriff Tucker said you'd give me a thumbnail view of the situation."

She found herself, haltingly at first and then with more command over her emotions, explaining the events, but deleting mention of Lassiter. Surely, she had enough to convince Blackbourne without breaking what cover Lassiter had as a visiting nephew of Sheriff Tucker. She mentioned the Galveston trip, D'Dee's death beneath the ferry, Adela's plunge from the Flagship Hotel, the satanic overtures everywhere she nosed about, the mutilations of the animals. She even told about the poppet and her concerns about Adela's brother, Trujillo, who was now the sole child in an abusive household. Somewhere deep in the pit of her stomach, she feared that Trujillo was the one in Emergency, probably suffering broken bones, lacerations or concussion.

After she'd completed her story, she realized she and Blackbourne had traipsed past Emergency, gone down further underground and were standing in front of the morgue.

"But . . . the morgue? Then . . ." She bit her bottom lip.

"Sure you want to go in?"

At her nod, he shoved on the double doors. He stood

before a shelf with his hand on the handle of box 11. Before he opened it, he turned toward her, and some emotion passed across his features. The look wasn't one of showing a crisis of conscience but more like an intellectual conundrum. She actually felt more comfortable with that more distant version of Blackbourne.

"This will be a shock."

Okay, maybe he did have a conscience. He was giving her a chance to back off from the corpse, a chance not to look on the Zeta boy's last visage, his pain. She pressed her lips together, felt the color drain from her face, but she remained rooted to the spot.

He raised a bushy eyebrow and nodded. A swish of well-oiled hinges reverberated in the quiet room, and a bagged body appeared on the waist-high gurney between Willi and Blackbourne.

With his hand on the bag's zipper, he intoned, "Came in still alive. Awful."

Willi noted the strain around his eyes, the tightness around his mouth, but found little sympathy for the man. A flush spread up and down her body, followed by an icy tingle. If he didn't unzip the bag soon, she'd faint before she knew the answer and could vent her justifiable wrath upon the Zetas.

"Mr. Laughton, out walking his dog in the back alleyways, heard a scuffling. He ran behind the city library and found the kid."

Willi nodded and swallowed bile. She willed the doctor to either unzip the bag or enclose himself in one and silently slip into the coldest of the metal shelves. Her teeth chattered; she clutched her elbows with her hands.

"Kid was carried to the city library from somewhere else. That's all Mr. Laughton told us." He lowered the zipper a few inches. "No way we could save the victim. This is the third botched job we've seen this year on teens.

They get scared and will go to anybody." His glance locked with Willi's.

He continued the procedure, finally revealing a head and torso, one which, through Willi's fog, was merely a hazy outline.

The odor of medications and antiseptics wafted up from the half-opened plastic, reminding Willi of the obnoxious smells of cleaning fresh-killed chickens in a kitchen redolent of the smells of Lysol and Mr. Clean.

Finally, she peered down at the corpse. For some seconds, which seemed to meld with time and last as long as a dramatic miniseries, she failed to focus, couldn't or wouldn't recognize the child—not Trujillo Zeta—before her. She laid a trembling hand on the damp curls on the forehead. A foul darkness wrapped itself around her shocked mind, the medicated mustiness enveloped her and she fell into an abyss of blessed forgetfulness. Her last coherent contact with reality was Blackbourne intoning, "There was nothing we could do."

"THOUGHT you was going to throw up everything but your toenails," said Elba as she assisted Willi into bed in the wee hours of the morning. "That there is your *third* visit to the hospital in about as many days. Gonna have to listen to me. You better be carrying that poppet. You been anywhere else lately just *two* times? That there'd be what you'd have to worry about next." Breathless, Elba paused. "You're worrying me worse than a tick on a dog, worse than a pimple on the backside of the circus's fat lady, worse than—" She wiped her forehead. "Whew. I got to sit a spell."

Willi's head hurt. She really didn't want to see Betty Norris in her mind's eye, but the vision of the girl floated there ad nauseum.

"Dr. Blackbourne said she'd had a botched abortion. That the idiot who tried finally realized she was too far into the pregnancy, and ended up doing a crude C-section to save her and the baby, but only the infant survived. At least that was what the note said which was found with Betty."

Elba fluffed the pillowcases behind Willi's head. "That'd sure enough explain all that table grazing she did. Lord, she could put on the feed bag, eat whatever wouldn't eat her first. I'd give anything to have her here now. I'd set a feast before the poor child."

Willi clutched the old woman's hand. "What if I could have said something to her to prevent this?"

"Too late for ifs, ands and buts. Couldn't have done nothing nohow. Young-uns get into that kind of trouble sometimes—not always—but sometimes make some bad decisions.

"And, at least, you know Betty didn't turn to those in that sick coven. She was trying to do right as she seen it. Poor kid. Didn't want them to have the baby to raise up in sick ways." Elba shook a finger in Willi's face. "Who knew she came to see you?"

"Hortense delivered the note, but anyone around could have heard her tell me. Caprithia Feather. Let's see. Paul Undel and Jerald Stanley. Miss Pinn."

"Which ones got an interest in this satanic stuff?"

"Hortense is so intense about it, she saves her hair and nails so no one can make a poppet out of them."

"Interesting. Go on."

"Jerald thought it would be wonderful to be named Beezlebub or Warlock or something like that."

"Mighty strange for a teacher, ain't it? Now I don't like that one bit. He's strong, too."

Willi rubbed her temples. "What does that have to do with anything?"

"Stands to reason some fella big enough to tie up that handsome investigator and get you up in a witch's cradle might be strong enough to scare a confused, lonesome and pregnant kid."

"But only Hortense stumbled on to that fact, and she wasn't absolutely sure."

"What about them others?"

Willi sighed. "Paul Undel and Caprithia Feather talk a lot about nothing, but otherwise are as quiet as mice. Neither one has mentioned devil worship."

"Them quiet ones are the most dangerous."

"Oh, I don't care anymore. I can't figure anything out. I've just caused harm rather than doing any good at all."

"Well, ain't we suddenly having us a fine old pity party? Betty's situation is tragic, no two ways about it, but this part of the tragedy only she controlled. She didn't share with nobody who the young man was so we can't expect no help for that newborn babe from no absentee daddy. But you, Miss Willi, aren't going to take that on your shoulders to worry about. No way are you going out there and figure out where that little bitty helpless thing might be."

Willi eyed Elba warily, "Sounds like you want me to go looking and—"

"Nope. That's not what I'm saying at all. I'm saying as how you need to get over your feeling sorry for yourself as there are others in worse situations than yourself. Maybe you ought to contact one handsome investigator fellow. Where in the hell is that Lassiter? What's he doing about this?"

Willi bit her bottom lip to keep it from trembling. "I don't know." The last word, much to her chagrin, ended on a wail. She licked her lips and tried for more calm. "And that's unfair. He's checking something out in Hallettsville, some connection. I'm the one responsible for this horror."

"Nonsense. Don't want to hear no more. You ain't no more to blame than cooties in spring, chiggers in summer nor cold sores in winter. Things just happen. Tucker is down to the hospital morgue. He's taking care of things. Here. Drink this."

The hot concoction down her throat soothed the raw edges of her nerves. She finally fell asleep, with Charlie Brown snuggled protectively in the curve of her knees. Nightmares of Betty swinging in a witch's cradle plagued Willi. She tossed, twisting the sheets around her until she awoke in a chilling sweat.

"AH-CHOO!" Bleary-eyed, willi stared across the sheriff's desk.

"Ragweed," he said apologetically. " 'Course if the dang blame air didn't have ragweed, there'd be something else." He rubbed his nose, more like a great tuber attached to his kindly face.

"So, Sheriff, what did you find in Betty's room?"

"Saw that altar you told me about. No cross. No diary."

"Damn."

"But Miss Willi,"—he opened a deep file cabinet, pulled out a packet of letters tied in gold cording and placed them on the desk—"these were beneath her mattress."

"Somehow Betty never seemed the type to carry on such a correspondence. That's quite a stack."

"Seven hundred and twenty-three to be exact." Sheriff Tucker handed them across the oak desk. "Already been gone over with a fine-tooth comb, so's you can touch them. Pretty strange letters."

After perusing a few, Willi had to agree. "Sort of a

loose-leaf diary. Notes to herself, some to 'Betty the Beautiful,' others to 'Betty the bearer.' " Willi sensed pain in and between the lines of Betty's meticulous penmanship. " 'Betty the bearer' is filled with self-disgust, confusion, hate. Poor kid."

Willi peered out the sheriff's office window. An overcast day. Nothing could be worse or more appropriate. The atmospheric change pushed against her chest. A storm brewed behind uncomfortable clouds on the horizon that threatened to disappear completely in the mist gathering in her eyes. She sniffed.

"Sheriff?"

Her voice betrayed her, changing an octave without warning. She tried again.

"Sheriff, this 'bearer' reference Dan and I discovered in Adela Zeta's room and these notes tie the girls' deaths together, don't they?"

"Yes, ma'am, I'm considering that pretty strong, but I have been since Quannah done brought me that little bitty cross from D'Dee's room."

"There was a diary, too."

"Oh? Quannah didn't mention it."

"Well, he didn't . . . I mean, I sort of borrowed . . . but, I lost it."

She told him in detail how the diary was lifted in the computer lab.

"It'll show up, Miss Willi. Mayhap in the hands of the killer."

Willi nodded and said, "The satanic cult references provide a thread, too."

"Seems like. Wonder what those girls did to get a cult which they was involved with so riled at them as to kill them?"

"You did check out that old house in the woods and

that horrible marble slab for traces of Betty's . . ." Willi swallowed. "For any trace."

"Got men doing that now, but not for anything related to Betty. Checking to see if there's some connection between what Quannah's searching for out Hallettsville way and our *problemos* here. Guess we should of done that soon as you and Quannah had your bad experience out there, but we was trying to keep things quiet until we had some evidence."

He rubbed his chin. "We done brought in the quack doctor who did the botched job. He admitted everything. Said he really didn't realize how far along she was—pretty dang stupid for any kind of doctor, you ask me—and he laid the baby on a blanket right beside her. He said he had wrapped it up good and warm, but there'd be no mistaking it when somebody found Betty. So—" Tucker worried his ear and changed the subject abruptly as if he couldn't face that idea at the moment. The abandoned shack seemed a safer subject. "Anyhoo, deputy at the shack radioed a while back and so far no luck at all."

"Who owns the land?"

"Some feller in Baghdad on the Bayou."

"Houston?"

"Yep, Miss Willi, but haven't been able to reach him. On a cruise. Has been all this month. He won't have anything to do with this here mess. Someone knew he wasn't ever around and took advantage."

For the first time, Willi noted the deep shadows beneath Sheriff Tucker's eyes. She smiled at his continuously red nose and his overall frazzled appearance. He no more cared for the idea of a murderer running free in Nickleberry than she.

He took out an orange-striped bandanna, rubbed his face, folded and placed the kerchief on the corner of his desk. He signaled one of the clerks by pressing a button on his phone. The young officer peered around the door.

"Coffee for me." He raised a bushy eyebrow in Willi's direction.

"Hot chocolate, please."

When the beverages arrived, Sheriff Tucker produced his small notebook and the stub of a pencil. Willi had never seen him with a new one and wondered if the Sheriff's Department received all the high school's rejects. A hundred or more three-by-five spiral notebooks, earmarked and labeled, were stacked neatly behind the sheriff's desk inside a glass case. The one on his desk would eventually be added to the collection. She wondered what he'd labeled the cover and asked.

"Haven't as yet. What might be the proper term?"

"For what?" she asked.

"Them witches. That name you kept calling them. What is it?"

"Wiccans." At the unspoken question in his eyes, she added, "Witches connotes to most people a female, although that's not really the case. Wiccans. I can easily envision males or females under that term. One wicked Wiccan loose in Nickleberry."

The sheriff removed an adhesive label from its backing and stuck the label on the front of the notebook. He penciled in WICCAN and set his pencil aside.

"Ah-choo!"

As if the sneeze had worked as his personal muse, he again lifted the pencil and squeezed another word in front of the first he'd written. When he finished, Willi reached out and turned the notebook toward her.

WICKED WICCAN.

Her glance locked with the sheriff's and she nodded approval.

"And we're going to get him for what he done to them three girls, Miss Willi."

She didn't think she'd ever been more fond of that weathered face, that bulbous nose and crooked grin. Unshed tears threatened to spill over. Finally, she had an ally who could officially assist with no more pretending. Relief flooded through her. Yes, damn it, the Wiccan behind the murders wouldn't get away with such atrocities.

She sipped her chocolate, peered at the desk and made circles on the top with her index finger. Now, with the air cleared and a cohort in the investigation, she felt strong enough to touch on a subject he had abandoned earlier.

"The baby?"

"Ah, yes, ma'am." He leaned back in his chair and belched behind his hand. "Pardon." Worrying his nose back and forth, he sniffed. "Can't say. Maybe someone— a Good Samaritan type—saw the little critter and took it for the night. Might be they'll turn it in soon as news hits. They just might not have wanted to deal with the girl dead and all. Folks do the strangest things, as you know."

"Sacrifice comes to mind."

"Miss Willi, Miss Willi. Mayhap, but let's not borrow no trouble. Whoever left the note wanted us to know the baby was okay. And if a coven's folks are responsible, they don't want babies nowadays for such as that. They want new members to raise up in their sick ways."

He pulled out another notebook and made a label with BABY NORRIS written on the front. "Two different cases at the moment. I figure they won't stay that way. But it's possible."

Well, he was probably right. She asked, "How's Mrs. Norris taking the tragedy?"

"She was out of town last night. Visiting a sister over in Lubbock. She's driving back. Ought to be here soon. In fact, right about now." He finished the dregs in his cup, placed his battered Stetson on his head and rose. Hitching his pants up, he replaced the orange-striped bandanna in his back pocket, and guided her to the door.

"No sense you suffering through this meeting with the mother. How about you taking those letters, notes, whatever, and seeing if you can make heads or tails of them?"

He placed them in a Winn-Dixie grocery bag, and walked outside with her. The swirl of dry dust from a passerby's car wheels dovetailed with the mist settling down from the spring clouds. "Mayhap we'll be getting another soaking rain."

"Oh, wait . . . I forgot." She hadn't mentioned the letters in the corner of Betty's message, delivered by Hortense. She showed him the telephone call slip.

"See? There's a *P* and a *U*." She shrugged and held the letters closer.

"Don't know. But it'll all fall into place. I'll put this with the other evidence on the Baby Norris case."

She paused, but didn't give voice to her next thoughts. She had an idea about those two letters. She'd go ahead and pursue that before going over Betty's letters.

"See you later, Sheriff."

He waggled a finger in her face. "You be getting some rest. Don't be worrying no more. I'm gonna see to this baby situation here, and Quannah's looking into something that'll be helpful about finding out about Adela and D'Dee. So, you just forget about it all."

She studied him with the most innocent look she could muster while nodding, headed outside, got in her car and studied the Texas road map.

"Where exactly *is* Hallettsville?"

CHAPTER
19

THE next day her morning calm was ruined with the Kackelhoffer sisters' predictions. Elba said, "Sure as Sunday follows Saturday, you're heading right into danger, Willi."

"It might behoove you to listen," Agatha added. "Both of us have seen the danger enveloping you, Sister in the Tarot and I in the crystal." Agatha touched her hot pink skirt and adjusted the green polka-dotted scarf. No wonder Sheriff Tucker was attracted to her. She looked like she was parading around in a half dozen of his colorful bandannas. "Sit for just a moment, Willi, please."

Elba tapped a gnarled knuckle on her cards. "Says you're a-going back to your childhood or maybe in danger from children."

"Yes, and . . ." Agatha shook her skirt. "Oh, I do hate to . . ."

Elba barked out, "If she was a-pouring gasoline on a fire, we'd tell her to stop. If she was a-driving on black ice on a Dallas freeway, we'd get her off. If she was fixin' to jump off Haliburton's Cliff, we'd grab hold tight. I don't want Willi shaking hands with eternity afore her time, Agatha. Now, dangblameit, tell what you saw in the glass."

"You were in a witch's cradle, blinded and suffocating."

"Maybe, most of this has already happened," Willi said, "like the witch's cradle—so we don't have to worry. Now, I have to—"

"No," Agatha insisted. "Another witch's cradle . . . and Brigham's nephew . . . well . . . he won't be able to help you. He's laid out on a slab of cold marble. His head, well . . . he can't help you."

Elba locked her arms together and hefted up her ample bosom. "That protective stone Quannah done give you and the protective poppet ought to keep you from harm . . . if . . . *if* you don't go sticking your nose where you shouldn't oughta. You got to honor what the spirits tell you through the cards and the crystal if you want to avoid things as they're now setting out."

Willi got up and hugged both the sisters. She pulled out Tunkasila and the good poppet, kissed them both and winked. "You can stop worrying. Now, I've got some errands."

"Where you getting off to now?" Elba asked as Agatha gently put away the cards and the crystal ball.

"Just to visit some of the teachers, maybe stop by and check on Aunt Minnie."

A few minutes later India Lou opened the apartment door for her. "Lordy, ain't it good to be seeing you, Willi." India Lou's face lit up in the grin no one could resist. "You stroll this here-a-way. Your aunt and Mr. Vivar done be setting out on the patio. Sure do hopes this storm holds off so they's can enjoy the evening air." She opened the French doors. "I'll just be getting another glass of lemonade and a plate of cherry brownies."

Willi stepped onto the vine-covered patio. A fan,

slightly askew and in need of oiling, creaked in cadence with a lone cricket. In the wicker love seat across from the glass-topped table, Auntie and Rodrigo sat holding hands.

Rodrigo rose, pulled out a chair close to them and held it until Willi seated herself.

Minnie chirped, "We were about to call you. Which shall we tell her first, my El Cid?"

Rodrigo took her hands in his own. "Whichever you wish, *mi paloma*."

Willi smiled. *My dove* certainly sounded romantic, even taken literally, and it certainly was romantic considering that half the Hispanic songs used the term to mean *precious* or *darling* one. Either way, from the expression on her aunt's face, nothing was lost in the translation.

"Rodrigo can't bear to go back to Tyler without me. He's moving into the Bluebonnet Apartments, too. Isn't that wonderful?"

"Yes, Auntie, it is, but, Rodrigo, what about your job as assistant superintendent?"

"It is well past my time to retire. I never had reason to before." He squeezed Minnie's hands. "Her illness made me realize how short life is and what is important."

Willi congratulated them and asked, "And the second thing?"

"Scuttlebutt," Minnie said, shaking her white curls. "Info about Paul Undel. Some cousin twice removed of one of the school board members passed this on. There's something about blackmail. Maybe he's being black-mailed?"

"Well, at this point I'd believe just about anything was possible. Did this cousin—?"

"—twice removed," corrected Auntie.

"Did this cousin twice removed give any details? For

example, who was blackmailing him and for what reason?"

"Take the bull by the horns, Willi. Most things in life are best if handled straight on. Go ask him." Auntie raised a forefinger. "Remember to come back and let us know the rest of the story."

When Willi got in her car, she had plenty to think about. She glanced upward. *Great. Here we go again.* The sky was gray and thunder boomed far away. Would it or wouldn't it rain? She needed time and a place to think about the rumors before approaching Paul. She wanted to mull over her find—the earring, and to her chagrin she was a mite nervous about the Kackelhoffers' perdictions.

She stopped at a small cafe north of town called Spacek's Bar-B-Q. Her folks had come there often, but she hadn't and couldn't imagine why she'd turned into the busted tarmac of the parking area. Ah, well, she was into following her nose, letting the instincts of the universe guide her this week. So, why not Spacek's? Ozzie would probably have horrible things to say about the rundown hole-in-the-wall. The screen door protested loudly when she swung it open. Each creaking step she took across the gray and gold speckled linoleum attested to the aging foundation. From an old jukebox the lyrics of "One Fool on a Stool" ended, replaced by the tones of Marty Robbins's "Begging to You."

All the corners were shadowed, which suited her mood and her need for anonymity just fine. Along the dark walls the gloom eliminated all but the outlines of the customers—silhouettes seemingly created with one of those erasable pens that left smudges. She slid into a corner booth boasting seats patched with duct tape, the stuffing obviously removed with each mending. She sank bottomward and wondered how she'd get out when the time came.

Amy Lee Grinlea, an ex-student, who after ten years

out of the classroom was still shy as a spring colt in its first thunderstorm, approached. Amy's nervous fingers tapped her order pad as Willi considered the menu. "The veggie plate, Amy Lee. And a tea."

"You want the corn bread or rolls, Ms. Gallagher?"

"Corn bread, please."

As lightning severed the skies, Amy Lee bolted away. The screen door banged behind Jerald Stanley. Willi ducked her head as the gentle rhythm of "Sweet Country Woman" came through the jukebox's speakers. Another flash of lightning zoomed through the cafe. Jerald came over and sat across from her. "Looking for a quiet place, Willi?"

"That was the original idea. I can't imagine this being the type of eatery you would frequent."

"You're right, I have a mission." Obviously not intending to share more, he pulled the metal napkin dispenser closer, glanced at his image and brushed a strand of his silver hair into place. "The devil seems to be orchestrating the weather lately, huh?"

"Interested in the occult, Jerald?"

"Just satanism. Considering what's going on lately, I prefer to be informed. You heard about Betty Norris?"

Willi sat straighter. "Her mother hasn't even been in to identify her yet. How did you—?"

Amy Lee skittered to a stop before the table and took his order. How had he found out what had happened to Betty so soon? She recalled his bloodred goblet, his caustic remarks about young brats. He'd certainly attracted his share of female adoration from the female students, especially emotionally hungry ones like Betty, perhaps also D'Dee and Adela. "Fraulein" 's chords burst into her reverie at the same time Amy Lee placed a basket of steaming corn bread and vegetables before her. Before she gamboled away, Willi asked for a tea refill.

Jerald helped himself to a piece of corn bread while
waiting for his own chicken-fried steak and salad. He
grinned at Willi. "I know about Betty because I spent the
evening entertaining a lady who happens to be a nurse on
the hospital staff. She was very upset. Said there was
nothing to be done, and poor little Betty didn't even say
a word." He tilted the napkin holder, wiped a crumb from
his full lips and smiled at his reflection.

Willi dug into her okra and yellow squash. Well, his
damned ego coupled with hormones certainly made him
equal to the task of impregnating one teen. Blast, she sus-
pected everyone of the most foul deeds. There wasn't a
shred of evidence he was involved in any way, just her
gut instinct.

Thunder rolled and boomed as an intro to "The Wabash
Cannonball." Amy Lee shrieked and bounded up with Jerald's steak and Willi's tea refill. The protesting door
squealed as a family of four left and Paul Undel walked
in, briefcase in hand. He headed for a booth across the
room.

"Should we wave to him?" she asked.

"And ruin the mission?" Jerald grinned. "I think not.
I've been waiting for this a long time."

She almost choked on her last bite of corn bread when
two Honors students—Andy Gates and Tina Blithdale—
walked in and headed for Undel's table. They didn't sit,
and Undel quickly handed them each a sheaf of papers.

"This is spring break," she whispered. "What is—?"

"Listen. Watch. You'll be a good witness." Jerald,
frowning, palmed his hair over his ears.

Andy Gates reached into his back pocket to pull out
his billfold and laid a number of bills in Undel's upturned
hand. Tina dipped her hand into her purse and came up
with a bulging envelope.

"What's going on here?" Willi whispered, although it was clearer than her retroussé nose in a magnified mirror. Life had truly turned topsy-turvy, and she figured that at any moment someone would erase her outline from the dusky wall and then none of this would have happened. She would not have just witnessed the demeaning of her profession, would not have been revolted by the exploitation of juveniles by someone in a position of power and trust. Willi slapped her forehead. Of course he wasn't surprised when he glanced at the papers in the computer lab. He meant to run off the English exams.

Andy and Ṭina slipped out the door. Willi wasn't about to let Paul do the same, but when she tried to get up the bottomed-out seat held her prisoner. By the time she'd scooted sideways across the duct tape, Paul had gone.

Jerald tapped her hand and picked up both checks. She frowned and slapped a bill on the table. He picked up the money, replaced it in her hand and closed her fingers around it. "Willi, I'm not a Paul Undel. I've been watching him for months."

"Your mission?"

"Right."

"Sorry. That action . . . uh . . . the money . . . was misplaced anger."

"I know, and certainly the anger is understandable. Now that we two have witnessed the transaction, we have to find tangible, physical proof through the computers."

Willi nodded. She told him about her confrontation with Undel and the open English test bank in the computer lab. "I guess you're right." She reached in her pocket and stroked the Teaching Stone. "Right action is needed."

"Sounds like a quote."

Surprised at herself, Willi nodded. "You're right. It's from a book about totems."

"Really?"

His one word sounded as if he were truly interested so she added, "Yes, Antelope Medicine . . . refers to right action at the right time." *Just because I want to go to Hallettsville now doesn't make that right.* "We need to go to the high school lab."

Somehow an uneasiness grew in her as she drove behind Jerald. Perhaps the white witches' crystal ball and card readings preyed on her mind along with the stormy evening, not to mention that niggling sensation that she'd be entering that rambling building with someone she didn't quite trust.

Nonsense. She parked, got out and squared her shoulders. There weren't any cradles or children right now at the high school.

Just as she set her foot on the first step, she paused. She wanted so desperately to go to Hallettsville. Why? A vision of Auntie and Rodrigo swam before her. She sighed. Her bent for a trip to south Texas didn't have a thing to do with the killings. It had everything to do with her emotions surrounding one Lakota-speaking investigator. She took another step up. *Not yet,* Winyan, *not yet* winged briefly through her thoughts. "Oh, shut up," she said.

"Pardon?" Jerald raised an eyebrow. "Are you all right?"

"I'm fine. Let's get this done. I *am* going to make a drive down south tonight, and nothing is going to stop me."

CHAPTER 20

HER heels, muted by the threadbare institutional
carpeting, felt heavier with each step Willi took. Following Jerald upstairs and down the hall to the computer lab,
she pushed her insidious thoughts to a corner of her mind,
promising herself to consider them later.

He unlocked the computer lab, turned on the harsh fluorescent lighting and invited her to sit beside him before
an IBM monitor. At the touch of a finger, the screen
blinked and a software menu appeared. Clicking a couple
of numbers, Jerald magically entered the test bank for
World History.

"So," said Willi, "you're in your own file. What help
is that?"

"We both know Paul is providing something worth-
while to the Honors students. Stands to reason it's something to do with grades. Some of the little snots would
sell their own souls for an 'A' on their transcript."

Willi agreed. "He might be selling exams."

"How do you know that?"

"I found a test in Adela's room. Exams dated for next
week. Now I understand the *P* and *U* letters on Hortense's
note."

"You lost me."

"She took a message from Betty Norris for me, before Betty was . . . uh . . . brought to the hospital. Hortense wrote those two letters in the corner. I believe we have someone who'll confirm the cheating scam."

"Willi, Betty's dead. Dead."

"I mean, through her letters Sheriff Tucker asked me to look through. Oh, blast. Jerald, what if those initials—?" Willi shouted.

"What? Don't shriek like that. It gives me goose bumps."

She put her hand over her mouth. Maybe she was telling Jerald too much, but too late now.

"Could Paul's initials in the corner refer to who Betty wanted to talk about in another way?" she asked. "Maybe he served as a middleman and convinced her to go to some sick hole-in-the-wall doctor for an abortion that went horribly wrong."

"Whoa, whoa. That scenario is a far cry from a cheating scam. If you have the letters, that's bound to come out in some way, but I think that's the wrong trail. More than likely she got together with another kid, Willi, nearer her own age. They do stupid things like finding some jerk that talks them into a cheap abortion. You know that. Tragic, but it happens."

"And all along I've been thinking Betty was concerned with a coven, Satan worship." Some of the letters did have "bearer" on them. It was all so confusing, so damned blasted confusing, like some nasty-minded spider was having a gleeful time crisscrossing all the threads into one sticky glob, just to catch Willi in the center. She walked toward the window and closed the blinds just as lightning flashed across her line of vision. The soft pitter-patter of raindrops sounded lightly against the window.

"I'm tired of the spring rains, and they've barely begun

for the year. Hadn't we better turn the computer off?"

"No problem," Jerald said. "There's a power surge protector."

She didn't pretend to understand the inner functions of the machines, but Mr. Andrews, the computer literacy instructor, had admonished her to turn the monitor off during a storm and unplug it from the outlet. She'd installed a surge protector on her machine at home, but still followed his advice. Some other reason why Mr. Andrews was so adamant hovered in her subconscious, but didn't surface. She merely shrugged and said, "Well, you probably know more than I do."

Jerald shot a look toward her that clearly indicated he certainly did. After a few minutes, she thought so, too. He manipulated keys until he entered every test bank.

"I imagined," she interrupted him, "that you had to have the individual codes to reach another teacher's files. Can anyone do this?"

He glared at her. "Of course not. How many average Joes learned PC programming? Most are only concerned with a particular software package and their own files, not with the computer languages and programming that software. I'm tutoring Lance in those in my spare time."

"You're a fake."

"What do you mean, Willi?"

"You really *do* care for the kids. You just don't want folks to know that. I promise not to ruin the reputation you've built up."

Jerald ducked his silver head of hair, grinned and said, "Be happy, have fun, help everyone. That's my motto, but you let too many too close at once and you get burned out."

"Emotionally?"

He nodded.

"Yes, I guess we've all been there." She certainly had.

Dan Oxhandler had helped her out of the doldrums, but didn't satisfy her need to be cared for, loved. All he wanted was a weekend partner to do the horizontal bop with him. *Enough. It's over with. Move on.* She pinched the bridge of her nose hard.

The gentle rain turned into a pelting tempest against the windows. Leaning against the cold pane, she trembled. Was Lassiter somewhere out at that compound, talking to the few Benjamites who were resettling there after the conflict? Thunder boomed and she blinked.

Quannah, in a wolf's skin and breechcloth, climbed up an embankment above the compound. Lightning flashed, highlighting his bronze skin. Knife in one hand, a feathered medicine shield attached to his arm, he raced down the hill. Wet mud gave way; he slipped, twisting and turning. His knife flew out of his hand and arced in the sky. Lightning hit it. Sparks flew overhead like great bursts of fireworks.

"*Winyan, I'm coming for you.*"

Down below, Willi looked up at him. The leather that had tied her spread-eagled to the stakes flipped away in the heavy wind. Free, she stood. Her headdress of raven and hummingbird feathers fluttered in the wind. She stroked the soft white doeskin dress, beaded about the neck and hem. Turning away from the crazed warrior yelling at her on the hill, she headed toward the compound's darkened tunnel.

"*No, Winyan. don't go down the dark way.*"

Silly brave. This was a tunnel.

"*Winyan, don't go. Heyokah waits.*"

Lassiter never could see what was right before his face. Lassiter?

Willi shook her head. She couldn't remember everything from *Animal Totems.* Hummingbird Medicine concerned laughter and joy, love and devotion. She concentrated harder. Raven was in the scene, too. Raven Medicine offered opportunities to enter the void—the darkness—to find important messages. She sighed. Why did the vision mentalgrams have to be contradictory?

The bright fluorescent lights winked on and off. She licked her lips and said, "Now, don't you think we should turn off the computer?"

Jerald raised his eyebrows a fraction of an inch, but kept his thoughts to himself.

Hours of bringing up directories menus and something Jerald called tree directories was too long for her. She yawned and pointed at her watch. "Eleven-thirty, Jerald, in the P.M. Let's call it—"

"Willi, look! I've got the proof. Mr. Paul Undel made a mistake. I knew he would."

On the screen a date, a time and an operator's name glared forth, pinpointed by the blinking cursor at the side. The operator's name was Paul Undel.

"I don't understand," she admitted.

"Paul doesn't teach biology. Yet he's filled out a date and time that he entered this file."

"Why would he do that?"

"Habit, generally a good one." He smiled and spread his hands toward the screen as if he'd personally created that most wonderful of all worlds—proof against Paul Undel.

"That explains one mystery."

At that moment the gods showed more than their cloudy underbellies. Lightning hit a pole outside, the lights flickered, the screen flashed and blanked out. Only seconds passed, and the fluorescent bulbs flared overhead again, but the monitor remained blank.

No date or time. No operator's name.

No proof.

"Damn." Jerald banged the top of the monitor.

Willi widened her eyes and innocently said, "Perhaps the surge protector—?" She allowed the question to hang in the frigid air.

"Damn it to hell!" He bent and peered beneath the table. Willi followed suit and viewed the red light indicating the protector was doing its job.

"Seems to me," she said after her subconscious unleashed the information, "Mr. Andrews said something about a power *supply*."

"What?" Jerald lifted his hand and banged it sharply against the table's edge. A few resonant expletives rent the air.

"Explain, Willi."

"A power supply," she repeated. "When the power goes out, the computer, I believe, stays on for a while until you can manually turn it off. Guess this"—she pointed at the battered machine—"doesn't have one of those thingamajigs."

Stone-faced, he quietly said, "Probably not, Einstein."

"No need to get nasty, Jerald. Besides, I remembered something else."

"You couldn't have shared all this information before?"

She used her sweetest voice to explain. "I didn't remember until the lightning sort of uh . . . jolted me." At that point she thought it expedient to move further away from Jerald and did so. She admired his self-control as he slowly turned in her direction.

"What else have you recalled?"

"These terminals are connected, tied, whatever, to a main computer—server, whatever—in Administration. If we . . . uh . . . you, rather, could bring up the information on one monitor, you could do the same with another monitor, provided the main terminal at the administration building wasn't knocked out, and provided that thingamajig under the table—the power supply, is working for some of these other computers."

His grimace turned into a smile. "Willi, you're wonderful. And more to the point, right." He stood up and stretched, walked to the window and peeked between the blinds. "Guess Zeus and his minions have had their fun. Storm's about over." He laced his fingers over his head for one back-creaking stretch and said, "I'll start again, now."

"Without me," Willi managed through a yawn.

"You're not heading on a road trip this late?"

"No, I guess not, but I'd like to be home before the witching hour. School starts again soon, right?"

"For some of us," he said in a way that boded no good for Paul Undel.

The county courthouse clock started striking its way toward midnight when Willi drove through town, heading toward home. The rain-slick pavement shushed beneath her tires, adding a counterpoint to the clock bongs. Thank goodness the city council hadn't changed the old clock for one of the modern digital ones. Just as the twelfth gong sounded, Caprithia Feather's house, darkened except for tendrils of light drifting up from a basement window and shifting shadows in the alley, came into view.

Willi slammed on her brakes. What had she seen? A pair of skinny legs, high-top sneakers? The sharp mewing of a cat startled her. Those blasted kids were headed toward Caprithia's backyard or the abandoned house across the alley. Willi started to stop and tell Caprithia, but the counselor had told her before that kids just played around and wrote graffiti on the building across the way. On Willi's list of priorities, that ranked about fifty-fifth right now. When the Feathers' basement lights went out, Willi figured Caprithia had heard the kids, checked on the commotion and locked her doors.

A block down from the Feathers', Willi pulled over, cut the engine, grabbed a flashlight from the glove compartment and sighed. Okay, maybe vandalism wasn't down there at *número* fifty-five. What was wrong with her that she couldn't let one little thing go by? Well, she wouldn't bother Caprithia or Mama Feather. She'd just sneak back and make sure the kids had gone across that back field, and then she could let the matter drop and not worry half the night about the Feathers being victims in tomorrow's headlines.

She shuddered as she entered the alleyway, paused and swallowed a lump in her throat. Purposefully, she loosened her collar, hoping for some relief from the light-headed fear threatening to destroy what little courage she had. She reached into her pocket and clasped Tunkasila.

"Do your magic, Grandfather, do your magic. Calm me, so I can think." Turning loose of the stone, she used both hands to hold her flashlight.

No sound emanated from the alleyway. Only a faint whiff of rotting garbage, properly covered in this section of town, reached Willi's nose. In response, she wiggled her nose trying to sniff air above that odor. Her sweaty hands almost lost their hold on the flashlight. She clicked the beam on. The flashlight slipped from her palms to roll down the alley.

"Blast." She stood still for a full two minutes while she counted with the traditional one-Mississippi-two-Mississippi method. At the conclusion, no lights came on, and neither of the Feathers called out.

She wiped her hands on her jeans, inhaled a steadying breath, picked up the flashlight and walked slowly toward the ebony shadows.

An old box atop the trash balanced precariously and rocked with each gust of wind. A scent, elusive but known to her at some deeper level of consciousness, assailed her.

She tried to distinguish the scent from the refuse, but failed.

Willi's flashlight beam flickered on the ground and across something familiar. She frowned, bent over, picked up the earring composed of tiny crosses and placed it in her pocket. Her stomach knotted. *How did Adela's earring get here? Did one of those kids drop it?*

"It's been a long day," she whispered to the wind. "A long day with too many unanswered questions." No one was near the abandoned domicile or in the backyard. She walked back to her car, feeling the tiny earring as if its weight equaled that of a trunkful of silver conchos.

She turned the radio on and station-surfed all the way home as she listened first to a golden oldie, then to a classic country station. Somewhere between "Yakety Yak" and "Chattahoochee," her mind simply shut down—down as in major vapor lock. As she'd told Jerald, it *was* too late to drive to Hallettsville, and besides, she had no idea where in blue blazes the compound was or who to see when she got there, but damn it, Lassiter would not get out of her mind. Maybe . . . maybe he wasn't in south Texas. Perhaps he was close, close enough so that he could . . . communicate . . . oh, ridiculous. She shook her head and hunched her shoulders before letting them relax to remove some of the tension.

In one pocket, she rubbed Tunkasila. In the other pocket, she fingered one of the inverted crosses from Adela's earring. Closing her eyes, she envisioned Adela standing in the field by the school. One earring jangled, the other one lay on the ground. Uh-huh. She'd picked it up.

In fact, Adela had constantly been playing with the broken earring, had lost a number of the crosses between Nickleberry and Galveston and generally complained about her mother ripping it out of her ear. Cold to Willi's touch, the earring brought forth questions without answers. Had someone else picked it up and dropped it in the alley, or had Adela herself before her death been one of the vandals visiting the abandoned building next door to Caprithia?

Suddenly, she wished one part of a daydream would come true. Maybe Lassiter would *come for her* and explain some of these things. She admitted it . . . she needed him. Beside her—arguing or winking, explaining or berating—she needed him. And as if on cue, the words ". . . I need you so now . . ." from "Turn Out the Light And Love Me Tonight" ended. She punched the button and the Platters sang the heart-tugging lyrics about being together at last at twilight time. She gulped past a lump in her throat bigger than Rose Pig and switched the radio off. When she lowered the window, the scents of fresh-turned earth, pines and lavender wafted over her as peacefully as a baby's blanket. She peeked out the window and up at the stars, winked and with that action somehow felt closer to one investigator. A calmness at his remembered touch on her cheek or shoulder stayed with her the rest of the ride home.

CHAPTER
21

DESPITE that calmness, she suffered through a troublesome night which left her totally unrested the next morning. She couldn't quite get Lassiter out of her mind. Was he in trouble? No, no. If anyone could take care of himself, he could. Agatha had cooked this morning, but Willi couldn't even recall what delicious concoction she'd made. All of Willi's senses seemed to be overloaded. She didn't quite remember her drive to the high school. Scary thought that was.

She paused beside the glassed-in high school office, took off her raincoat and shook it out before folding it over one arm.

From inside the office, Paul Undel yelled, "Liar."

Jerald Stanley waved computer sheets in Undel's face. Principal Wiginton shut his door and drew the blinds.

Blast, she couldn't see or hear anything now. Hoping Jerald would give her the scuttlebutt when he left, she waited upstairs in the teachers' lounge by the mailboxes.

While waiting, she pinched the bridge of her nose and rubbed eyes as uncomfortable as organdy, that transparent muslin with a stiff finish.

Shadows.

She trembled as frames of the evening replayed across her mental projector: Undel's hand holding students' money, disembodied legs running in and out of the shadows, a rain-drenched alley.

That elusive scent she couldn't quite place bothered Willi, too. Well, obviously brooding about it wasn't going to bring it to the forefront with a name attached.

Groaning, she envisioned three faces: D'Dee, Adela and Betty. Angry tears sprang to her eyes, washed away some of the scratchy sensation and trickled down one cheek. Briskly, she wiped her face.

Finally, Jerald entered the lounge. Grinning, he said, "That's one son-of-a-gun who won't be teaching this morning."

"Fired?"

"Right out on his cheating heart."

He grabbed his mail, glanced quickly through the envelopes and threw them into the wastebasket.

"Needless to say, you located the proof again."

"Right. Thanks to you, Willi. The computer info helped, but the clincher was when I nosed around in his files and found names of particular students popping up many times."

He paused, filled his red goblet with lemonade and gulped as if he'd been in a desert instead of an air-conditioned office. "Five minutes with some of the kids, including the two we saw at the cafe, and they confessed."

He loosened his tie, finally taking it off. "Too formal and stuffy for today," he said by way of explanation as he leaned toward Willi. "These rainstorms aren't clearing the air at all, just leaving a heavy mugginess in their wake."

An aroma, soft and clinging, drifted from him when he

unbuttoned his top shirt button. He grabbed his grade book and sauntered down the hall.

Willi gasped and raced after him.

"What is that aftershave, that scent you're wearing?" she asked breathlessly.

He laughed, smoothing his silver hair. "Expensive item, I bet you thought."

She held her palms up. "Well, Jerald, you're the only teacher with a crystal Waterford goblet."

"The *scent,* Willi, is Johnson & Johnson."

"A new men's fragrance?"

"Johnson & Johnson *baby powder,* Willi. Not what you expected, is it?"

"No, not at all," she whispered to his retreating back. *Baby powder.* The scent that had wafted lightly toward her in the alley.

Blast it, she still felt strongly that he was involved, and if so, then the scent of Johnson & Johnson baby powder tied him in somehow. Of course, all his smooth words, his show of honesty and concern for students could be the absolute truth.

Right, and Texans don't use jalapeños in their chili, spit Red Man tobacco or wear their spurs inside the bar. And all of those struck her as honest and down-to-earth sincere—an adjective that didn't seem to hang well on Jerald Stanley.

She ran to class, but even so couldn't outdistance her thoughts. Jerald had been at the high school when she entered the alley, hadn't he? Of course, that's what *he* said. Less than five minutes were required to reach the Feathers' home from the high school.

Jerald could have been in the alley a minute or two after her, if he'd followed immediately. Certainly, if he were guilty, he would. The wicked Wiccan had given many warnings and seemed to know every step she'd taken in the investigation. That could also explain the smell of baby powder surrounding the space between Caprithia's Victorian house and the abandoned building.

Unless . . . unless there was a baby. Blast Elba and Agatha and their frightening predictions. No, she couldn't blame the white witches entirely. Betty Norris, after all, had been delivered of a child who had not yet been located. She collided with two students at her class door, apologized and forced her thoughts to first-period English.

Her lecture and demonstration on Shakespearian theater unraveled without mishap throughout the morning classes. Third period she called roll and paused.

"Trujillo Zeta," she repeated and peered uneasily at his empty desk.

"Hey," Lance said, "like the dude's been down about his sister and all."

David, a smart-mouthed jock of the type that thought everyone should love his every opinion, said, "No, hey, man, the reason he ain't here is the bad weather. If we weren't seeing the baseball videos today, you know, this woulda kept me home."

"Back to the Globe, fellows." Willi narrowed her eyes and got the class back on task. As soon as they were into the written assignment, her mind followed an old track— the one where each rail led back to the mutilations, the killings and the Zetas.

Trujillo had never missed a day of school. He'd received a perfect attendance award for each semester since he started two years ago. With Adela's death his home life might be topsy-turvy, but a week had passed since spring break, the funeral was over and he hadn't seemed the type to dwell on a problem without seeking help if needed.

Also by third period the news of the cheating system and Paul Undel's part in it had spread from the office and through the classes as if the information were a virulent disease. As the sick news traveled the corridors, students and teachers alike were aghast, perhaps fearing the virus might spread to other victims, those innocent of the Honors cheating scam.

Her uneasiness about Trujillo didn't abate despite tremors caused by the Paul Undel scandal or her attempted concentration on the Globe and Shakespearian actors. As far as she was concerned something was definitely rotten in the state of bronc riders and Texas Rangers. Lassiter or no Lassiter, she was determined to stop the evil and corruption which had spread itself over Nickleberry. She prayed she wasn't too late for Trujillo Zeta.

Fourth period, Willi's conference period, came just before lunch, which allowed her almost two hours. Picking up her purse, she headed for the office, checked with Principal Wiginton and proceeded to the Zetas'.

As she rushed up the steps of the tract house, she paused, pulled her raincoat tighter and wiped moisture from her face.

Someone inside yelled, "I'll give you something to cry about, boy."

Willi, cupping her hands around her face, peered in the window beside the door.

"I told them nothing, *Papá*, nothing. I swear!" Trujillo cowered in a corner of the living room.

Mr. Zeta brandished a belt and lowered his arm for another whack across his son's shoulders.

Gasping, Willi stabbed at the doorbell. She peeked through the window again. Mr. Zeta and Trujillo were not there.

She plunged her thumb on the buzzer and didn't remove it until Mrs. Zeta arrived at the door. She opened the door only as far as the chain would allow.

"Wanna go through my *niña*'s room again, *sí*? Told

you to take care of my Adela. Look what happens to her."

Willi's stomach roiled and guilt spread over her shoulders, but she stood her ground. "I want to see Trujillo. He wasn't in class today. He's never missed it, and I was worried about him."

To her surprise, Eva undid the chain and opened the door. "He had a little accident. He'll be in his afternoon classes." She walked toward the hall to the bedrooms. "Trujillo, come, *niño*."

The boy, all deadened eyes and pale skin, advanced into the room. "Ms. Gallagher."

Other than the dazed look, he seemed fine. No marks on his face. He buttoned the cuffs of a long-sleeved shirt and tucked in the tail. His legs in the jeans, torn at the knee and thigh as fashion dictated for teens, didn't tremble. He spread his feet, Reebok-clad, and stood solidly, defying her in his stance to say anything about what she'd seen.

"I'm glad he's feeling well enough to go now. I'll give you a lift, Trujillo, if you don't mind stopping at the Burger Beef for lunch first. My treat."

"Fine, Ms. Gallagher."

Eva grabbed her handbag, stuffed her hand inside and clutched some bills. She shoved them toward her son. "*Aquí.* You pay for your own. You owe her nothing."

To Willi she said, "This coming, showing concern for him, it don't make up for my Adela, you hear me?"

If Sheriff Tucker hadn't shared his information about the Zetas' track record, Willi would have thought the woman was sincere.

"*Mamá,* don't."

Knees trembling, Willi left with Trujillo close behind her. The drive to Burger Beef was silent.

While he ordered, she made two phone calls, the first to the school, the second to Elba.

"Yep," Elba said, "that investigator fellow called. He sure enough did. He has a right pleasant voice, don't he? Why, he could melt the inside of an igloo, maybe turn a certain English teacher's insides to warm honey, might even—"

"Elba."

"Anyhoo, he has a nice voice. 'Course, it would have been more pleasant if the phone weren't garbled and crackling what with all these rain showers we been having."

"Elba, what—?"

"I seen the preacher's wife down to the market this morning, too. She wanted to know if he'd called you. She was buying strawberries for the Sunday school picnic. Got to admit she was some curious about you and him."

"Elba, what did Lassiter say?"

"Oh, he said to tell Willi, that's you, he found the connection from Hallettsville to Nickleberry, and for you to be careful. I done told him Agatha and I been warning you."

"What was the link?"

"The phone had loads of static. See? There it goes again. I called the phone company. Jimmy Tate will be checking it soon."

"Did Lassiter say anything else you understood?"

"He sure did."

"And, that was—?"

"Faculties. Something about your faculties."

"My facul—? *The* faculty?"

"That's it. That's what he said."

"Thanks, Elba. Later."

She allowed Trujillo to finish his double malt and cheeseburger before asking, "You were sick this morning?"

His brown eyes searched her face.

"You know, Ms. Gallagher. You saw."

"I'm sorry. I couldn't be sure if you'd seen me before I rang the bell. Why?"

"Why does my *papá* beat me? He needs no reason." He paused and supped noisily on his malt.

"Would you like to talk? I don't want to push you. I . . . I feel at a loss about how to ask you . . . this."

She waved her hands ineffectually. She shook her head and began again.

"I called the school. You don't have to go today."

"The school? You tell them? Now, everybody will know."

"Just the counselor, Trujillo, just the counselor."

Trujillo's eyes grew wide. He sighed and laid his hands quietly in his lap.

"This I wish you had not done, Ms. Gallagher. This is very bad."

"No, we'll help you. Is there somewhere you'd like to be now? Someone you'd like to talk to?"

His response surprised her. "The sheriff, he's a friend of yours, *sí*?"

"Sheriff Tucker. Yes, a good friend."

"I need an *amigo*. I *must* talk to the law. So I kill the one stone with two birds."

"Two birds with one stone. Yes, Trujillo, we'll go. May I ask *one* question . . . or *two*?"

He narrowed his eyes and his jaw muscles worked, but he said nothing.

"Your parents came from Mexico, but your records say you were born here, yet . . . yet your verbal skills tell a different story, and my first question is—"

"I know your question. The Trujillos, they adopted my sister and me. We been here in *el Norte* for maybe little over two years. Many before us, they adopted. Easier to get us into their ways when we have no one to turn to

here. I was lucky that I got to meet the grandmother—
the real *abuela* of Eva Zeta. She make the difference in
my life. I talk to the sheriff. He will know how to stop
them."

"Yes, he will. My last question. Were you in the alley
between the boarded-up house and Ms. Feather's home
last night?"

"*Sí,* Ms. Gallagher. I was walking last night, saw you
stop your car and tried to scare you away when I see other
kids up to no good. Do not go near the old abandoned
house or alley."

"Why? What's there?"

"That was the *third* question, *sí,* and I am very tired."

"Okay, let's go."

She slammed on her brakes in front of Sheriff Tucker's
office. Before she could ask another question, Trujillo
jumped out, shut the door and stared back at her through
the open window.

"Don't get out, Ms. Gallagher. I think on the way over
here. It is easier for me to talk to the sheriff alone. You
go back to school. Really, it's okay."

She remained long enough to see him march through
the door. She made an illegal U-turn and headed back to
Nickleberry High. Tucker got information. Lassiter got
information. Damn it, she was the one who'd gotten the
ball rolling on these murders. Now she couldn't get anything out of anyone. Well, one tidbit. Those crazy Benjamites of Hallettsville, those cultists responsible for
fifteen or more ritual deaths in the name of Satan, had
one of their active members employed at Nickleberry
High.

One of the *faculty.* That had to be what Quannah's garbled message meant.

With Paul Undel out of the picture, Jerald Stanley
moved to the top of her list. Jerald and his bloodred

goblet, his interest in the occult, and that scent of . . . baby powder.

Willi shivered and reached into her pocket to caress and draw comfort from Tunkasila. Blast it, he wasn't there. Now, where in Hades had she left that stone? This time a cold chill prickled along her spine. Could some sick mind use Stone Person's Medicine against her in some horrible way like they would use nail clippings or strands of hair? In her mind's eye she pictured a black arts altar with the stone and her photo in the middle. Flames suddenly burst forth, blackening and curling the picture until only her eyes stared out to see Tunkasila break into dust particles.

"No," she whispered, wishing for the thousandth time she wouldn't drift off into such mental meanderings.

The cold chill pierced through to her guts. She bit her bottom lip. Maybe she shouldn't go on. Maybe the killer had grown tired of warnings. Maybe the next time, as Elba and Agatha said, she'd not get help. An immobilizing fear gripped her in its embrace. For the first time since she'd heard Adela and D'Dee discuss *all that blood,* she touched her own core of vulnerability, her own fear of mortality.

Shutting her eyes, she breathed in deeply and out slowly.

Quannah's voice reminded her, *It's an inner knowing. Find the quiet and the answers will come.*

Her panic had been brought on by the discovery that Tunkasila was missing. She opened her eyes. Someone knew the stone had become a talisman, a protection for her. Blast him to hell. Playing mind games with her, was he?

Her heartbeat slowed. She calmed. Now that she *knew* this, she could handle the doubt that had seeped beneath her defenses. Anyone could have seen her holding the small stone, rubbing it and placing it back in her pocket.

No, it wouldn't be hard to guess she treasured the stone. She nodded. Yep. Anyone on the faculty would know. Jerald Stanley remained at the top of her list, but she added another name to run neck and neck with him.

Hortense Horsenettle.

CHAPTER
22

WHEN the last class bell rang, willi attended a Principal's Advisory meeting which lasted until half past five. Her dress heels were pinching her toes, which made her less than in charity with anything the principal might have said. She hoped it wasn't important, because she hadn't had her mind on anything except the murders. Another couple of hours, and she had worked her way through the grading of two sets of essays. Proud of herself for staying focused on a project other than the local crimes, she smiled.

Taking a well-deserved break, she wrapped her hands around a steaming cup of tea and relaxed in the upstairs teachers' lounge. Staring out the floor-to-ceiling window, she considered the ever-threatening cloud banks, gathering for another deluge if she was any judge, and she mused about the events that had catapulted her through the last two weeks. Were the girls' deaths tied in any way to Trujillo's beating?

"Probably not," she said aloud and peeked over her shoulder to see if anyone else was in the lounge. Add the trauma of Adela's death to the frustration of having to deal with an alcoholic in the family, and the strain proved to be too much. Probably hitting the boy was one way—albeit a sick manner—Mr. Zeta relieved it. Eva Zeta quite obviously used to slap Adela at the slightest provocation, and yet she claimed she loved the girl. Alcohol was Eva's demon, no doubt. The night before the Galveston trip was a prime example.

Lightning glittered in the most distant clouds, but the nearer ones turned loose a gentle cascade of rain which pattered against the picture window. Willi jumped up and startled a cockroach the size of the *Titanic*. He scuttled beneath the sink where she had set her cup, then came out again to wave his antenna.

"You," she said. "You're a lowlife. What do you think about the Zetas?" *Great, Gallagher. Now you talk to cockroaches.*

Titanic scuttled farther out on the counter, inspected a crumb near the sink and climbed on top of a cup.

"Nasty creature. You'd probably understand this sicko killer."

The control, the power was so intoxicating, he killed simply to maintain silence about his area of authority, the coven, cult, whatever. She tapped her fingers on the tabletop.

Titanic, startled, jumped into the cup, scampered up and over the side. The wind outside increased, and the rain turned into a slashing monster, demanding to break inside the glass barrier.

"Hortense might have overheard the girls' conversation in the library," Willi said to Titanic. "She ever sees you, she'll grind you up for some spell or something." Titanic raced down the inside of the stainless steel sink.

Who else had overheard the girls talking that day before the fatal Galveston trip?

"Caprithia Feather had fluttered by, too."

Willi yawned. She had waved to Paul Undel and Jerald Stanley before getting stuck with the Native American books, which she now had to admit had added something very special to her life.

She rubbed her temples. This wasn't getting her anywhere, other than nearer to a headache and possibly an asylum, in particular the floor for those who talk to the animals.

She trudged back to her classroom to finish the last two sets of essays. Two hours later, she laid aside the final one. Blast if she was going to drive home without a break first. She returned to the lounge, gazed out the window at a darkened sky with a moon sliding in and out of a filmy curtain of clouds. The hard rain had abated, but she wouldn't bet her last nickel that she'd seen all of the storms for the evening. She sipped absently at her tea, which had grown cold as the weather outside and as deadly calm as the center of a hurricane.

She kept gnawing at that word *power*.

Why?

The chanting heard in the Hall of Horrors echoed through her mind. She whispered the words to the slate-colored view before her.

"Blood and magick, origins of power, I will bend thee to my will, blood and magick, origins of power."

Absently, she brought the cup to her lips, missed and spilled a drop on her silk blouse. Well, damn. That's what she got for getting back into proper professional attire again. Painful toes and a bigger cleaning bill.

She shivered and, setting the cup down, rubbed her arms. That repetitious chant held the answer. If only she could plumb beneath the surface. Who was filled with passion, wanted power over others? Left a poppet as a calling card warning not to meddle? Left decapitated roosters dripping blood? Who was strong enough to tackle her and tug her up and into the witch's cradle?

One of the Zetas?

She disliked wrapping her thoughts around such a seedy and sadistic pair. She pushed away the cold cup of tea. The buzz and whir of a vacuum cleaner alerted her the janitorial staff had arrived. One fellow paused at the lounge door.

"Howdy," he said, "I cleaned in here already. You mind turning off things before you head out, ma'am?"

"No problem."

"Ma'am?"

"Yes? Is there something else?"

"Don't forget to unplug the coffee machine. Mighty nasty out tonight. Just heard about two wrecks out on Licorice Lane. Another one, too. Somebody plowed right into one of the telephone poles near the hospital. Anyhow, drive careful."

"Thanks, I will."

"Good night." He moved off down the hallway.

She tapped the end of her nose in that something-just-clicked-in-her-mind pose. Material she'd read and events she'd witnessed collided.

"Titanic, where are you? How can I solve this mess without someone to talk with? Evidently, Lassiter has deserted the case. Sheriff Tucker won't reveal the juicy tidbits anymore. I'm trusted only up to a point, you see."

The roach crawled out from the sugar bowl and dumped the contents into the garbage.

"Uck. Well, I asked for that." She eyed him warily. "We're discussing the Zetas. I'm wondering how they got such high and mighty lawyers every time to get them out of the previous charges."

Okay, community leaders were in charge of covens or cults, and those groups in turn revolved within a network of professional lifelines. When a cult member landed in trouble, the network brought lawyers in from Fort Worth, Dallas or Houston to clear them. The cults protected their own. She bet the leaves in the bottom of her teacup she was right.

A cloud obscured the moon. Wind whistled eerily around the empty building. She had to get home.

"Sleep tight, Titanic, and may the bug spray not get you tomorrow."

When he disappeared, she grabbed the sugar bowl and dumped the contents into the garbage. Setting it in the sink, she filled it with hot, soapy water.

She rushed to the office downstairs and cajoled a janitor to let her in to use the phone.

Elba fussed and snorted through the receiver.

"Dangnab right I was worried. It's almost midnight. Along with Tarrant and Johnson counties, Nickleberry County is under a tornado alert until three in the morning. Grading papers, weren't you? I ain't the only one walking the floors. That good-looking Indian is looking for you. He's as worried as a preacher with Sunday chiggers, as frantic as bulls before castrating, as troubled as only a man can be about his woman—and that's a heap of distressed."

"He is?" That thought brought a pleasant rush of adrenaline.

"He's done gone, though. Left me, Agatha and your auntie, with all the real worry. Worried as an astronaut with air sickness—"

"Okay, Elba, I get the pic—"

"—as a parson without his Sunday-Go-to-Meeting collar—"

"Elba, that makes *five* comparisons. No more, and—"

"—as worried as a chicken without a roost."

"Make that *six*. I suppose I deserved them all for causing so much concern. I'm heading home right now."

She drove through Nickleberry on a route that took her past the Feathers' home again. Déjà vu enveloped her as she glimpsed some darkly clothed figures. They ran down the alley beside the abandoned building. She spotted sneakers, jeans. Teens. Two nights in a row? What in Hades was going on?

She bit her lip. She'd promised Elba, but . . . but it would only take a few minutes to investigate.

No light floated out from Caprithia Feather's basement windows. No Sweetpea skulked in the shadows. Willi drove a block farther and parked in the First Methodist Church's lot. Checking the batteries in the flashlight, she carried it in one hand. When she stalked across the wet concrete parking, her dress heels alternately clicked on the surface or splashed through puddles, but were muffled when she walked over two lawns before reaching the alley.

Inching her way along, she turned on the flashlight only in the darkest corners. Whoever was in the abandoned building wasn't going to be forewarned. The odor of refuse overwhelmed her. Her stomach revolted in a quick flip-flop as she sternly chided herself.

Passing beneath Mama Feather's room, she strove to tiptoe, a stupid maneuver when wearing heels. She overbalanced, landing in a pool of liquid rank with vegetable matter. Then and there, she disgraced herself, throwing up quietly beneath Mama Feather's bedroom window. Like Titanic, she scuttled toward the darkest shadow.

"Oh, God." Hose torn, blouse ruined and muck-tasting mouth.

A lamp, perhaps a small night-light, glimmered through the window. She wiped her mouth, feeling suddenly refreshed and alert with the exception of the bile burning her throat. She scooted back, managing to knock over only one box.

The thing must have been filled with BB pellets. The cacophony of sound brought Caprithia to the window. The light shining through her wispy hair created a halo around her concerned face.

Willi could not, despite her nagging conscience, bring herself to the woman's attention.

"It's nothing, Mama, nothing," Caprithia said as she shut the window.

Willi waited, mentally counting to sixty at least four times. She really had to find something better to do with her life than sit and count in nasty alleys. Deeming it safe, she eased herself up by pressing her back against the wall. A breeze touched her cheek. She swallowed and stepped forward after carefully scanning the area with her flashlight. This time she kept the beam in front of her every step. At last, she rounded the corner of the abandoned building.

She located boarded-up windows, one broken water spigot and a hole gouged in the side of the house. The hole had sheet metal screwed into place over most of it. She circumvented the entire house and decided neither Sweetpea nor Titanic could have skimmed beneath the slab foundation of the structure. Damned kids must have skedaddled across the field behind the two houses. There wasn't anywhere else to go.

She squinted in that direction, but only made out forms of the orchard's trees. She stood for a moment to savor the sweet smells of apple blossoms and lilac bushes. The man in the moon smiled crookedly at her and she grinned. She sighed, retracing her steps. Shining the beam at her watch, she grimaced. Uh-oh. Now she'd have to listen to another tirade about worry from Elba. She wished the moon a peaceful night before she stepped back into the alley for the return walk to her car.

A rat scuttled into the shadows. More scuffling sounds

followed in its wake. These noises were far too loud for one small rodent.

Was that someone behind her?

Instinctively, she reached a hand to her sore spot. Damn all demons to Hades, she wasn't going to get another knock on the head without a fight first. Her heart beat erratically, doing a quicksilver tempo between a cha-cha-cha and a mambo. For a moment, it stopped beating and was just a painful muscle of excruciating agony, riveting her to the spot, making her lose control as she grabbed her chest. The flashlight dropped to the ground. The plastic casing shattered and the light went out. Only the eerie illumination from the moon highlighted the area. She peered into a face hidden by a cowled hood. Billowing, black sleeves rose in the air. The scent of baby powder wafting on the breeze was at strange odds with the silken rustling of the robe.

Was that a scepter, a club?

Screaming, Willi raised her arm to ward off the blow. Her attacker was quicker. Pain cascaded from her right temple and down her neck. A similar jolt to the chin knocked her down. Her knees buckled. She crumpled into the alley's refuse, old cat food and pea soup. Just as the pall of blackness crushed her in its folds, voices swirled around her: *Winyan, wait. Be aware. Remember Raven's lessons . . . children . . . gagged and blinded . . . don't go messin' where you shouldn't.*

THE inky darkness didn't abate when she opened her eyes. An insistent pain radiating from her right temple tattooed itself into her brain. She groaned. Her breath came in short gasps.

Why couldn't she breathe?

Heart pounding against her chest, she opened her mouth

to scream again, but only a strained moan escaped. The pain was too intense. No one could endure this agony, so she must not be here. This was a nightmare, one of her more horrible imaginings. She'd awaken. Oh, God, let her awaken.

Her arms must have been pulled from their sockets. Her senses heightened by fear, she swore she could hear tissue ripping, cartilage tearing. Damn, she had her eyes open. Tears streamed from them. She blinked.

Why couldn't she see?

A faint odor of cat food and soured vomit swirled around her. Panting like an expectant mother against the pain of contraction, she managed not to faint. Another scent, more prevalent, grabbed her attention. Leather. Dusty and old.

Her whole body swayed and turned in space. With each movement, hot flames prickled her joints. A creak of leather against wood and a distinct tilt when she attempted to squirm sideways confirmed a gnawing fear.

The witch's cradle.

No, not again. She was going to die.

Perspiration slithered between her shoulder blades, drizzled between her breasts and cooled against her clammy skin. She shivered. The sadistic bastard had tied her arms above her this time, rather than close to her body. Wiggling her toes, she touched the edges of her swinging coffin. Hot tears stung her cheeks.

Quannah won't be there to help you this time.

Elba and Aggie were right. No, no . . . that might mean he was dead? They'd said something about blood all over his head. She whimpered at this thought. Even Elba wouldn't know where she was. Fighting a losing battle against the sharp, steel slivers of pain going down her back, she screamed.

Low laughter joined her screams. She was losing her

mind, becoming hysterical. She twisted her head, shook the sweat from her face and bit down on her bottom lip.

A soft titter matured into a cackle surrounding her world of stifling darkness. An unseen hand twirled the witch's cradle. Willi drifted on a nebulous wave of nausea. Something inside the cradle skittered up her arm. Without sight, she imagined the worst. Titanic's cousin. No, not in a coffin. Much more horrible creatures inhabited coffins. Bile rose in her throat at the thought of a maggot on her flesh. Her skin crawled.

Guttural laughter erupted. Rough one moment and breathy the next, the sound defied her limited faculties. The harsh voice penetrated the rawhide binding her.

> *Blood and magick,*
> *Origins of passion,*
> *Origins of power,*
> *Blood and magick.*

"What . . . do . . . you want?" Willi managed to push the question past her burning throat.

"Power."

She should know that voice. The person's identity hovered in her mind like a persistent housefly, right before one's eyes but impossible to catch.

"What do you want . . . with me?" she asked. She had to keep him talking, mustn't faint or let him know how weak she was.

"Peace. Peace for our circle. Your curiosity and persistence could be unhealthy. Troublemakers within our circle have been disposed of. Leave well enough alone. You could end up like one of the bearers."

"The *bearers*?"

"Yes, new bearers of our Crow's cross. Betty Norris was one."

Bearers. The plural.

Within the confines of the rank leather and dust she coughed. *Think, damn it, think. Keep him talking about anything.* "The marble slab in the shack? Is that where you . . . sacrifice the . . . bearer?"

"We don't sacrifice those we spend such time to train. We do honor them with an animal bloodletting over their newly consecrated bodies."

"Honor?" Willi gasped out the word.

"Yes, the circle honors the newborn—new blood to bring the magick—to bring the power."

"Would that include Betty's baby?"

Silken robes rustled, sending the scent of baby powder circling even inside Willi's leather prison. In an angry voice, the Wiccan said, "Never *hers.* The Lord and Master's. She tried to hide the birth, and almost succeeded. If one of our own had not seen that bungling doctor leave the wrapped baby, we might have lost it forever. Now, we'll baptize it during the full moon renewal festival."

"Your . . . master is the Devil . . . Satan?"

"Naturally."

How could this person, witch or warlock—wicked Wiccan—take the life of a young girl so lightly? As if her thoughts had penetrated through the cradle, the Wiccan answered.

"Betty was an acolyte. She gained importance only for the gift of power her youth could give to the coven. Her death was unfortunate, but not of our doing. Her pregnancy and delivery of a healthy child bestow special powers on all in the group."

A picture of Jerald Stanley holding his bloodred goblet rose in her mind's eye.

"But you convinced her and the other girls to slowly become as warped as you. You make the young ones sacrifice the animals, and no telling what else."

She tried to scream the words, but her effort fell pitifully short. Was that a sigh from the Wiccan? Willi strained to hear.

A swish of robes, a distinctive step.

She'd gone too far. The same hand that had shoved D'Dee beneath the ferry and had shoved Adela from the hotel was going to torture and kill her. She'd be as helpless as a packinghouse carcass. The Wiccan shook the cradle. Shafts of agony twisted down Willi's arms. Groaning, she managed not to scream.

She thought about calling Jerald by name, but that might enrage him more, entice him to kill her because she knew his identity. No, no, she must keep quiet. Let him think she knew nothing.

He twisted the cradle again and chanted. The Wiccan spoke in that horrible, raspy whisper at the end of the litany. "Silly, silly girls. Once one has served the Master, one belongs. Forever. They thought the circle was a pastime to be dropped when they lacked courage in their first test. If girls don't have courage, they should stay where they belong—at home in the family nest."

Something about that last phrase caught Willi's attention. Striving to push back the pain, to clear her mind and to remember, she struggled to pull the momentary insight to the surface. The critter inside the cradle slithered across her neck. Goose bumps rose on her shoulders and arms. She shivered so hard her teeth chattered. A spider? Her shivering increased, and she shook like an addict with hallucinations. The tiny legs teased the skin of her neck. It was a spider and she couldn't knock it off.

Find your Sacred Breath.

Concentrating on drawing air in slowly and letting it out slower, she calmed herself. She had to keep him talking.

She whispered, "The puppy, the kitten."

"A delightful ritual. The girls didn't like the *blood*. Power-giving blood! They disdained the magick!"

Willi drifted between moments of intense pain and nebulous horror. Minutes passed or perhaps hours. She slipped in and out of consciousness.

At one coherent moment, the Wiccan said, "What's that? Someone coming? No more warnings. I've had to dispose of so many bearers because of you. Ah, that's it. You'll become the bearer for the circle. We'd have to keep you in the cradle for months, until we knew you had grown to love our ways. Think, Willi, think about it."

"You *think* about it. I'm . . . I'm not the only one who knows who you are." She prayed the bluff would work.

"Your investigator friend? You don't need to worry anymore about him."

"Not just him. Others have found out."

"Ridiculous. No one in the circle really knows *me*. I've the power and the magick." A rustle of long sleeves, a swish of a robe and at last, "Remember, dear, don't meddle." He swung the cradle so violently it crashed against the wall.

Willi snapped her head up and screamed. Finally, a welcome blanket of pain-numbing darkness wrapped around her.

CHAPTER
23

ALONE at last, Willi cried, "Help!"

Only a whisper escaped her. A phrase floated to her consciousness.

Find your Sacred Breath.

Impossible. Every breath ripped her apart.

Stop it, Gallagher. Concentrate. Focus.

Damn Jerald Stanley. She had to try something, anything to fight against the pain, the fear gnawing away inside her like a rat at a corpse's cold guts.

Sacred Breath.

Okay, she *could* do that. Focusing all her strength on breathing slowly in and out brought a surprising lift to her spirits. Despite occasional sharp pains, she persisted, trying to remember. *Be aware*, the animal totem text insisted. *Be aware*, Quannah told her. Put your wishes out into the universe, into the Great Void, and all your totem guides, all Wamakaskan would work to manifest your needs. But, first . . . what was it she had to do first? Oh, yes. She had to give thanks, sincere-total-belief thanks for the help *before* it arrived. Her prayer was simple: *Help*.

Inhale. Exhale. Again, and once more. Her eyelids

closed, pain lessened and a feeling of peace settled around her. *Pilamaya. Pilamaya ye.*

"ᎩᏍ! ᎩᏍ! woof! ᎩᏍ!"

"Charlie . . . Charlie . . . Brown?"

A wet muzzle snuggled beneath her ear. She reached out and touched wet grass. Light blazed across her lids. She tentatively opened one eye and peered up into Elba's face, creased with worry. When she turned her head again, Charlie Brown licked her.

"Dang nab it, girl," Elba fussed. "I didn't think you was ever going to wake up before you hit Gabriel's shore. I got the nervous wigglies. Why, I just as well might have been a pea in a hot skillet, one of Redenbacher's popped kernels . . . oh, forget it. Lord have mercy on these old bones."

Squinting, Willi said, "Sorry."

Sunshine cascaded over her. She smiled and splayed her fingers against the warm soil and grass. Tears mixed with the dirt. *Pilamaya. Pilamaya ye. Thank you, thank you.*

Elba busied herself by pillowing Willi's head on an old sweater. She heaved her ample frame up and waved to someone outside of Willi's vision.

Agatha's cheerful voice responded, "Tea's coming."

Willi, spread-eagled on the grass, closed her eyes. The breeze lifted torn pieces of her blouse, tickled her legs inside the shredded hose and caressed her face. One shoe dangled from a toe.

Charlie Brown now lay on the frizzled edges of her hair right beside her cheek. She didn't even have the strength to pet him.

Agatha bent down. She looked like one of those distorted depictions one sees when looking into a spoon bowl. Willi giggled. Spasms of pain radiated from her diaphragm outward.

"Poor child is near hysterics. Can't blame her after the last week," Agatha said.

Elba supported Willi's head and Agatha made her sip chamomile and catnip tea through a straw. When she finished two glasses, the sisters allowed her to sit up.

She said, "Sheriff Tucker. Got to tell him. I know who . . ." She choked. "Blast Lassiter, tromping around in Hallettsville while I almost get sacrificed. No, no, he's not okay. You said I'd be in that damned witch's cradle and he . . . and he . . ."

Agatha calmed her. "He's fine. Called a couple of times for you, in fact. The visions and cards present strong possibilities which can occur if right action isn't taken. Guess you've partly done that because, as I said, he's fine."

Willi's head swam and she blinked. "But I found out who the killer is. Let's go."

"Take it easy," Elba admonished. "You're going to hurt right smart for a while and have a skull cramp that'd kill a good-size horse. What you just drunk ought to take the sizzle away for a bit."

Moving cautiously, Willi sat up without shafts of pain— as Elba said—sizzling through her. She looked at the tea pitcher and raised an eyebrow.

Elba interpreted the look. "Never you mind what all was in my special blend. You don't ache, and that's what matters right now."

Somehow Elba and Agatha managed to boost her into Elba's old pickup. They propped Charlie Brown and her one shoe in her lap. With a sister on each side of her, she managed to stay more or less upright.

"Where?" asked Willi in the comforting haze created by the tea and probably something David Blackbourne wouldn't approve of drinking while driving.

"Where? Good question. Where were you come midnight?" Elba grunted. "*Be right home.* That's what you said. And me with the Tarot deck before my eyes. Seeing danger all around you. Hoped you'd have sense enough to come on home. But, dang nab it, no. Midnight come and went. I put supper back a dozen times all told."

"But, Elba—"

"Don't but me. I was worried sick."

Uh-oh. Willi knew what was coming and braced herself.

"Sick as a drunk belching hot Budweiser beer, sick as a baby's first yellow poop, sick—"

"Elba," Agatha interrupted, "Willi doesn't need to hear such as that now."

Willi asked, "How did you find me and where?"

Agatha looked at Charlie Brown sleeping in Willi's arms. "That silly pup. At first light this morning, he ran between my legs and out of the house when I arrived to help Sister with the mopping."

"I wasn't in no mood to do no mopping," grumbled Elba.

Agatha threw the ends of her green polka-dotted scarf over her shoulder, where the morning breeze caught and fluttered the ends out the window. "Anyway, we ran after Charlie Brown. Sister was mad at first. We ended up at the hermit's shack."

"Nasty, evil place," said Elba. "That stuff gives white witches a bad name. Nasty." She shook her head.

Willi couldn't tell if Elba merely shook her head because she'd been unable to come up with more comparisons for *nasty*. "You went inside?"

"Sure enough. That pup hung back like he didn't want to enter."

"I declare," Agatha said, "his hackles, small as they are,

stood up on end." She placed a hand over her heart as if it were fluttering like the scarf in the wind. "He edged inside and stood beneath that witch's cradle. He barked himself into a sick frenzy."

Willi petted the soft mound resting on her lap. No wonder he was so tired. He'd done a good morning's work for such a tiny fellow.

"Soon as I seen that cradle, I knew." Elba gripped the steering wheel tighter. "Got you down as fast as I could. Agatha can't do no heavy lifting."

Willi considered short, round Elba. "I'm surprised you could handle the weight. Thanks, Elba."

"Oh, weren't nothing much. You volunteer at the Senior Citizens' home a day a week, you learn how to lift a lot of weight. To tell the truth, lifting down that contraption was a sight easier than moving them contrary-minded old codgers."

"Then," Agatha said, "I walked back for the pickup and called Brigham. Told him about all that yellow crime tape around the place. Someone trampled it to pieces dragging you there, I guess. He and his nephew had been looking in town around the high school and asking everyone about you since early this morning. Brigham said to apologize. If he'd had both those cradles instead of just the one taken in immediately, you wouldn't have had this horrible experience."

"Thanks. Both of you, thanks."

Elba snorted. "Best get some rest before Sheriff Tucker and that handsome buck arrives. Maybe you can pretty yourself up and—"

Willi yawned.

"Act like you ain't interested if you want, but you ain't fooling no one."

Getting out of the pickup, Willi frowned. "I wish I'd had Tunkasila."

"Sorry." Elba stomped up on the porch. "That's that protective stone the good-looking investigator brought you with them wildflowers, huh?"

Willi nodded and headed inside and upstairs.

"But she don't care for him none, does she, Agatha? About like strawberries don't like cream or—"

"Sister, don't be a pest."

As it turned out, Sheriff Tucker had to wait until almost evening before Willi awoke from the comforting embrace created by Elba's brew. Even awake the feel of being in the throes of a nightmare surrounded her. Chanting. Alley cats, painful shoes. Black-robed figures carried goblets spilling over with blood.

Finally, she brushed the remnants of the nightmare away, dressed and actually strolled down the stairs. Only small stabs of pain pricked her shoulders. She would have to commend Elba for her concoction of special herbs and . . . ninety proof.

"Hello, Sheriff," she said, entering the living room.

Sheriff Tucker hid his bulbous nose behind a red and white polka-dotted handkerchief. His eyes shone as he reverently folded and placed the bandanna in his inside jacket pocket. "Gift from Agatha," he offered.

Willi nodded. "Polka dots being her favorite design and you her favorite man, it makes sense."

"Uh-humm." Sheriff Tucker cleared his throat. "Thank God you're okay. Feel up to talking now?"

"Yes. Let's sit out on the porch."

She led the way, shaded her eyes and studied the sheriff's cruiser. *Humph. Lassiter couldn't stand to be shown up on a case, huh? Didn't have what it took to face the music.*

Elba brought a fresh pitcher of iced limeade and corn pones with a side dish of jalapeño sauce for dipping.

"This here is good for what ails you. It'll clean the grit

out of your craw, the wax out of your ears and the crap—"

"Ah-choo!" Sheriff Tucker flourished his bandanna and sneezed again.

Willi looked aghast, turned away and smothered a giggle. Sheriff Tucker's sneeze sounded suspiciously contrived.

Elba, miffed, left them with the limeade, the corn pones and the early evening stars.

"Well, might as well tell me, Miss Willi." Shaking his massive head, he pulled at his ear.

"I was stupid. I saw kids running down the alley again and was determined to find out why." She continued her tale. "A cowled figure hit me with something—a staff, a billy club—and the next thing I know . . . I'm hanging in that . . . that awful Witch's Cradle." She could still only think of the thing with capital letters as if that helped signify the grand horror of the experience. She moaned and continued, leaving out nothing, knowing from experience that Sheriff Tucker would accurately fill in the blank spots anyway. "Jerald Stanley is . . . the most despicable . . . the most . . ."

"Mayhap, Miss Willi, but let's go one step at a time," he said. "So, might be we'd find your other high heel shoe in the alley?"

"I suppose it would have to be unless the Wiccan discovered the shoe and threw it away."

"You feel mighty sure it's this Jerald Stanley."

"No one else left, is there, unless we want to seriously consider Hortense?"

"Quannah sure enough thought she might be responsible. Checked her out against the records out there in that Hallettsville mess-up."

"Oh, really? Guess that's why he had her name on my notepad."

"I wouldn't know about that. His contact did hint as

how there was two connections between them sorry Benjamites and Nickleberry. Yep. Kinda sad."

He dipped a corn pone into the jalapeño sauce, held his other hand cupped beneath it and brought it to his mouth. After licking his lips, he said, "Hortense lost family in that situation."

"Oh, no. One of the cult members who got shot?"

"Nope. There was a negotiator, a first cousin, the poor man them sickos burned at the stake. Awful way to go." He shook his head so hard his jowls quivered.

"And the other connection was Jerald Stanley, wasn't it?" She leaned forward. Her curiosity couldn't be denied one detail. "Wasn't it?"

"Quannah, he's checking on that very idea right now."

"Oh? But, I'm the one who . . . uh . . . well, got the ball rolling to . . . find the killer. Shouldn't I be in on the final . . . whatever?"

"Mayhap your noggin wouldn't be so dang bumpy was you to have kept that cute little nose out of the way. Quannah can handle this last matter. If everything gels, then I'll be arresting a real nasty piece of work tonight." He ate another corn pone and followed the hot sauce with a drink. He squinted at the stars.

"Mighty fine night to arrest the sorry jerk. Folks don't mind going in on a cold, drizzly day or a freezing snow-filled day, but they sure hate to lose a clear starry night of freedom."

Tugging his ear, he continued to grind out the words. "I want this fellow to see them pretty stars twinkling and know he'll only be seeing them from a barred window from now on."

Willi asked, "Did Trujillo Zeta visit with you?"

"Yep." His sad hound dog eyes looked reproachful as if accusing her of prying secrets best left hidden.

She arched her back and rubbed her shoulders.

"Guess you've suffered enough to deserve all the answers." He dabbed a corn pone in the jalapeño sauce and sampled the duo. "Whoo-whee! Got the pepper that time." He wiped tears from his eyes. "Mighty good."

"Trujillo Zeta?" she asked when he'd finished half a dozen and gulped down another glass of limeade.

"He cleared up some things. Hard for him to do, too. His folks—even though not blood—it's what he calls them. Guess they were better than what he had in Mexico. Anyways, they're part of a coven, have been ever since he came here. He thinks Eva was forced into it. Mayhap, that there's why she drinks. But he says the old man enjoys it. Gets a power kick out of making folks do sick things. Seems he's one of the special higher-ups. You done told me that sicko explained all that to you."

"Yes, Jerald has been a part of this horror since he was a child himself. You never know about people."

"Yep. Damn sicko. Wives of these men—creeps, not men—bore children for the coven. Might be they're trying to get these young girls to start, or—like poor Betty Norris's situation—use an unfortunate teen pregnancy for their own ends. Tell a girl in that condition that everything will be taken care of, her and the child, and nobody is to know nothing, and sure a young kid will grab at that kind of straw."

"The *circle*," Willi said. "uses these babies for new members which they control from Day One."

"You got it. Sick."

"Wicked."

"I done some checking with some of my *compadres* in Fort Worth and Dallas. Even called one down in Houston. Facts. They know what's going on but can't get tangible proof."

"Then, Mr. Zeta was going to make Adela a bearer of the Crow's Foot cross for the group."

"Right. She and the Oxhandler girl, being the newest members, were to go through some initiation at the next full moon. Might have been something worse than the initial experience of killing the puppy and kitten." Sheriff Tucker worried his left ear around.

"That's why the Crow's Foot cross lay beneath her bed, to discover the truth."

"Mayhap. The Zeta girl found out the night before you all left for Galveston that her stepdaddy was going to make her go through with a full initiation. She flat told them she wanted out, and she and D'Dee knew something to get them out no matter what he did."

"But, the Zetas weren't on the Galveston trip. They didn't push D'Dee off the ferry or Adela out the hotel window."

"No, ma'am, they didn't. But, they let the leader of the coven know, by dang, and it's my bet he was on the trip."

"Jerald Stanley?"

"Looks that way."

"The baby, sheriff? I guess Betty's baby is hidden with one of the members?"

"Must be."

"And Trujillo is safe?"

"A ward of the court and in protective custody at my house."

Willi yawned and stretched. The effects of Elba's tonic were a taking a long time to dissipate. An owl hooted in the distance and she shivered.

"Getting nigh on to time."

"Beg pardon?"

"If you feel up to it, we'll go check on your shoe, Miss Willi."

She paused no longer than a heartbeat before answering. "I'd love to, but I don't think Elba will ever let me out of her sight again."

The screen door swung open. "Dang nab right. Get this on to ward off the chill." She offered Willi a sweater.

Willi said, "I'll be fine with Sheriff Tucker, Elba. I don't want you worrying."

"I'm not going to." She waddled out to the patrol car and shuffled herself into the backseat. "Can you turn the siren on?"

Sheriff Tucker winked and opened the cruiser's front door for Willi.

When he reached Nickleberry proper, he parked next to her car in the church parking lot.

"More likely, Sheriff, you'll find Jerald at the high school in the computer lab or at home or . . . maybe that old building." She thumbed toward the abandoned house next door.

"Quannah said to meet him here."

The three got out. Elba and Willi followed Tucker up the front steps of the Feathers' Victorian house.

Willi pulled on the sheriff's sleeve. "We shouldn't pester them. Those poor old ladies have had enough bother to last them a lifetime."

She pointed down the alley. "That's where I was hit over the head. I think the creep hides somewhere in that old building next door."

"Mayhap, but Quannah said he'd meet me at the street. He ain't there. Miss Feather might tell us if he went on by hisself. Now, you calm down, or I'll make you both hightail it home. We're going to take this slow and easy and get all the facts." The sheriff took off his hat.

Caprithia, breathless and red-faced, came to the door. "Sheriff. Willi. Why, hello, Elba." She ran her fingers through her hair. "So sorry. Had to bathe Mama and move her back to bed. My, my, my. It takes my breath away sometimes."

"May we come in, Miss Feather? Got a few questions you might help us with."

"Well, it's late. Mama has had so much excitement. I've called you the last two nights about those kids."

"Yes, ma'am. We need to find out about them."

"Well, dear me, dear me. For a few minutes, then."

He sat beside Caprithia in the parlor filled with potted plants.

Willi eyed the corner. The spiderweb, hidden by the evening shadows, swayed in the breeze coming through the high window.

Elba looked uncomfortable in one of the Victorian chairs. "Hate to have to dust this place. More knickknacks around here than in the Nickleberry Museum."

A moment later, Mama Feather called out in a frightened voice. Sighing, Caprithia started to get up.

"I'll go check on her," Willi said. "She's used to me by now."

"Mama Feather?" She shut the bedroom door and approached the bed. "It's Willi Gallagher."

"Wilhelmina. Come sit here. What's going on?"

"Sheriff Tucker and Caprithia are . . . visiting . . . a few minutes. Don't worry." She patted the soft hand closed over the covers.

"Ought to check on the noises. I been complaining to Caprithia. Neighbors have a new baby. Cries all the time. They aren't feeding it enough. Caprithia told me the cats were carousing. Cats don't carry on during the day, do they, Wilhelmina?"

Willi inhaled, hoping nothing of the anxiety she felt showed in her face or voice. "How long have you heard the baby?"

"Last two, maybe three, nights."

"Where exactly do you hear the baby?"

"Sounds crazy. That's what Caprithia calls me. At first,

I thought the crying came from next door, but then I thought it might be from the alley or our cellar." She sighed and asked for a lemon drop.

Willi edged one over the old lady's cold lips.

Mama Feather smacked greedily. "Guess I am crazy. She says I have been since her papa changed his religious views. He used to take her to the cellar, you know."

"Caprithia's father?"

"Oh, dear, I'm wandering in the past again. It's time for my bath."

"Caprithia just gave you your bath."

"No, no she didn't. Did she?" Mama Feather pouted, but then smiled. "That nice Jerald Stanley came to visit me today. Told him about the baby. He was angry. Doesn't do any good to get angry, does it? Hiram never cared if I got upset or cried or yelled. Satan took over Hiram's life. I couldn't do anything about that. But, then, he held my hand."

Confused, Willi rubbed her temples. "Your husband. I'm sure he did hold your hand. That's sweet." Unreasonable fear edged into her mind and her heartbeat increased an extra beat.

"No, no, Wilhelmina, Jerald Stanley. He held my hand. Told me the noise was the cats, too. So, you think cats?"

Willi's mind was speeding along as fast as her heartbeat. She suddenly remembered where she'd heard someone talk about *awesome power*. It had been on the Galveston seawall. Undel? Hortense? No. Caprithia and Jerald. It had been one of them. Now, Jerald Stanley had been by here, perhaps to find out if the Feathers had heard the baby across the alleyway.

Willi blinked. "I'll check it out. How do I get to the cellar?"

"At the end of the hall outside my bedroom. Gray door. Light switch is on the right. Be careful. Steps are mighty old. Older than me." She chuckled at the thought of that possibility. "Wilhelmina?"

"Yes, Mama Feather?"

"She liked going down in the cellar, liked those chants and such. I couldn't stop them."

Willi paused. "She? Caprithia?"

The old lady snorted. "That bubble-popping girl came by to visit, too."

"Betty? Jerald took Betty down to the cellar?"

"Betty Grable was a pinup queen. Pretty little blonde."

Great, the old lady wandered from one decade to the next and back again faster than a jet flight to Austin. "I'll go check."

First she peeked into the parlor. Sheriff Tucker was indicating he'd like to look around outside while Elba kept Caprithia company.

Willi tiptoed into the hall. Glancing over her shoulder, she paused. Perhaps she *should* tell Sheriff Tucker. Nah. The man had enough on his mind. Quannah should have been on time and met them at the street. Shame on one Lakota-speaking nephew for giving the sheriff extra cause for worry.

Willi turned the doorknob. This might be a wild-goose chase. Probably turn out to be one of Sweetpea's paramours with her litter.

CHAPTER
24

WILLI opened the weathered wood slowly. She stepped inside, shut the door and reached for the light switch. The glow from forty-watt bulb lit the middle of the vast room, but didn't penetrate the shadows. Thanks to her Hush Puppies, she walked silently down the old treads, finally coming to rest on an ancient red brick foundation.

Soft mewing from her right caused hairs on her arms to rise. A fussy baby's whimper or that damn Sweetpea? Allowing herself time to adjust to the gloom, she hesitated. When she could determine shapes, she advanced. Her hand brushed against a piece of wood. She grasped hold and swung it up into the light.

A baseball bat. That could come in handy.

A long workbench in the middle of the room took up most of the space. A tarp, black in the murky shades, was draped across the tools. Sitting atop the canvas was a Stetson hat.

A . . . familiar . . . hat.

"Lassiter's?" she whispered.

Her heart skipped a beat. What was his hat doing there? She considered the tarp-covered table closer. The poor illumination from the swinging forty-watt bulb left this area pitch-black. Perhaps, what was underneath the tarp wasn't what she thought. But . . . *his* hat. He'd never be without it unless . . .

No, impossible. The sisters said he was okay. Sheriff Brigham said so, too. The bat fell from her limp fingers and hit the floor, rolling into the shadows. With one swipe of her hand she knocked the hat to the floor and pulled the tarp back.

"No, oh, my God, no."

Once strong and virile, now cold and very dead, he lay on a carved altar. His head with his face mercifully turned away had hair matted with blood as dark as the blackest raven's wing. Blood crusted around the knife, still embedded to the hilt in his chest. One hand clutched at the knife, fingers frozen in the death rigors.

Willi fell to her knees. Hot tears hit her cheeks, but they'd never, never . . . wash away this agony.

Her mind could not grasp the scope of the tragedy or the pain ripping her apart, much worse than the physical torture she'd endured. She could envision twinges of misery eating her flesh, taking bits of her heart into an endless hole. She scrabbled across the floor for the Stetson. Clutching it to her, she sobbed, crying so long, she was only a shell around the hole of grief, dried and empty, never to be filled.

Visions and phrases floated around her.

Thong-tied ponytail lifting in the sea breeze.

"Oh, God."

A strong hand wiping a tear from her eye. Warm smile and mischievous wink. "Loose lips sink ships, Winyan."

Her lips? Had she poked her stupid, curious nose in, said something to the wrong person? Tears dried on her face.

A frigid breeze wafted against her cheek. She blinked. Every movement was in slow motion. There was no reason to hurry anymore. Nothing left to care about. The world was black, ugly and evil. She glanced at the knife. The forty-watt bulb moved in the slight wind and light glinted off the hilt.

Studying the weapon for a moment, her mind curled around a fast way to end her pain, a way to take her dry shell to another less painful shore.

The wind whistled through the cellar, but suddenly stopped blowing when there was a loud thud and click.

What was that? Not the upstairs door. Oh, what in Hades did it matter? Her mind kept revving up for life although her heart crumbled into that horrible hole inside her.

The breeze came from an outside door into the cellar. His killer had escaped! Blood pounded against her temples. She scrambled up. Averting her face, she threw the tarp back in place.

"Won't . . . get . . . away with it. Not . . . this time."

She beat her fist into her other hand and the hat she clutched. She inched her way into the inky shadows in the direction from which the wind had come. A huge shape loomed before her. Goose bumps skittered over her, tightening her scalp. She gasped. The features weren't clear in the murkiness.

"You won't get away with—"

He reached toward her.

She raised her hand to ward off a blow.

He grabbed and held her up against his chest. He wrapped his hand over her mouth. His large fingers covered her nose, too.

She struggled to breathe and hit out at him with the Stetson. She would not be dragged and placed in that leather chamber of horror again, not be tied on a cold slab like . . . Lassiter. She twisted and executed a quick upward knee to his groin.

"Damn . . . you . . . Gallagher."

That *voice*.

Chills played hopscotch along her spine. She stared back at the tarp, back at him and went limp.

"But, you . . . your . . . black hair . . . you." Her mouth, like a fish gasping for breath out of water, worked soundlessly.

Pulling his Stetson out of her grasp and slapping it on his thigh, Quannah spat out, "*Winyan*, wasn't it enough to use your warrior spirit on my hat?" He caught his breath and got halfway up, holding his palms against his knees. "Great Coyote's balls, I've never had such senseless, stupid things happen. I know you're in my path so that I can learn something, but what the hell that is, I can't imagine. Gallagher, would you wipe that damned grin off your face?"

"Not you?" she asked inanely and pointed to the slab.

"Despite doing your damnest, no. Great Eagle, you got a lot of fire in that knee. Hell."

"Who, then?"

"Jerald Stanley, I'm afraid."

"But his hair is silver, and—"

"Dried blood in this light is black. It's him. Next time look at the face, Gallagher."

"He's the Wiccan, so—" Her world tilted off-center. All this time she'd been so sure, but not positive. "You had to kill him?"

"No, Gallagher. Jerald was snooping in the wrong place at the wrong time. You two related?"

Glass crashed to the floor. Jerald's body, shoved off the altar, landed at their feet. A caped figure with a gun raised at chest level rose from the other side of the table.

Quannah leapt in front of Willi.

A spit of fire glared along with the muffled sound of a silencer.

Quannah groaned and grabbed his head. Blood seeped down his temple. He collapsed into her arms.

The Wiccan jumped over the slab. Quannah pushed himself up, but before he reared back his fist, the creature landed a blow on his chin.

Willi opened her mouth to scream. A neat left uppercut knocked her head back.

The next few moments were confusing while she struggled against him. When she could clearly grasp what was happening, she was sitting in a chair back to back with Quannah. Her hands were tied to the chair rung and to his wrists behind her. Rough hemp chafed her wrists. She twisted just enough to see Quannah's profile. They seemed to be alone.

"It'll be okay, *Winyan*. Don't worry."

"Your head?"

"Still there. He didn't wound you?"

"No," she said. "Nicked my stubborn chin. What do we do now? Scream?"

"Won't do any good. Look at the walls. That's special soundproofing you're seeing. Maybe someone might hear us through Mrs. Feather's bedroom air vent, but I doubt it."

"I suppose this is one of those things you've been investigating while you *weren't* in Hallettsville?"

"I've been *there,* but kept getting these messages you were into deep trouble."

She decided not to mention her own revelations and asked again, "What do we do?"

"Depend on the allies and watch for opportunities."

"Allies?"

"Two types. One are the animals—your personal totems or one of the helpers." He chuckled. "If the need arises, I'll be Opossum. You be Badger—the stubborn side of the Medicine of Badger."

Frowning, she asked, "Badger?" She tried to think of what the particular totem might have to offer. Badgers could see what others couldn't in the dark. They got in small openings where few could go. But none of those qualities seemed to suit the immediate problem.

She repeated, "Badger?"

"Just be yourself."

"*Pilamaya ye,* Lassiter." Recalling her vision of the wolves while in the witch's cradle the first time, she asked, "Totems could be like shadows or . . . reflections . . . of an animal?"

"Yeah, like me. The big, bad wolf."

Damn him. In her mind again. "Two types you said."

"The two-leggeds. Uncle Brigham and whoever knows you're at the Feathers'. Someone does know, right?"

"Elba and your uncle came here with me. I'm just a heck of a lot confused about what's going on."

"Me, too. I thought Jerald was responsible for the deaths. Some investigating, huh?"

"Don't feel badly. Until tonight he was tops on my list, but I think I know . . . who. In fact, it has to be, although it makes no sense."

"We have time, Gallagher."

She scooted, trying to find a more comfortable spot on the hard chair. "Two questions, first."

"Okay."

"Sheriff Tucker told me Hortense had a connection to the Hallettsville satanists. Who was the second connection? Jerald?"

Quannah moaned and sucked in air.

"Oh," Willi said, "don't talk if you're in pain."

"The link was Trujillo Zeta, Adela's father, Trujillo Sr., not her brother. Zeta was an emissary, a goodwill ambassador, who often went to the gatherings there as a local representative. He isn't our killer. He'll do just about any low-crawling thing the mind can conjure, but he won't murder." Quannah shifted, grasped her little finger with his, and wiggled it. "Second question?"

"Uh . . . I was wondering. That name . . . *Winyan* . . . what exactly does that mean?"

Leaning his head back, he chuckled. "Worried about it, are you, Gallagher?"

The chuckle changed to a guttural laugh.

"Lassiter?"

"Shush. Wasn't me."

The quality of the air changed, becoming harder to breathe. Willi licked her dry lips and trembled.

"Badger. Remember," Quannah whispered. "Allies are nearby and on the way. We must stall."

A cowled figure stood in front of Willi. "Who are you?" Willi asked, although by now she was ninety percent sure of the identity.

"The one you call wicked, *the* Wiccan, dear." Strong square hands slapped a billy club on an open palm.

Silken robes swished. The Wiccan trailed cold sleeves against Willi's face in passing. Circling around them in a slow, stately walk, the Wiccan sighed and returned to the darkest shadows.

Willi narrowed her eyes and decided it was time to use some of that Badger Medicine. "I remembered that moment on the seawall."

An angry swish of robes met her words.

Pushing onward, Willi said, "Power. You were in awe of the ocean's *power*. Just like you told me while you had me dangling in that horrid contraption. *Power* and *control* are what you want. Mama Feather was really talking about you, not poor Betty, when she said you liked studying the occult with *your* father in the cellar. She wasn't wandering in La-La Land about that tidbit, was she, Caprithia?"

"My, my, my. So you have figured out my less illustrious identity. I warned you so many times. I liked you. Odd for me to like a woman, to have a friend." The tone of voice changed to a breathless twitter. Caprithia strolled in front of her and bowed. "Behold, the coven leader," she said, pulling back the robe's cowl.

Quannah sat up straight. The back of his head lightly touched Willi's. When she turned sideways, she viewed his bronzed skin. Perspiration flowed down his temple.

Caprithia glared at him. "I didn't tell *you* to look." A resounding slap landed across Quannah's face. His head jolted back against Willi's. "Badger," he whispered.

"Ow!" Willi's eyes teared up. "Huh? Right, right." Just keep her talking, keep her feeling as comfortable as if they chatted over a cup of tea.

"Wasn't your father a leading member of the Baptist or Methodist Church all his life?"

"We Wiccans must lead two lives until the coming of our Lord and Master. Yes, Papa was a fine deacon. Very respected."

"We can get you some help, Caprithia. You don't have to do this now."

"Of course, I do. When one leader dies, he must be replaced. That's why I chose to do a special ceremony with the coven. So exciting. The oil-covered bodies. The flames dancing over us. Then folks coupling. Drums beating a fast tempo. I danced close to him once, and no one saw the needle enter Papa's neck."

"You killed your own father?" *Oh, great heavens, the woman would do anything.* Willi's bottom lip trembled.

Quannah groaned.

Willi peered around. "Lassiter?"

He slumped in the chair, but his hands twitched.

"Lassiter?" Damn the man. He'd lied. He was hurt much worse than he'd said.

"Oh, don't worry, dear. Maybe this way he won't feel anything."

Fear clutched Willi's heart. "What? What are you going to do to him?"

"My dear, really, I wished you no lasting harm. You gave me a few hours' peace now and again from that old woman, that leech upstairs. But, you will, along with your investigator friend and the baby virgin, have to be taken care of somehow. Such a pity I didn't realize in Galveston what trouble you were to be. I could have settled matters there, but we'll devise a plan. Not to worry, dear, not to worry."

"Caprithia, you can't get away with that. The sheriff and Elba are right upstairs."

"No, dear, they believed the tale I convinced Mama to relate to them. Even now, they're on their way to the hut, thinking you've remembered something important you have to find there. Your curiosity has certainly played into my hands quite well." She cackled. "By the time they realize that's a false trail, you'll be gone."

Willi closed her eyes a moment to center herself, found that elusive Sacred Breath and focused on Caprithia. "You've always been fair, Caprithia, so you will keep your word, right? You said you'd satisfy my curiosity."

"Satisfy your curiosity? Certainly." Caprithia snapped her fingers. "You have more questions. We still have time."

"Why . . . uh . . . *why* didn't your mother stop your father or at least keep you from being pulled into the group?"

"Mother turned a blind eye. These things happened and that was that. One did not ruin the good name of one's family by advertising the eccentricities of one's husband

and daughter. You know, dear, I was fond of Papa, but I never had any power. I wanted power *over* him." She swished her robes as she bent over a box where a sweet cooing sang from the depths.

Sweat broke out on Willi's upper lip.

Quannah, in a painful nightmare, twisted violently, groaned and settled again.

Caprithia said, "I have the power over life and death, but, really, dear, I prefer to give joy with life. As long as I control the giving. Sweet, sweet, sweet, don't you think? But, those girls, weak insignificant creatures, had discovered who I was, *really was,* and threatened Zeta and me. Me!"

She patted her bosom. "No reason to be upset. I've taken care of them." She cooed softly to the baby before picking up the wiggling bundle. She held the bundle toward Willi. "The Lord Satan would be pleased with such a fresh new member, would he not? Beautiful, isn't she?"

"Betty's baby?" asked Willi.

"The gift to our Lord. Yes. He would have been pleased, but we'll have to pass her along to another county or state due to you and your meddling. Perhaps, after she's had training for some years, she can return to her home coven." Caprithia peered toward the outside door. "We must start soon."

Quannah jerked. "Sure you want the child to come back? She'll be a damned sight prettier than you, old hag."

Willi gasped. "Lassiter?"

Caprithia tightened her lips. She walked away to replace the baby in its makeshift cradle.

"Lassiter," Willi whispered, "what happened to *your* Sacred Breath? Let's not get her agitated, okay? Think about the allies."

He shifted, almost pulling his chair away from her. "Exactly, Gallagher. The ally is Opossum." He jerked upward and slumped again. "You're Badger. Get her upset."

"Ow!" Willi's wrists, bruised, throbbed each time he moved. "Caprithia, I guess you've probably lost a lot of power the last few years, right?"

"What . . . do . . . you . . . mean?" Caprithia twirled a-round.

Willi gulped, trying to come up with words that would agitate as Quannah obviously wanted. "I mean it's a shame folks judge a woman on her graying hair and advancing years, isn't it? I suppose the members prefer someone younger and more . . . vital . . . with more . . . uh . . . *power*."

Caprithia bared her teeth in a sickly smile. "I decide what the group wants. I control who does what. I dictate who to do spells for or against, who we terrorize, who we allow to go their way. I choose who pickpockets at concerts, who steals what, who does a drive-by and where, who gets drugs, who doesn't. Those troubled students meet me next door whenever I send the message. To them I reveal the powerful and regal side with a little help from makeup and wigs. They tell me they're afraid the counselor next door will turn them in for coming down the alley."

She laughed. "The counselor is the incognito persona, the Wiccan is the reality. And none of them—none—think of me as old." Both hands clenched together, she swung with full force, her intention obviously to smack Willi, but instead she hit Quannah on his wounded shoulder. The impact sent both Willi and him to the floor. The rungs of the ladderback chairs broke.

Quannah pulled his hands from behind his back and rolled to his knees. He grabbed Caprithia by the legs, jerking her down. Entangled like writhing snakes, each struggling to become the victor, they both scrambled on the floor.

Willi, still tied to her chair, pulled herself up to her knees. She wrestled one arm free, then the other. Kicking the chair away, she fell face forward, reached out and grasped the baseball bat. Standing, she stood back from the squirming figures. The tangle of bodies left her little to strike at.

Caprithia finally freed a hand to get to the billy club around her neck. Willi moved in. The bodies twisted. She brought the bat down and smiled as it cracked against a skull. Quannah stood very straight for a moment, looked quizzically at her and toppled over.

The robed figure rose.

Willi cringed. "Oops."

Billy club raised, Caprithia chanted her *magick and power* litany and lunged.

Willi swung the bat upward, grazing Caprithia on the chin. She swung again and connected with the side of Caprithia's head. Blood spurted from a deep cut. The Wicked Wiccan slumped to the floor.

Heart racing, Willi gasped for air. She leaned on the bat. Sweat poured between her shoulder blades.

The cellar door creaked open.

Zeta, her helper?

A frigid draft filled the room. The coldness clutched around Willi's heart, squeezing it. In slow motion, she faced the man. She raised the bat, spread her legs in a stance to give more leverage to the swing and said, "Come and get it, you SOB, I'll knock your damned lights out."

"Mayhap," Sheriff Tucker said, "you could give me a reason for having to do that, Miss Willi."

Sobbing, she dropped the bat and ran into his arms.

Elba helped Quannah sit up.

Constantly glaring at Willi, Quannah told what had happened.

Willi filled in between her sobs. Sheriff Tucker wiped her tears with a crisp white and red striped bandanna. "Now, my nephew ain't gonna hold a tap or two against you, Miss Willi. Mayhap, if that crazy sicko ain't awake yet, you can show us this newborn filly."

Willi pointed to the corner.

Gently, as if he were handling the last Texas-born baby, Tucker held it close. In his huge hands, the bundle seemed pitifully tiny. "Ain't new babies something, Miss Willi? Another hour and we're gonna have to find somebody willing to give a 3 A.M. feeding, ain't we?"

BY noontime caprithia, divested of hood, coven and power, sat in a cell. She was telling tales of her innocence and saying the coven and its actions were mainly brought about through the many illegal efforts on the part of the Zetas. Eva and her husband had been brought in as accessories. They each claimed the group's actions were caused by Caprithia Feather's materialistic maneuvers. The mess would be fun for the Nickleberry lawyers to sort out.

Mama Feather remained quite calm throughout the ordeal. Arrangements were made for the retirement home which she thought was the Hotel Chez Noveau. She sucked lemon drops taken from the competent hands of Nurse Bennett, a no-nonsense young woman who kindly took in and gentled Sweetpea.

After recounting events to Auntie and Rodrigo with India Lou Aiken listening in, Willi needed rest not induced by drugs. But first she had to read Betty's letters. Having set them aside for a moment, she dozed in one of the rockers on the porch. Charlie Brown ran up with a folded note between his teeth. She grabbed it. "Bad doggie. Give me that." She opened it up and read:

" 'I'd rather die than continue with this bearer mess. Too late to get out. Too late. What's going to happen to me? To my baby? I want to die.' "

Willi sighed. Betty had gotten her wish. Baby Norris, now in the care of the Foster Children's Department, would be okay. Willi folded the note and replaced it in the stack, rested her head against the rocker back and fell asleep. In only minutes, a nebulous nightmare awakened her. The only emotion left over from the dream was one of great loss, similar to that felt when she'd discovered Quannah's hat in the cellar. Her heart flip-flopped against her ribs.

A tear trickled down her cheek. Quannah reached out and with one finger wiped the tear away.

She gasped and rubbed her eyes.

He winked. The bandage on his head made him look a lot like Jean Lafitte. "Didn't mean to startle you. You were into some serious snoozing. Just came to say good-bye."

Lassiter was leaving? No, the nightmare was over, and he was supposed to stay. "Good-bye?" She clutched the rocker arms.

"Got an investigation down the road. I'll be visiting Uncle Brigham this summer if caseloads don't get too heavy." He tapped a finger on her head, and tapped his own. "If we're in one piece, *Winyan,* I'll take you to a Pow-Wow."

She sat up straighter. "Pow-Wow?"

"That's better. Don't ever lose that curiosity, Gallagher. It becomes you."

"Thanks."

He raised an eyebrow.

She giggled. *"Pilamaya ye."*

He stood, straightened his new Stetson at a jaunty angle and grinned. Splaying his fingers across his chest, he said,

"I do not want to buy a new hat this summer, Gallagher. No chasing the bad guys, okay?"

He held a hand out to her.

She clasped it and rose to stand beside him.

"Close your eyes, *Winyan*." Keeping hold of her, he reached into his pocket with his other hand and placed something in her palm.

The warmth of it told her before she opened her eyes, and she yelped, "Tunkasila."

"It was in the baby's blankets."

"Really?" She nodded. "Protecting."

"When you were in the witch's cradle, the Feather woman must have carried the rock back home in the folds of her Wiccan's robe without knowing. Now," he said, staring with such intensity she almost wanted to look away, "you keep it near you until this summer."

He took her chin in one hand and rubbed a finger along her bottom lip.

Her breath quickened. His eyes dilated, mirroring her own. *This moment must be frozen in time.* The breeze caressed her cheeks and lifted his dark ponytail.

Quannah brushed a quick kiss across her lips and stepped away. "My bet is you'll know the answer to your question before I see you again."

"What question?"

He backed away, stepped off the porch and got into his Rover. Leaning out the window, he yelled, "Later, *Winyan*."

"Uh . . . Lassiter, wait."

He sped off. The Rover's wheels spewed up gravel. His laughter sounded over the grinding of gears and speeding tires.

"*Winyan*. Blast you, Lassiter. You bet I'll figure it out. By this summer, you hear, Lassiter?"